SANCTUARY ON FIRE

BOOK 2 OF THE SANCTUARY SERIES

NIKITA SLATER

PREFACE

Dear readers,

Thank you for purchasing Sanctuary on Fire. This book picks up where Sanctuary's Warlord ends. The Sanctuary series is a trilogy with each of the first two books ending in a cliffhanger. If you haven't read Sanctuary's Warlord, then you'll want to go back and read that one first. I hope you enjoy this book. Thank you for reading!

Nikita Slater

It's 2073, the world has become an apocalyptic nightmare, falling under the onslaught of a virus that turns humans to their most basic primitive selves. Survival depends on well-fortified cities called Sanctuaries. Places where government, education, medicine and food is all carefully controlled. These Sanctuaries are ruled by Warlords, men that are often cruel and brutal.

My name is Taran and I'm married to one such Warlord. Like his contemporaries, he is often brutal, his methods difficult for me to understand. As a rebel leader my entire existence thus far has been to improve the plight of the people, to create equality throughout our Sanctuary. But over the course of weeks and months my marriage to the Warlord has become a partnership, a gradual understanding of each other. I love him, desperately and without reservation. I've had my entire family stolen from me, the thought of losing him is unbearable. Yet, we live in a cruel world where more people die than survive.

In an act of violence, I have been forced to leave my husband and my Sanctuary, driven into the desert where

Primitives rove the land looking for new victims. In this lawless land, I have finally come face-to-face with my worst nightmare; a Primitive. No one can survive the Death Kiss without turning. From birth, I've been taught that a bitten human is a dead human.

And I've been bitten...

ONE

TARAN

"Diogo – "

Time stands still as I sit on the dusty ground, my hand over the wound on my neck. Blood drips slowly from Diogo's knife, falling in gruesome drops, reminding me of the ease in which he just took a life. She was a Primitive, a zombie, and she attacked me.

Then the import of what's happened hits me. I've been bitten. By a zombie. I'm going to turn, probably in a matter of minutes, if not seconds.

My gaze creeps up the man standing over me. Strong, savage, brutally handsome. My husband. A zombie killer. It's his job. He protects the city and his people by taking out any threats. I've become a threat. And I know what he does to people that've turned. I'd been told in gory detail how he stabbed Victoria Greystone through the heart. He held her as she died, then he cut her head off, ensuring there would be no chance that she could turn.

I look him in the eyes, searching for the love he'd promised me. I see none. I see nothing at all. His gaze is bleak, flat, dead. Just as I'm about to be.

I hope to find a flicker of love in his expression, or at the very least, indecision. But I see none of that in his face. As though our time together is erased. I'm the enemy. More now than I ever was. The undead.

A sob erupts from my throat, the sound sharp and dry, loud in the stillness surrounding us. The cacophony of noise as Diogo's people and the mercenaries fight the Primitives seems to have died away. Or maybe we're out of hearing range.

I don't want to die.

The decision to run hits me hard, driving another rush of adrenaline through my veins. I dig my fingers into the ground beneath my body, burrowing my fingers into the dirt. Just as Diogo's hand lifts, as he raises the knife, I throw the dirt up at him, aiming for his face. In the split second it takes him to blink and turn his face away I'm on my feet and running. I race full tilt into the foothills, my feet hitting the ground so hard dust flies up with each step, choking me.

If there's one thing I'm good at, it's running. I've been running my whole life, training for this moment. I pelt forward as though my life depends on it. Because it does. Diogo was about to kill me. My husband was about to cut me down in the dirt, his remorseless gaze steady on mine. Terror lends wings to my feet, driving me ever faster.

I know I won't get far, that this was a doomed flight. I'm about to become a Primitive. And when that happens I'll turn back around and launch myself directly at the first person in my path. The husband I've come to love, more than my own life. Suddenly I'm running for a different reason. I have to get away from Diogo before I turn, before I become a danger to him.

This thought distracts me. I stop watching where my feet land and glance back over my shoulder as I round an outcropping of rocks. He's directly on my ass, his long legs easily killing the space between us.

My feet tangle in a scrub brush and I go down in a heap, my body hitting the dirt. Automatically I roll with the impact to stop injury. I land next a tree, dazed, pain shooting through my leg. I groan and reach for my ankle, probably twisted by whatever I tripped over. I don't have a chance to get up again, in a matter of seconds Diogo is on top of me. Standing over me.

Only this time the look on his face isn't cold and emotionless. It's anguished. Finally, an emotion, but it's not satisfying. We're being torn apart. He's gutted by what he needs to do. The thought of his love gives me the strength I need to lift my chin, to look him in the eyes and say, "Do it, Diogo."

The anguish switches to fury as his intelligent brain rapidly searches for a solution, for a way out. I see the moment he loses that hope. He knows what he has to do, and it's destroying him.

"Taran," he whispers my name brokenly, almost pleadingly.

I can't help him. It breaks my heart seeing him this way, but my heart won't stay broken for long. In a moment he'll kill me, separate my head from my shoulders and I'll cease to be. Unless he hesitates too long, giving me time to turn. If that happens, I won't be me anymore.

I can't allow that.

"Just do it, Diogo," I beg him, my voice breaking as I speak. "I can't run anymore, and I don't want to turn into one... of them. I'd rather die by your hand than live as the walking dead."

Tears drip down my face, but I keep my hands down, allowing the wetness on my cheeks. Showing Diogo that I won't defend myself. When still he hesitates, I whisper, "I don't want to turn."

A shudder racks his body and I can see the moment he decides. The death in his eyes. But this time, it isn't the lack of emotion. It's my death I see, his death. Because he's going to follow me. I know it. He's said before that there is no Sanctuary without me.

He lifts the knife and I force myself to watch him, to give him the strength he needs. He swings, the blade arcing down at my neck in a blurred rush.

TWO

DIOGO

8 MINUTES EARLIER

Grief hits me like a punch to the side of the head. A knife to the heart. A tearing in the soul. I freeze, standing over my wounded wife. I will myself to move. To drop to my knees in front of her and take her in my arms. To comfort her in her last moments of life. Instead I'm stricken, staring at her as time stands still, insulating us in a bubble of terror.

I want to reach out to her, call her name. The seconds tick by in my head, each precious moment lost to the over-whelming grief as she slowly turns. I look for signs. Look for the telltale red in her eyes as they turn hazy, turn inward, toward the Primitive. I glance at her hands, splayed out in the dirt. When she turns, they'll curl inward, into desperate claw-like devices. Soon she'll be writhing on the ground as every atom in her body changes. Twists into something new, reverting to her most primitive self.

Her hands twitch, digging into the dirt beneath her. It's beginning. I tense, lifting my knife, expecting her to launch herself at me, the nearest human. I wonder how I'll react. Will I have the guts to take the merciful path, cut her down before she turns completely, every part of the Taran I know erased and taken over by a hungry beast? Or will I leave her execution to my men? The people that have my back. Do I have it in me to allow another to touch her? Even with a blade or a bullet?

No. She belongs to me; her life and her death. If anyone must end her, it'll be me. Even if it means killing myself at the same time. She deserves more. She deserves the best. She deserves for her husband to escort her into the afterlife with all the love in his heart.

But before I can bring my blade down, killing her in a single stroke, she throws handfuls of dirt up into my face. Reflexively I turn my head to the side, avoiding the blinding sand. When I look back she's already running away, tearing hellbent across the desert toward the next outcropping of rocks.

I admire her speed and agility, even as I follow, chasing behind her, my longer legs rapidly eating up the distance between us. She's fast, arms and legs pumping in a blur, but she's no match for my strength and speed. I follow her, heart pounding in fear, knowing what I'll have to do when I catch her.

She zigzags past pathetic skeletal desert trees, their branches reaching toward her but never catching her. Briefly I wonder why she's running from me instead of launching herself at me, snarling, spitting and ready to take a chunk out of my flesh. It takes seconds, minutes at most for a new Primitive to turn. But, though her back is to me, she's not showing any Primitive characteristics. I know it's wishful thinking. That I'm clinging to the hope that maybe she wasn't bitten deep enough, hard enough, to turn her. I'm wrong though. I saw the blood streaming over her shoulder. The bite was deep and penetrating.

I've never seen a person survive a zombie bite. They all turn. Always. Every damn time. She doesn't have a chance.

Another wave of grief nearly drives me to my knees, slowing me down and lengthening the distance between us. I'm gutted by the thought of losing her. I've found the person that can centre me, provide my conscience, fight me, love me and stand with me. I've barely gotten the chance to know her and now I'm about to lose her.

She darts behind an outcropping of rocks and I follow close behind. As I round the corner, I'm surprised to find her sprawled in the dirt. She's tripped. She rolls onto her back, cowering against the side of a sun-scorched tree, her hand sliding down her leg to clutch at her ankle. She turns wounded eyes up at me, tears filling them.

I stand over her once more, caught by indecision.

Her eyes reach mine and the desperate fear fades to resignation. She tilts her chin up and nods. "Do it, Diogo."

Her voice is rough. I can feel her terror. Fear of me, fear of turning. Taran is a free spirit, always flying on the wings of her convictions. She's always known her direction, even when I captured her and twisted that direction toward me. Now she's lost, knowing she doesn't have much time.

"Taran." I say her name like a prayer. Despite what's about to happen to her, she is my love, my everything. She's a saint in a world of sinners. She doesn't deserve this end.

Understanding flickers through her grey eyes and she gives me the saddest smile I've ever seen. "Just do it, Diogo," she says tiredly. "I can't run anymore, and I don't want to turn into one... of them." Her gaze flicks past me, then travels up my body to meet mine. "I'd rather die by your hand than live as the walking dead."

Tears burn in my throat and I have to force breath through the constriction. It hurts to look at her. To see the tangles of her dark red hair tumbling around her shoulders, the blazing intelligence in her eyes, despite the fear threatening to overwhelm her. The torn dress. Her small hands balled in her lap as she forces herself to give up the fight and face me, Sanctuary's Warlord, with a brave face.

"I don't want to turn," she whispers pleadingly, a tear trailing down her face and dripping off her chin. She chokes on a sob.

I nod and lift my knife, willing myself to do this for love. To stand strong, to not weaken. I will not leave her to turn. Will not leave her to my men. She deserves more.

I stare at her, taking in her bright eyes, now an intense blue-grey with shimmering tears. I've no doubt the grief on her face mirrors that of my own. She's ready. I will do this, then I'll lay down my arms and walk away from Sanctuary. Without her I have no reason to stay. No cause to protect a city that doesn't hold my Desert Wren.

As I bring the knife down, she closes her eyes, hiding her last thoughts, her last emotions. In the few seconds before I strike, I count the minutes since she was bitten. Seven. Maybe eight. Definitely not less.

I've never seen it take more than four minutes for a person to turn completely. Usually it only takes two or three minutes and during that time there are obvious signs that it's happening, signs that Taran isn't exhibiting.

I twist to the side, slamming my knife into the tree just a hairsbreadth above the crown of her head. She gasps as it thuds into the wood, her eyes flying open in surprise and her hand jerking up to her neck, clutching it as though expecting to find a gaping wound. My blade bites so deep into the trunk that it breaks through the brittle wood. The tree groans and the top half falls, toppling over next to

Taran. She cringes, burying her head in her arms, trying to protect herself.

I ignore the thud of the tree hitting the dirt next to us and drop to my knees. I grip her arms and drag her up out of her crouch. She stares at me in shock, her breath coming out in shallow gasps, her face white.

I search her features, waiting. Waiting for the first signs of the Turn. Seconds tick by, minutes, as she sits in a slump, allowing me to manhandle her. Nothing happens. She blinks steadily up at me.

I look at her wound, maybe it's not as bad as I thought. But it is bad. Her delicate flesh has been torn, teeth marks are buried deep into her throat, blood still dripping steadily from a bite that badly needs medical attention. It's a gruesome sight. Her flesh was penetrated by a Primitive. Yet here she sits, the same Taran as the one I've spent weeks getting to know.

"You haven't turned," I say, unable to hold the gratitude and awe back as I speak. "8 minutes, Taran."

She blinks, and few tears trickle unheeded down her face. She blinks several more times, rapidly as she takes in the meaning of what I'm saying. A river of tears now make tiny wet paths down her cheeks.

"I haven't turned," she whispers back to me, the same awe I'm feeling reflected in her voice.

THREE

TARAN

I'm not dead.

I haven't turned into a Primitive.

I want to be grateful, but I'm too stunned. Shock is stealing the warmth from my limbs leaving behind tremors. I'm shaking, chilled to the bone as Diogo twists to look over his shoulder. I turn my gaze behind him, but I see nothing. Then he's tearing the bandana from his neck and wrapping it around mine. Pain slices through me as his knuckles brush against the bite. I flinch but he holds me still while he knots the end, securing it. I reach up to touch my neck, but he drags my hand away.

"Don't touch it," he growls, his hand tight around mine. He leans forward until his nose almost touches mine. "No one can see this bite, understand?"

I frown, trying to understand, but I'm dizzy with pain and exhaustion is beginning to seep in. I'd watched a friend die, climbed the wall and ran across the desert, then was attacked by a rabid horde, followed by an almost deadly reunion with my Warlord husband. All of that after a very stressful dinner party. It had been a long day.

He touches the collar of my dress and I look down. The white material is soaked in blood. My blood, the Primitive's blood. Diogo unbuttons his military coat and tugs it off his broad shoulders. He wraps it around me, pulling my arms through the sleeves before buttoning it back up as far as it'll go.

He grips my good shoulder and searches my eyes. I know what he's looking for. He still thinks I'll turn. I still feel like myself, but I don't know what it feels like to turn, so I can't reassure him.

He glances behind him again, then turns back. "No one can see the bite." When I just stare at him blankly, he gives my shoulder a hard squeeze and growls. "Do you understand what I'm saying to you, Taran? Repeat the words."

I swallow, wetting my parched throat and say, "I understand."

"What do you understand?" he demands.

I give my head a little shake, trying to clear the cobwebs. The shock is starting to lift, clearing my mind. "I have to keep the bite hidden." My voice sounds foreign to my ears, scratchy and painful. I lift a hand to my neck, but he slaps it again and grabs my hand, squeezing hard.

His voice is rough with intensity when he speaks. "If my men see the bite, they won't understand. You'll be killed on the spot. No questions, no time to think about it. Don't talk about it, don't touch it again."

I shudder and nod my understanding. They'll kill me, the way Diogo was about to, the way he should have. "I'll be careful, Diogo."

He grips my arm and stands, pulling me to my feet. I clutch him as a wave of dizziness hits me. He doesn't wait for me to recover, he starts walking, pulling me with him. As soon as I put weight on my right ankle pain shoots up my leg and it gives out. I start to pitch forward, but Diogo turns swiftly and rights me before I can fall. He looks at me questioningly.

"I twisted it," I explain, shifting all my weight to my left leg.

"Fuck," he snarls. He sheaths his knife and drags me against him, stooping to slide an arm around my waist and pinning me to his tall frame. He pulls his sidearm and starts forward, dragging me with him. "I can't carry you. I need to keep at least one arm free. There could be more Primitives heading toward the fight. They'll have heard those gunshots from miles off."

I don't say anything, conserving my energy. I hobble as fast as I can, tripping against Diogo's side as we move back toward the cars and his men. Tears of pain leap to my eyes, but I do my best to hang onto them. I need to be tough now, need to not be any more of a burden to Diogo. As we walk I realize the area has become eerily silent. Which means either our side won, or the Primitives took everyone out and then scattered, looking for more fresh meat.

My heart leaps into my throat as we round the rocks and half-dead trees, entering into the clearing with all the vehicles. I nearly vomit at the sight that greets me. Bodies are scattered across the ground, heads and limbs severed. Next to a vehicle, the driver's door is open as if he tried to climb inside to safety. Another man lays in a pool of blood, his throat ripped out. Gaping wounds to his back tell me he was attacked by a Primitive and didn't survive long enough to turn. I move away, tucking myself tight against Diogo.

Men stand near vehicles at the head of the rock formation. I realize most are wearing military uniforms, while the ones that aren't are on their knees in the dirt, hands behind their heads. I try to search their faces for Xavier, but everyone is in various stages of dirty, bloody and beaten. Then Diogo drags me past everyone toward his jeep. I twist around, but he opens the door and shoves me inside, closes the door and stands next to it, blocking my view. Or blocking their view of me.

"Cruz," he snaps, drawing the attention of his second-in-command. He jerks his head and Cruz strides over.

The front of Jorje's uniform is splattered in blood and it's been smeared up the side of his face and into his hair as though he ran a bloody hand through it. I swallow the bile rising in my throat and lean back in the seat forcing myself to breathe long and slow. Diogo places his arm over the door frame and fills the opening completely with his big body. With Diogo now fully in the way, I'm unable to see Jorje and he can't see me either. I shudder as I realize what would happen if Jorje discovers my injury. We need more time to pass without me turning before we can tell anyone.

They hold a low-voiced conversation that I can't hear and then Diogo straightens away from the door and says loudly, "Take the prisoners back into the city. Move quickly, make sure you avoid Primitives. You don't need to be fighting them with a band of Outsiders in your custody."

"Yes, Commander."

Diogo strides around the vehicle. Jorje's gaze lingers on me, taking in his Commander's jacket, dwarfing my much smaller frame. A frown lingers on his face for a moment then he steps away and heads back to his men, shouting orders at them to secure their prisoners and head back to the city.

Diogo slides into the driver's seat and fires the jeep's engine. He hits the gas so hard the tires spin in the dirt before we start moving. Diogo looks utterly terrifying, his face is set in harsh lines, his shoulders stiff and his knuckles white on the steering wheel. My actions have created a gulf between us. The last thing I should do is bring attention to them. Still, I have to know what happened to my ex-husband.

"Diogo? Did you see Xavier back there?" I speak softly, already cringing in my seat, knowing what his reaction will be. "Was he captured, or... or... ?" I leave the sentence hanging, unable to finish it.

Diogo turns glacial eyes to me, his condemnation stabbing at me. Then he turns his gaze back to the desert, declining to answer. His eyes move constantly, all around us, through the windshield, my window, his, the rear-view mirror. He's looking for Primitives. I look too, but I don't see anything. Dusk is rapidly falling and I realize it's only been a few hours since the explosion, since I climbed the wall and ran through the Sonoran desert. Since the attack.

I twist in my seat, glancing behind us. Several cars are following well behind ours, dust clouds puffing up in every direction. Diogo's military.

"How do you feel?" Diogo asks, surprising me. I know he's furious, but his fear for my well-being is taking a front seat, for now.

"I feel... I feel okay, I think. No changes that I can tell." I start to lift my hand to my neck and then drop it, remembering his insistence that I not touch the wound. "It hurts a lot though. The bite. And my ankle too."

He nods, his sharp eyes taking me in at a glance, but he doesn't say anything. I feel cold despite the heavy jacket wrapped around me. He blames me for leaving the city with Xavier. Maybe blames me for Garrett's death, if he even knows. As I think of Garrett, the tears start. A good man, doing his job to protect me and losing his life in the process.

This day has been too much, all of it. The loss of friends, of conviction. The loss of Diogo's regard. I turn my head to the side so he can't see me as I weep. I've broken the trust Diogo and I built between us and I don't know if it can be recovered.

FOUR

TARAN

As we approach the city gates, Diogo lifts his radio and calls in, asking for a Doctor Bishop to meet him at the Tower and to come prepared to treat a patient. Someone responds. No one ever seems to ignore the Commander's requests, so I have no doubt that the doctor will be on Diogo's doorstep when we get there.

As we drive from sector to sector, waiting for guards to open each gate, I begin to drift off. The trauma of the past hours combined with the warmth of Diogo's jacket is dragging me into unconsciousness.

"Taran." His sharp voice jolts me and I straighten in my seat. "No sleeping."

I frown as we arrive in Sector One and head straight for the Tower. I'm not sure why I can't sleep. I was bitten, not hit on the head. But I suppose I look as dirty and bloody as the other survivors at the scene of that massacre. Maybe he doesn't want to take any chances. Maybe I shouldn't. I might've hit my head while I was scrambling around, fighting with the Primitive. I touch my head and tentatively slide my fingers around, looking for a tender spot. I don't find a bump, but I do find dried blood. I feel nauseous as I remember the blood that had sprayed from the Primitive Diogo killed to save my life. I drop my hand quickly.

As we approach the building, I see an elderly man waiting outside. He nods toward Diogo as we pull up. He steps back as we pull up to the curb and then reaches for my door, opening it for me.

"Mrs. Fuentes, I assume?" he says, holding his hand out to me.

I glance nervously at Diogo, who isn't reacting with his usual protective arrogance whenever someone tries to touch me. "It's alright, Taran," he assures me. "Doc Bishop is my personal physician."

I take his hand and allow him to help me from the jeep. I'm forced to grip the door handle, wincing, as I put weight on my injured leg. The doctor peers hard into my face, stooping a little so he's on my level. He's a tall, thin black man, probably in his eighties. His dark brown eyes look me over with sympathy and kindness.

He clucks his tongue and says, "Looks like you've run into a bit of trouble."

I try to respond, but truthfully, I don't know what to say. Diogo told me to keep the attack secret. I shrug. Diogo comes around the jeep, takes my hand from the doctor's grip and lifts me into his arms. He strides into the building while the doctor trails behind.

"You okay to take the stairs?" Diogo asks without looking back. "I can have a man sent over for the manual lift."

"I'll be fine, son." The doctor's response sounds amused as he follows us into the stairwell. Several floors later he's still trailing behind us, barely out of breath and not once asking to stop for a break.

"How old is he?" I ask Diogo in a whisper.

Diogo flashes me a quick look, his mouth softening into a partial smile for just a moment. "Eighty-two," he says. "Been my doc since I took the city. He attends my soldiers. Used to be a military surgeon around the time of the Great Fall."

I gape at Diogo's shoulder, wishing I could see past him to the doctor. Meeting people his age is extremely rare. The harsh conditions, lack of medication and illness usually kills people at a relatively young age.

Diogo enters the apartment and carries me straight through to the bedroom. He places me gently on the bed and steps back. The doctor is a few minutes behind us, having slowed down around the 15th floor. He comes through the door, trying to catch his breath.

"My walking regime is nothing compared to those stairs," he says jokingly and sets his bag down on the end of the bed. I realize he climbed all those floors with his heavy medical bag.

"She's been bitten," Diogo says bluntly, his arms crossed over his chest, massive biceps bulging with threat.

The doctor straightens, his mouth dropping open in shock. His dark eyes look me over and this time I see a combination of pity and fear. "Bitten," he says in a hushed voice. He doesn't ask for clarification. He knows exactly what Diogo means. "And she hasn't turned yet?"

I flinch at the 'yet' and cringe back into the pillows behind me. No one has heard of a bitten human surviving the experience. I should be either dead or turned.

"As you can see," Diogo confirms.

"How long ago?" The doctor busies himself once more with his bag, setting some of his things down on the bed next to my legs.

"About half an hour." Diogo's sharp eyes take in every move the doctor makes.

"I need you to be specific, Commander. Her life depends on your answers."

Diogo growls and shoves an agitated hand over his head as though he thinks the doctor is threatening me instead of helping. "More than half an hour, but less than 40 minutes."

It seems shocking that so little time has passed since I was bitten, it feels like hours. If feels like days since Xavier grabbed me and took me over the wall, fleeing into the desert to meet with those Outsiders. But really, it's only been hours.

The doctor takes a breath and moves toward me. "Let's have a look."

Diogo steps in front of him, blocking his path. "You breathe a word of this to anyone and you will die, slowly and painfully. Your family will be turned from the city and I'll make damn sure the last thing they experience is the bite."

I'm not sure if threatening the man who is about to administer to me is the best idea, but I keep my mouth shut. Diogo fears for me and when he's concerned, his feelings take the direction of rage. Apparently his doctor knows this as well. He places a hand on Diogo's shoulder and says, "She's going to be fine, son. But I need to tend her. She's likely in shock, which can kill almost as fast as a bite if left untended."

Diogo grunts and steps to the side, allowing the doctor to settle himself next to me on the bed. He reaches for the collar of Diogo's jacket and says, "Do you mind if we remove this?"

Diogo reaches for me, helping to lift me, the doctor

tugging the jacket off while I lay helplessly. I don't feel like an invalid, but I'm happy not to have to move. My body feels battered in the worst way and the doctor is right, I'm probably still in shock.

His fingers are gentle on my neck, but after examining the bite he lets out a low whistle. "This thing goes hallway around your neck; she was going to tear your throat out."

I swallow hard at this news. I hadn't really thought about it, but yes, the marks feel deep and they are in the front and back of my neck. If Diogo hadn't taken her head off she would've killed me. He must have superb control to have been able to kill her in one stroke without touching me with the blade.

The doctor pours antiseptic on some gauze and wipes the wounds. I flinch and my eyes water as the antiseptic hits the open wound, but I hold any further reaction in so Diogo doesn't separate the old man's head from his body. When he finishes, he drops the gauze. It's bright pink with my blood. He places another piece of gauze over the wound and tapes it to my skin.

"You need to check her ankle, and then the rest of her," Diogo says coldly from beside the bed.

"Her ankle?"

I struggle to sit up straighter and pull my leg up the bed. "I twisted it while I was running."

He nods and turns to attend my foot. The pain shifts from my neck to my ankle as he probes it. "No broken bones," he announces. "Stay off it for a few days and it'll be good as new."

Silence falls. We're all thinking the same thing. I was bitten. What if I still turn? What if I don't have a few days?

Doctor Bishop turns back to me and takes my hand. "If

you were going to turn, you would've done it by now, Mrs. Fuentes."

I nod and speak past the lump of fear in my throat. "Taran, please," I tell him. "And how do you know that? We've all been told that a bitten human is a dead human. No exceptions."

He nods and scratches at the dark whiskers on his chin. "Call me Bishop," he says warmly. "And yes, we used to know that. But we also used to know that a bitten human turned into a Primitive within seconds. Minutes at the most. Necrotitis Primeval rushes through the system, changing the very basic cell structure of its victim and it does this with each beat of the heart. Each time blood passes from the heart to the torso, to the extremities, it carries the virus, changing everything in its path. The only known method that slows the process down is freezing."

He pauses for a moment letting his words sink in. I already know this, having seen the virus in action, but it's quite another thing hearing it from a medical professional. He squeezes my hand and smiles. "You would have turned by now if you were going to turn. I'm completely confident in this assessment." He looks to Diogo and then back to me with a teasing glint in his eye. "The Commander will keep an eye on you and let me know if you suddenly have a craving for raw meat. Taran?"

"Yes?" I whisper, tears are gathering in my eyes.

"You aren't going to turn." He looks into my eyes with a gentle reassuring expression. "Trust me."

I blink the tears away. I'm not going to turn. This is the first moment since I've been bitten that I've allowed myself to believe that I won't turn. I thought maybe it was just taking longer to go through my system. That something within me would trigger and I would become a mindless zombie in the blink of an eye. But the doctor is right. It would have happened by now, each beat of my heart would have forced the change.

"Thank you... Bishop." I smile weakly at him.

"It's my pleasure, Taran." He stands and turns to Diogo, his voice growing stern once more. "You need to keep a close eye on her," he says as he gathers his things. "Not because there's a chance she could turn, but because she had some serious shocks today. And though she seems to be doing well now, delayed shock could still set in. Watch for signs of rapid pulse and breathing, nausea or vomiting, enlarged pupils, dizziness or fainting."

"You stay and watch over her," Diogo growls. "Make sure none of that happens."

"I can't stay, there are wounded coming in," Bishop says, picking up his bag and turning back to us. Diogo has come to stand next to me. I gape at the Doctor. I've never heard anyone refuse Diogo before. I'd be more amused if this wasn't about me. "Your wife will be fine," he assures Diogo. "She's in remarkably good shape considering what happened. Help her get cleaned up so the scrapes on her arms and legs don't get infected, then tuck her in and let her sleep for as long as she wants."

"You said I should watch for signs of shock," Diogo snaps angrily, letting his agitation at my condition show. "How will I know if she's gone into shock if she's asleep?"

"By the time you clean her up, get her something to eat, and get her into bed, you'll know. Delayed shock is unlikely. This is just a precaution."

When Diogo opens his mouth to argue I reach out to take his hand, tugging his attention down to me. "I'm fine, Diogo," I say softly, trying to give him an earnest look. "I just want to sleep. It's been such a long day and I'm exhausted."

He nods and then turns hard eyes on Bishop. "You stay by your radio and you come back here immediately if requested."

"Of course, Commander." His voice is kind considering Diogo is being rude. I suppose he's had a lot of years of handling our Warlord.

"And you'll come back to see her tomorrow," Diogo insists.

"Nothing can keep me away." He winks at me. "She's the most pleasant patient I've had in a long time. You soldiers are all stoicism and gruff answers, but I've never seen such a lot of children when it comes to injuries. You'd think a sliver amounts to gangrene."

I laugh out loud, some of the tension draining from my shoulders. Surely Bishop wouldn't be making jokes if he truly thought I was in danger.

Diogo walks the doctor out and then returns. His face is still set in rigid lines as he lifts me from the bed and helps me remove my dress and panties. He goes over my entire body, his fingers brushing along my skin. His face becomes grimmer with each scape and bruise he finds. As he kneels at my feet, his hand just barely resting above my swollen ankle, he says, "You will never again do something this reckless."

My heart beats faster and I look him in the eye, promising, "I won't."

He rises, standing over me, his hands sliding to my bare waist and holding me upright. "No, Taran. You won't be tempted to do something like this again, because I will make sure that you have no reason to do it."

"What does that mean?"

"It means that I will be removing your reason to leave. I will remove Gunther, and I will destroy the rebellion."

I stare at him, trying to decide if he means what he says. But with a sinking heart, I realize, I already know. Diogo always tells the truth. If he says he's going to destroy the rebellion, then that's what he's going to do.

"You don't understand what happened." I need to get him to listen to me, explain why I left.

"No, you don't understand." His words are quiet, dripping in ice. Almost worse than if he was yelling at me. "I don't care what happened, Taran. What I do care about, is what almost happened. And it won't happen again."

FIVE

DIOGO

Taran doesn't speak again as I take her to the washroom, strip my own clothes off and then take her into the shower. She stands silently while I wash first her, then myself. Cleansing us of dirt and blood. I run my fingers through her hair, untangling the waves and leaving the strands to cling wetly to her body. I'm careful to keep the water away from her bandage as much as I can, tipping her head back so the water streams away from it. I kneel at her feet, washing all the way up each leg, paying attention to each scrape. I keep her in there for several minutes longer than necessary, warming her with the hot water she enjoys so much. I'd noticed the tremors wracking her small body when we were in the jeep, driving back to the city. Her teeth were chattering, despite the warm desert evening and my heavy military jacket.

When we finish, I dry her off and then carry her back to the bed. Her eyes are already fluttering closed as I tuck her under the covers. Her breathing is even and steady. I'm about to turn and leave when her voice reaches out to me, sounding more vulnerable than I've heard before.

"Will you stay with me?"

I don't hesitate. I turn back to her and climb into the bed, gathering her tight to my chest. She sighs and relaxes against me, sliding her hand under my arm and over my waist, clinging as she falls asleep. Though I am furious with her, I won't deprive her of the basic human contact she craves. Taran so rarely reaches out for the things she needs, for me, that I'm loath to deny her. She can hate me in the morning, when she discovers exactly how small her world has shrunk. When she finds out the fate of her ex-husband.

I hold her for almost an hour, watching her face in the flickering light of a lantern. I will never get tired of looking at her. Her beauty is deceptive and easily overlooked, but the expressive mobility of each emotion as it flits across her delicate features lights her up. Creates an unmistakable energy and beauty that ripples out from her and ensnares the people around her. Her kindness, drive and determination cap her fragile beauty, giving her a strength that legions will follow.

But first, they must follow me. And my wife must fall into line with my way of thinking before I'll allow her to interact with the people of this city. She's far too persuasive, too ingenious to be allowed loose until I know that she'll fall in with my way of thinking.

I touch her brow with my fingertips, feeling the smooth, resilient skin. Then I press a light kiss in the same spot before sliding from the bed. She continues to sleep soundly, oblivious that I've left her. I stretch my arms over my head, testing sore muscles. Then I pull on a pair of jeans and a shirt. I leave the bedroom, but not the apartment. I won't likely be ready to leave my wife's side for quite a while. Trust has been lost and I'm not willing to subject myself to the wrenching feeling each time I find her gone. If she has to spend the rest of her life shadowing my footsteps, then so be it.

I'm standing in my kitchen, eating a tomato and cucumber sandwich when someone knocks on the door. I open it to find a tired looking Stryker on the other side.

"Cruz sent me to report, he's tied up on the rebuild. Got another one of those?" Stryker nods toward the half-eaten sandwich I'm holding and pushes past me, heading toward the kitchen.

He picks up the half cucumber I left on the counter and takes a bite, then tears a chunk off the bread and stuffs it into his full mouth. I don't admonish his serious lack of manners. He looks as rough as I feel. His blond grey hair lays in matted tangles down his neck and his thick beard is streaked with dirt. He probably hasn't eaten since our botched dinner party and working the wall is a consuming job, especially during times of high security.

"So report," I grunt and wave him toward the table where the lavish dinner spread has disappeared, leaving the surface bare.

Stryker grabs a tomato and another chunk of bread before following me and dropping his big frame into a chair. It creaks underneath him. He's about as big as I am. All of my military elite are big men. Powerful symbols of the Authority that rules our city.

He chews for a minute before speaking. When he does, his words are grim and to the point. "I've been supervising the wall since the explosion. The sound attracted Primitives from far and wide. We were attacked on all sides, but most heavily at the explosion site. We had over a hundred of 'em attempt the wall. We took every single one out. None made it inside the city." He swallows half the tomato in one bite, juice soaking into his beard. "Cruz is still on the wall rebuild. Thinks it'll take weeks for us to get a decent barrier back up and months before it reaches the same height and strength as its predecessor."

I grunt my acknowledgment, not surprised. The original wall took years to build and when I took over as the New Tucson Sanctuary's Warlord I had sections of it strengthened and rebuilt, the effort a massive undertaking. The wall goes up over 90 feet at its strongest point and is topped by razor wire and sharp metal posts that jut out toward the desert. It's mostly made up of failing infrastructure, concrete, buildings, roads, cars. Whatever's most likely to withstand the test of time.

"The rebels?" I ask shortly.

He nods and finishes his tomato before speaking again. "Cruz put Boss on roundup duty. He's gathered about fifty known rebels and has a team out searching for more. We'll start interrogating the detainees in the morning."

Alder Bossman is a young and hungry soldier, always ready for the next big job. I rarely give him big jobs, believing that his eagerness might also be his downfall. A man who doesn't expect death doesn't know to watch for it. And Bossman's youthful arrogance can too easily lead to his death. He is the right man for this job though. He takes his responsibilities seriously and doesn't fail when given a task. He will round up every known person involved in the rebellion and send them to processing and then interrogation. He doesn't fuck up. No one in my elite military team fucks up. The consequences are devastating and final.

"Who did we arrest in the desert?" I lean back and cross my arms over my chest. "Looked like Outsiders from the brief glimpse I got, but more organized. They were already engaged when I arrived. Seemed to be holding their own."

"Mercenaries from what I can tell." Stryker finishes up

his meal and wipes his palms across his thighs, dusting off the crumbs.

"Mercenaries," I repeat. It seems like an outdated concept, but I suppose it makes sense. The next logical step for an Outsider is to seek people similar to themselves. Men that don't fit into society, don't affiliate with a Sanctuary. Wild, untamed, unprincipled. Coming together to create their own kind of lawless roving band. In a way, I can relate to them. If duty didn't ride my every decision, I might be inclined to walk away from Sanctuary. Become an Outsider.

"How many?" I demand.

"Six in custody, four killed. I was told there were nearly fifty dead Primitives at the site."

Good odds. They must be skilled fighters to make it out of such a heavy Primitive attack with six men. My guys arrived after most of the Primitives had already been taken out. We helped clean up the few stragglers.

"Anything else?" I ask Stryker. So far I'm happy with the report.

He shakes his head, but then hesitates before saying, "How's the wife?"

I narrow my eyes at him, trying to judge his interest.

He lifts a conciliatory hand. "Heard she made it back to the city, but you called for Doc Bishop. Just want to know how she's doing."

I grunt. "Fine. A few scrapes."

He nods knowingly. "That wall must be a bitch to climb over. Never done it myself. No point, got my wall guard to do it for me. Doesn't look like a pleasant prospect though."

I snort my agreement. The truth is, I've never attempted to climb the wall either. Why would I? But the fact that my tiny, agile wife has done it dozens of times fills me with pride. Her endurance and determination to succeed is unequaled. Though she'll not be doing it again.

Stryker's gaze is sharp on my face. "If you don't mind my asking, why did you never marry before, Commander? Man of your age and position should have an heir, should be working on his fifth or sixth child."

I'm not surprised by the question. Stryker is about the only person that can get away with asking me personal questions. I've learned to value his counsel; his advice is usually as good as clean water. Men my age are almost always married. Whether happy or not, it doesn't matter. In order to flourish, our society must reproduce. As Warlord I'd have my choice of any woman either already living in Sanctuary or coming in as a refugee.

I'd never been interested though. Sanctuary itself has become my constant companion, the yoke of my existence. With the city as my burden I haven't taken the time to consider female companionship. And the few women that might've piqued my interest didn't hold it for long.

"You calling me old, Stryker?" I deflect the question. "Why did you never remarry after San Antonio?"

His gaze drills into me and I feel almost uncomfortable under the intense censure I see there. "I'm no bigamist, Commander."

I frown, trying to follow his logic. "How do you figure?"

"My wife is still alive. She's out there somewhere. Won't desecrate what we had by remarrying."

I sit motionless for a moment, absorbing the deep trauma that seems to have shaped Stryker's life. I don't get close to people, don't listen to their individual stories because I can't do my job effectively with their voices in my head. Yet here I sit, Stryker across from me, asking for his story. I know it's Taran's doing. She's changing me. Making me more receptive to the plights of others.

"Your wife, she was bitten?" I ask, encouraging him to speak of it. Styker's story isn't uncommon and he was forthcoming with the information after he made it to our Sanctuary. He was taken in because he had a lot to offer as a good soldier, a good defender of the city.

"Yes," he confirms. "Changed right before my eyes, while I was busy cutting down the bastards that'd done it. I watched as her eyes turned wild and her hands turned inward, curving into claws. You know what it's like to watch someone you love become a fucking demon, Commander?"

I didn't, but I'd come so close that his story chills me. Every word drives home how close I'd come to losing Taran. "Tell me."

His eyes darken in pain and he hits the table with his fist, almost subconsciously. "Turned in less than a minute. My beautiful Abrielle became unrecognizable. First thing she did was turn around and join the attack. Tried to kill me. I cut them all down except her. It wasn't easy, hacking away at them without hurting the woman that used to be my wife, but I'm skilled, I managed. I killed them all until there was only the two of us left. But there was no logic left in her brain. She kept attacking, kept launching herself right at me. I tried to appeal to whatever was left inside, tried to reach her human side. Get her to stop."

"Nothing worked," I finish for him.

"No." His voice, his eyes are haunted and now I can see the grief etched into his face.

"She attacked herself," I say, knowing what she would've done next. Primitive's are predictable in their behaviour.

He nods absently, his gaze cloudy, turned toward the

past. "When she couldn't get to me, she turned on herself. Tore the flesh off her face. I could see her skull through the bloody trenches she'd burrowed."

"You didn't kill her."

"No," he confirms, then falls silent, not speaking again.

Now that I have Taran I understand completely. I might not have gotten it before, but now I do. After today, nothing in this world would induce me to kill my wife. Not even the Death Kiss. If she were to turn, I'd lock her up, keep her living a half-life. I'd give her what she needs to survive as a Primitive, maybe selling what's left of my soul in the process. Then, when she was ready to go, ready to meet the final death, I would join her.

I wait, giving Stryker time to collect himself. After several minutes have passed I say, "Dismissed."

He nods, the harsh lines of his face softening. He wants this conversation over as much as I do. We've both learned something about the other tonight. I've confirmed why Stryker hesitates before each kill. He's searching the faces of every Primitive, looking for his lost wife. And he's learned something from me. I love my wife as deeply as he loved his. She's become my single vulnerably.

He places one hand on the table and rises to his full height, waiting for his orders.

"Secure the wall, eliminate any remaining Primitives. If it's quiet at 06:00 then you can go home to bed. Tell Jorje to continue wall supervision until the same time. He can find someone good to relieve him. If Boss is done in the slums he can take over. I'll be at HQ in the morning, interrogating the prisoners."

He nods his understanding and turns to leave but pauses halfway to the door. "Commander."

I don't speak, and he doesn't seem to expect an answer

from me. He continues, "I should've killed her." He runs a hand over his head and then through his beard. A nervous habit. "My wife. It would've been a mercy. Instead I left her to whatever horrors those creatures are subjected to after they turn. My biggest regret."

He leaves without another word.

SIX

XAVIER

Everything hurts.

I'm laying on the floor of a cell in Sanctuary's military headquarters. I'd tried to stay standing, then sitting. Tried to preserve my dignity for when the boss comes to see me. As the hours passed, so did any drive I had to maintain a dignified front. Eventually I slumped to the floor in a heap and then slid into my back, the most comfortable position I could manage with ribs still bruised and broken from the beating Fuentes had given me.

Despite my grim predicament my thoughts linger on one thing; Taran. What happened to Taran?

The last I saw of her was when I shoved her into one of the mercenary's cars. Then I was attacked from behind, taken down to the ground and nearly bitten. It took all my strength to save myself. Somehow, I got the upper hand, twisting until I was on top, straddling the Primitive trying to kill me. Reaching for the rifle that I had dropped in the dirt, I slammed it under the zombie's jaw and pulled the trigger. As his head exploded I thanked fuck that the weapon landed so conveniently close.

I didn't have much time to think about it though. Another Primitive launched at me, having successfully eviscerated its previous victim, one of the mercenaries. I crawled underneath the vehicle and out the other side, leaving the Primitive to slam itself into the side of the car while I ran through the scrub brush trying to get away.

I didn't make it far before I was detained. Only this time it was one of Fuentes' men, Jorje Cruz, sitting in his vehicle staring me down. I turned on my heel and ran in the other direction, only to come face to face with another Primitive. I didn't have enough time to protect myself, thought I was gonna die in that moment. Didn't though. Cruz was hot on my heels, following close behind me in his gutted, repainted Honda Civic. He hit the Primitive, throwing it up on the hood and then driving over it. I ducked as the car swerved to miss me, spraying dirt everywhere.

Jorje Cruz pulled himself up into the window frame. "Get the fuck in, Gunther, or I'll run you over next. Leave your weapon in the dirt, hands behind your head."

I didn't have a choice. I'd been arrested by Cruz on the spot. Told him I could fight, could help him take out any threats we encountered. He'd looked at me coldly and cuffed me to a bar he'd installed on his dashboard. Then he proceeded to kill more Primitives as we'd made our way back to the main clearing. He didn't say a word. Just did his job. I must admit, the man was impressive. His face was set in stone, a never changing expression as he shot the head off every Primitive we passed.

After we arrived at the mercenary camp I searched every face and every dead body, leaning as far out the window as I could while still cuffed to the interior, looking for my wife. Not my wife. My ex-wife. I wasn't given an opportunity to look thoroughly though. I was kept in the vehicle and monitored by a guard. The soldiers knew who they had; realized they'd managed to take the rebel leader into custody.

No one answered my questions after arriving back in the city. For all I know, Taran could be lying in the desert dead, her flesh being eaten away by whatever predator happens upon her.

Regret pierces me. Taran didn't deserve any of this. She's a pawn. She's always been a pawn; from the moment I took one look at her fourteen-year-old defiance and made her my wife. She was a youthful, charismatic dreamer that I used for my own ends to further the rebel cause. As the years passed, my admiration for her grew, but so did the distance between us. She's independent, idealistic, headstrong. I'm a realist, I don't suffer fools and I'm not a patient man. I didn't have the patience to woo a young woman realizing her potential and growing into herself, an incredible and principled young woman. It wasn't until I lost her, when she fell into Fuentes' hands, that I realized how much I love her.

Now I don't know if she's alive or dead. And no amount of shouting at my guards will give me the answers I want. I know, I've been trying for hours.

A door slams somewhere in the building and I hear footsteps approach. I ignore them. A dozen soldiers have come and gone, looking at the rebel leader behind bars. Watching me at my lowest point, not saying a word. I comfort myself by believing that I'm a martyr for the cause. But that soft voice in the back of my mind, the one that sounds like Taran, tells me otherwise.

A metal door slams shut and sharp voices reach my ears. I ignore them. They're nothing to me. Not unless they're either deciding my fate or telling me what happened to my wife. My ex-wife.

I look over as two guards walk past. "Hey, I want to talk to your Warlord," I call to them.

They ignore me and continue past, leaving the cell area. They've been ignoring me since they locked me up. I would've thought Fuentes or one of his minion's would want to interrogate me right away. It makes good sense from a war perspective, interrogate the prisoner while they're low, exhausted and beaten up. They should also be finding out if I have another attack planned. In short, they should be torturing me for information. But it would seem no one wants to touch me without the Warlord's approval and, as far as I know, Fuentes isn't even in the building.

This is what makes me anxious. Did something happen to Taran? Is that why her husband is missing? Is he distracted by his wife?

Pain slices through me at the thought of him marrying Taran. I didn't want to give her up, but I knew eventually it would happen. Figured she would fall in love and move on from me. Didn't figure it would happen this way. Part of me has always held onto the hope that I could make it work with Taran. But the years passed us by, each new one bringing in a new set of problems I had to deal with. There was never any time for us. My fault. She deserved better than me. She deserves better than Fuentes. My time is limited now. Diogo and his men will torture me for information and then have me publicly executed.

Before that happens, I will find a way to atone. To make up for my many shortcomings. Give Taran the life she always deserved. A family to love.

I fall asleep, thoughts of Taran haunting my dreams. I'm not sure how much time passes, but when I wake it's with the certain knowledge that I'm not alone. I've spent most of my life being hunted by the Authority. I can smell military a mile off.

I struggle into a sitting position, pulling myself back until I'm leaning against the brick wall of the prison. Diogo is sitting in the centre of my cell on a metal chair he must've brought it in while I was sleeping. I'm a little embarrassed that my enemy managed to get so close while I was vulnerable. But my exhausted body is trumping the hyperawareness that has become a part of my daily life.

"Fuentes," I greet him, attempting to swallow my hostility so I'm more likely to get an answer to my next question. It sticks in my throat for a second. I'm afraid to hear the answer, but I can't live without it. "Is Taran... is she?"

His dark eyes turn even darker, becoming chips of ice as he spears me with his lethal gaze. "She is none of your business." His tone suggests that I might live longer if I never speak of her again. Of course, I was never one to take the easy path.

His use of present tense and the fact that he hasn't killed me yet for taking her outside the wall tells me she's still alive. I pull a leg up painfully and rest my arm over the knee. "What happened to her, is she hurt?"

He just stares at me, refusing to give anything away. No anger, no revenge, nothing. His face is set in stone. After a moment of silence, he says, "You will tell me if there are any other rebel plots to take out the wall, or any other part of the city. I give you this one chance to speak."

I blink in surprise and then force myself to readjust my thinking. Every thought had been for Taran, none spared for the fate of the rebellion I'd spent so long nurturing. Completely unlike me to think of a single person over the cause that has taken up my entire life. Of course Fuentes would be focused on the security of his city.

In a rare moment of humbleness, perhaps brought on by the beating he gave me a few weeks ago and my current incarceration, I admire him. It doesn't matter that his city was brought low or that I stole his wife and took her from Sanctuary. He is first and foremost the Warlord. Brutal, cold, efficient. He won't let me get under his skin.

"No."

"No?" he repeats.

"I'm not saying a word until you give me something. I want to know how Taran is. Better yet, I want to see her." I'm courting death by asking to see his wife, but I have nothing to lose. I'm going to die. Before that happens, I need to talk to Taran. The only indication of his displeasure is the barely perceptible tightening of the grooves next to his mouth.

He stares at me for a moment, maybe thinking about his response. Then he stands, picks up his chair and leaves the cell, not speaking again.

"The prisoner is yours." I say, stopping by Jorje's office. He sits back in his chair and stares at me. "I want any and all information on the rebellion. You have my permission to take whatever steps are necessary to get the information. Don't kill him yet."

I don't wait for an answer. I don't need to. Jorje will do his job, he'll get what he can out of Gunther. Before I leave though, he calls out to me.

"We got someone in lockup you should know about." I turn back to him and raise a brow in question. "Picked her up as a known rebel and you have her flagged in the paperwork as a friend to Mrs. Fuentes. Name's Emery Bailer."

I nod and consider him for a moment. I'm eager to get back to Taran. I've vowed not to go anywhere without her, yet in her weakened state I wasn't able to bring her with me. I placed a guard in the apartment and another on the outside of our door. I didn't want to pull resources from my security team, but Taran's safety is more important.

"Where is she being held?" I ask.

"I had her segregated from the other female prisoners

and put her in interrogation room three when you came in. Figured you'd want to talk to her."

I grunt my acknowledgment. As usual, Jorje is correct in his assumption. He may not approve of Taran, or of my taking a known rebel as a wife, but he'll do his duty to his dying breath.

"I want any information you get out of Gunther right away." I turn and leave his office, heading for the interrogation rooms.

Emery Bailer sits in a chair, her hands cuffed to the table in front of her, her back straight and her eyes on the door. Despite the undoubtedly uncomfortable position, she looks as steadfast and resolute as the last time I saw her. When she recognizes me her expression becomes worried. Her eyes dart behind me, searching for Taran. I take the seat across from her. I'm reminded of Taran's interrogation. Of leaning over to take her hands in mine and threatening her.

I wonder how this interrogation will go, how Emery will respond. She'll have to be careful with her words, and, depending on her answers, I may be able to help her. For Taran's sake. But first and foremost, I need answers. We are not on the same side, we have different agendas, and my role as Warlord has to come above her friendship with my wife. She's high up in the rebellion and I'm the Authority.

Still, I feel protective toward her, an extension of my feelings for Taran toward the woman that took her into her home and cared for her like family. "Are you alright, Ms. Bailer?" I ask her.

She narrows her eyes, perhaps trying to divine my thoughts from the simple question. Then she sighs and shifts in her chair. "I'm worried about Taran," she says, looking at me sharply for a reaction.

I don't give her any. Instead, I say, "I need information on the explosion. Were you part of the plot to bring the wall down?"

A flash of fear shows in her eyes, giving her a haunted look. Then it's gone, and she sits in silence refusing to answer. Is she afraid of the consequences should she be found guilty of being implicit in the rebel plot? Or is something else frightening her?

"The explosion was extremely effective, Ms. Bailer. It'll take months to get enough of the wall back up to keep the Primitives out."

Again, the flash of fear, and, if I'm not mistaken, regret. Fuck. She must've been involved somehow. Not something I want to hear. I want to find a way to get Taran's friend out of police custody, or, if that fails, a lighter sentence. But it's starting to look like she's guilty.

"W-was anyone hurt?" she asks tentatively, allowing the regret from her eyes to leak into her voice.

She was definitely involved.

"Tell me about the bombing," I say softly, keeping the accusation from my voice.

She flinches at the word 'bombing,' then lifts her eyes to mine. There are tears in them. "It wasn't supposed to happen this way. I was told that you were keeping Taran prisoner, that she was extremely unhappy and had nearly killed herself trying to escape from the Tower. You refused to let her come home and I couldn't visit."

Though I keep my face wiped of expression, anger rushes through me at the lies being spread about my wife. Though I have placed restrictions on her movements, she is not my prisoner. I will do anything to ensure her happiness. I don't tell Emery this. I don't have to explain myself or my relationship. Instead, I say, "Tell me what happened."

She nods and shrugs her face into her shoulder, wiping a tear on her sleeve. She composes herself before speaking. "I was told that we had the opportunity to get Taran back, that she wanted to come back into the fold. It was a dangerous plan that involved taking Taran over the wall to meet with some people that could protect her. I wasn't privy to the entire plan. By the time I'd started voicing my doubts it was too late."

"Too late for what?"

"The plan was already in action. A woman, a rebel with more extreme tendencies than most of the rest of us, was on her way to the wall with a bag full of explosives. Directly after the explosion, news reached us that the men were heading into the foothills to meet with... with... Taran." She avoids saying Gunther's name, not knowing that I'm well aware of who took my wife.

"You're wrong," I say coldly.

Her brow wrinkles in confusion. "Wrong?"

"There is something you could've done. You could've come to the Authority with your story. You could have prevented that explosion."

"I didn't know it was a bomb meant to blow up the wall! I was told it was just a small distraction, so we could get Taran out of the Tower and out of the city."

"What kind of distraction do you think is going to be good enough to take my attention away from my wife?" I ask, allowing her to hear my impatience with her willful naivety. "It wouldn't take anything less than a full bomb and the shattering of our main defense against the Primitives to swerve my attention from Taran."

She shudders and drops her eyes, her shoulders slumping under the weight of her complicity.

"One of my men was killed by a horde in the desert.

Ripped apart limb from limb and then shot to save him the misery of turning. He was killed defending the city from the Primitives attracted by the explosion." She lets out a sob that shakes her thin frame. "Two people have been reported missing. I was told that they were last seen near the western wall, prior to the explosion."

She gasps and lifts tear-filled eyes to me. "Wall guard?" she asks.

"Civilians."

I turn away from her and leave the room, the sound of her sobs following me.

I hadn't expected to wake up alone. Though I tell myself that Diogo is an important man and he has an important job to do, especially in the wake of the explosion, I'm still disappointed. I roll out of bed, groaning in pain as sore muscles stretch. I test my ankle as I stand up, using the bedframe for balance. It's still tender but I can walk without too much pain. I limp to the washroom where I brush my teeth and then sit at my desk and run a brush through the tangles of my hair. I smile wanly at the wild fluff I've made of my hair, then I look at myself. Really look at the dullness of my eyes, the paleness of my features, the dark rings under my eyes.

The smile drifts from my lips as I take in the last twenty-four hours; the elite dinner party, the explosion, the desert, the attack. Dead people everywhere, Primitives and humans. A lump forms in my throat and I shudder, dropping the hairbrush back on the desk. I change into a pair of long pants made of soft material and a shirt with a high collar. All good quality. Only the best for the Warlord's wife.

I fluff my hair over my bandage and open the door,

catching the attention of a soldier on the other side. I stand for a moment staring at him, not sure what to say or do. Finally, I whisper, "I'm sorry."

I'm not sure why I'm apologizing. I didn't startle him, I didn't ask for him to be here. But something about the cool assessing look he's giving me forces the words from my lips. I'm uncomfortable under his scrutiny.

"What's your name?" I ask, strengthening my voice and standing straighter. "I assume you're the new guard."

"Yes, I'm Garrett's replacement," he says, his eyes moving off me to stare at the wall. Waves of chill accusation hit me. Does he blame me for Garrett's death? Maybe he should. Maybe I should've realized the explosion was a distraction and that we'd be ambushed. Maybe there was more I could've done for Garett. He'd been my guard, but also a friend. He was a good man.

But Garrett's death doesn't change our current situation. If he really is replacing Garrett then we'll be spending a lot of time together.

"Your name?" I prod him, trying to sound more like a Warlord's wife.

"Grayson Truss, ma'am."

Though he looks anything but welcoming I decide to proceed as I would with anyone assigned to work with me. "Nice to meet you, Grayson." His shoulders stiffen when I use his given name. "I'm absolutely starving. I think I'll grab something to eat. You hungry?"

I don't wait for an answer. I turn my back on him and limp toward the kitchen. As I reach into the cupboard, looking over the canned fruit, I glance over my shoulder confirming that he followed me in. A scowl gives his already fierce features a truly frightening look. I shudder but continue to act as though our meeting doesn't faze me.

"You okay with pears?" I ask, frowning at him as though this is the most important question of the day. "We appear to be out of the peaches."

His terrifying expression melts for just a moment as he readjusts his viewpoint. I wonder if he was expecting hostility from me? What has he heard of me? Definitely that I'm a rebel. Did he assume that would make me difficult? I smile to myself. I like to consider myself pretty easy to get along with. When there's a disagreement, I tend to show my feelings in actions.

"I'm fine, ma'am."

"Oh good, I didn't know where I was going to get a can of peaches at this time of night," I say, purposely misunderstanding his meaning.

I make a fuss out of opening the can and splitting the pears into two bowls. He makes a sound as though to reject my offering, but I shove the bowl into his hands, pick mine up off the counter and head toward the door leading to the roof.

"I'll be upstairs," I tell him. "I'd rather be alone right now, but I understand if that's not an option."

Sure enough, he follows me up. My guess is that he has orders not to let me out of his sight. Maybe for my protection, or maybe because Diogo doesn't trust me. I try to tell myself it's probably a combination of both. I stand right next to the ledge of the rooftop, gazing out at the dark city, wondering where my husband is. The wall? The police station?

When will he come home? And what mood will he bring with him? The easy comradery we shared is gone.

I lift my fork and eat the pears, forcing the tears back as I wait for him.

NINE

DIOGO

Exhaustion beats at me, seeping through every part of me. I've spent the night with my soldiers, checking on the wall rebuild and sitting in on interrogations. The work is endless in the wake of an attack that could bring our city down if not dealt with properly. By the time I return home, I'm satisfied that we won't fall if I take a few hours for myself.

The need to set eyes on my wife has been riding me strong throughout every interaction. I almost wished I'd brought her with me, but she needed the calm and rest only our home can provide.

I do a quick search of the apartment on my return, but don't find her or her guard. I take the stairs up to the rooftop three at a time, throwing the door open when I reach the top. Though I don't immediately see her, I'm relieved to find her guard.

"Truss," I snap, still searching for her sleight figure. "Report."

He jerks his chin toward the greenhouse. "She woke up an hour ago, had something to eat and went to work in the shed."

I absorb the words, some of the tension releasing form my shoulders. She's in the greenhouse. She hasn't disappeared on me again. My men are too skilled to let her slip away from them. That's how I know Garrett had done his job. The only way he would've allowed himself to be separated from her was through death. Still, I'm anxious to lay eyes on her, reassure myself that she hasn't been harmed.

"Fall back to the main door," I tell him and walk away, leaving him to follow my order.

I find Taran by the back wall of the greenhouse, on top of a stepladder, peering into the bird's nest. I'm about to speak, but before I do, she twists and glances over her shoulder. The look on her face stops me short, steals my breath and makes my heart pound in a way no battle can possibly do.

The smile that lights up her face is radiant. It steals every exhausted shadow from her lovely features and makes her more arresting than ever. She lifts a finger to her lips in a hauntingly beautiful motion and then beckons me closer. Helpless in her thrall I walk on silent feet to the nest. As I approach, she reaches for me excitedly, taking hold of my arm, curving her hand around me, and drawing me in. A feeling of home rushes over me as my wife voluntarily, eagerly, touches me. I've known, almost from before meeting her, that Taran was the one for me. But this moment, her touch, our silent connection despite the events of the past days, has convinced me that I will do anything to protect this fragile feeling blooming between us.

I stand just slightly below her, the two steps on the ladder giving her a slight advantage. "Babies," she breathes, pointing into the nest.

As if on cue, I hear the tiny flutters from within the straw and mud bird house. The miniscule cheeps indicating life from within. There are four baby birds, freshly hatched. Probably sometime last night while we were out in the desert. The mother wren has left them, likely seeking food so she can, in turn, feed her babies.

"They're so ugly," Taran giggles, turning shining eyes toward me.

I laugh, the sound rough after a long sleepless night. I wasn't expecting to share such a perfect moment of peace with my wife. Not after the events of last evening. Not after the arrests and interrogations of my night. The feeling is such a relief that I forget my anger, forget the gulf that has built between Taran and me, and I slide my arm around her waist. She leans against my side and we watch together as the hungry little beasts cheap helplessly and open their mouths for sustenance.

She turns her face towards me at the same time as I reach for her head, sliding my fingers into her silky red hair. Her eyes slide shut and a smile curves her lips. I tug her face to mine and take her mouth in a kiss meant to be gentle. About two seconds later gentle intentions go out the window as Taran deepens the kiss, turning on the ladder to press her breasts to my chest. The feel of her soft body pressed full length against mine is intoxicating, chasing away the lingering effects of exhaustion. I wrap my arm around her hips and drag her closer into the cradle of my body.

She gasps as she slides from the ladder into my embrace. Holding her lips a few inches from mine she says in a breathless voice, "I enjoyed being taller than the Warlord."

I chuckle against her mouth. "Your ego has always been taller than mine, Desert Wren."

She glares in fake anger. "That's because I'm better at pretty much everything than you!"

"Not everything." I squeeze her hard until she's gasping and wriggling in my arms. "I'm stronger than you."

Her eyes flash and I can see seriousness replacing our playful banter. "Stronger isn't better, Diogo. You think that strength equals survival, but you're wrong. People need so much more than a strong leader, strong army, strong defences."

"You're simplifying my words, Taran. If I thought the only things humans needed was strength then I wouldn't have chosen you to be my wife." She growls her annoyance at that, pricked by my reference to her diminutive size. "Humans also require intelligence, speed and the ability to reproduce." I know I'm poking at her philosophies but arguing with my wife is one of my secret joys.

She smacks her palm into my shoulder. "Trust you to ruin a perfectly pleasant morning with your Warlord bull-shit. Put me down, I want to go inside!"

While I anchor her firmly against me with an arm around her waist, I take a handful of her hair and force her face to mine, my lips hovering over hers, her intoxicating scent of wild freedom beating at my senses. She's stiff in my arms, angry at the turn our meeting has gone, but I can feel the heat from her. Feel the rapid beat of her heart against my chest. She wants me as much as I want her.

"I will never let you go, Taran. Will never put you down. You belong to me forever."

I take her mouth hungrily, sweeping away any resistance with my tongue, teeth and lips. When she tries to jerk away, probably to continue our argument, I turn her face back to mine and deepen our kiss until she's forced to concentrate on taking gasping breaths every time I allow her room breathe. I explore her mouth as though it's the first time, memorizing her again and again, feeling the moment that I nearly lost her. That moment gives a desperate edge to my sensual attack.

Almost as if she feels my switch from punishing kiss to devoted exploration, she wraps her arms around my neck and clings to me, returning the pressure of my kiss with equal fervor. I slide my hand from her waist to her thigh, hoisting her up, encouraging her to wrap her legs around me. She clings to me as I push her back against the ladder, placing her ass on one of the rungs so I can reach between us.

I grip the collar of her shirt. My shirt, I note with amusement. It fills me with pleasure that she has chosen something of mine to sit next to her skin, despite having many new outfits to choose from. As I release the buttons, my fingers brush against the bandage on her neck. She jerks back, her hand automatically coming up. Her face crumples for just a moment before she can smooth her expression. I catch the moment of pain though and it cools my lust like nothing else can.

Moving the collar of her shirt to the side, I inspect the bandage, making sure that it's still firmly in place. The sight of the tape against her beautiful skin erases what was left of my ardor. Not that I mind fucking my wife while she's inca-pacitated, far from it. But never in pain. Not unless it's the delicious kind of pain that only I can inflict on her.

As if sensing my reluctance, she shrugs my hand away and burrows closer into my chest, kissing the edge of my jaw. "Diogo, I want you," she says breathlessly.

The pressure of those soft lips against my unshaven skin and her beautiful voice begging for more, sends a cascade of pleasure through my body. I crush her to me, careful not to grip her neck as I take her hair in my hand once more. I tip her face up to mine and stare hard into those stormy intelligent grey eyes.

"No, Taran," I admonish her. "Not until you've healed."

Emotion flickers behind her eyes as she tries to decide if she should push me to get her own way. This is one of the things I love about her. The sharp intelligence that weighs her decisions. She won't fight a losing battle, but she might try to find a way around it. I cut her thinking off before she can make a decision.

"If you persist, then I will be forced to wait until you're healed, spank you until your ass is on fire then fuck you."

She tilts her head to the side, thinking, a mischievous look in her eyes. "I might like that."

"I promise you won't." I kiss her hard on the lips and then step back, lifting her off the ladder and placing her on her feet.

She leans to the side, favouring one over the other.

"How is your ankle?"

"Getting better," she says.

I grunt my doubt and slide an arm around her waist. "Lean against me."

She does as I say and I walk with her to the door. A flutter of wings has us looking back. The mother wren flies down from the hole in the roof to her nest. She glares reproachfully at us as her babies begin to cheep louder, begging for food.

Taran grins. "Sorry mama bird. Next time we'll take our activities away from the nest."

I usher my wife out the door and into the dry desert morning. We stand for a moment looking out over the city. Taran stares toward the wall explosion. She can't see anything from this vantage point, but the sorrow etching her face speaks to her feelings. She looks up at me, her eyes cloudy.

"I didn't know this would happen. Any of it."

"I know," I tell her. "People died as a result of the bombing. Both inside Sanctuary and out. You value life too highly to have ever agreed to such a plan."

A sad expression still creases her features, but her voice is relieved when she says, "Thank you for believing me."

I hold her close for a few minutes, content in our unity. I have my wife by my side, full of life and healing from her injuries. Which is enough, for now.

"Let's go to bed, I need some sleep before my next shift."

"I'm not sleepy," she complains with an edge of teasing to her voice.

"Then lay with me while I sleep."

I don't give her a choice. I lead her down the stairs to our bed.

TEN

TARAN

The sound of raised voices wakes me up. I sit, pushing the wild tangles of hair out of my face. I'm groggy, unable to focus for a minute. I must've been far more tired than I thought when Diogo brought me downstairs. He helped me take my clothes off, then laid me down and kissed his way down and then up my body. Not in a sexual way, though I was plenty turned on by the time he finished. His exploration was sensual, worshipping. He kissed each healing scrape, kissed my hipbones and ribs, the arch of my feet, the tip of my nose and the top of my head. Then he turned me onto my side and pressed his lips against the birdcage tattoo on my back.

A possessive reminder of my place in his life? I don't know, and in the moment, I didn't care. I felt safe and satisfied, drifting to sleep in my husband's arms.

"Pardon my disrespect Warlord, but this is important. I must insist." The emphatic voice, raised in agitation, draws me from my comfortable bed.

I pull on my clothes, neatly folded and placed on the

bench in front of my desk. I'm about to run a brush through my hair when I hear Diogo raise his voice in anger. I'm shocked. I don't think I've ever heard him shout, and I've given him plenty of reason. I drop the hairbrush and rush to the door, fearful that there'll soon be a bloodbath on the other side if I don't intervene.

Doctor Bishop is sitting at the table, his face smooth and serene as the last time I saw him. Diogo, on the other hand, looks ready to kill the older man. His dark eyes are narrowed in fury and his rigid posture with a hand resting on his knife suggests my fears were not unfounded. I step between the two men and smile at the doctor.

"Bishop, so good of you to stop by," I exclaim. "Are you here to examine me again?"

He nods, shifting his gaze from Diogo to me. A smile creases his face and he reaches for my hand. I give it to him. "Among other things," he says enigmatically. "Let's have a look then."

He stands and presses me into the chair, then pulls another up. He lifts the bandage with clinical precision and looks at the wound. I wince as he presses his fingers to the edge of the bite wound.

Diogo leans in. "It looks bad," he grunts.

I roll my eyes while the doctor rebandages it. "She tried to rip out my throat. I didn't expect it to look good."

"It's healing quickly," Bishop interrupts. "Has a nice pink look to the edges of the wound. It'll scar though." He looks up at Diogo, concern etching his rugged features.

"Do something about it then," Diogo says bluntly.

Bishop raises an eyebrow before leaning forward in his chair to lift my leg and examine the ankle. "There's nothing to do about it. We aren't equipped for cosmetic surgery, and even if we were, I'm not a cosmetic surgeon. She'll just have to live with the scar. Now, Taran, how does this feel."

"Very little pain," I murmur as he presses his fingers against my ankle bone.

"Good, the swelling has gone down. You should be walking around just fine by tomorrow."

Before I can thank him, Diogo interrupts. "What do we need in order to remove the scar? I'll send some men to Sacramento Sanctuary for supplies."

The doctor sighs and sits back in his chair giving Diogo a stern look. "I appreciate your concern, son, but she's going to scar. Period. By the time your men get back with a doctor and supplies, the wound will be well healed. The skin would have to be cut away and re-grafted."

"I don't want that!" I say appalled.

Bishop pats my knee. "You don't need it. You'll heal up beautifully, with a few little marks as a reminder to run faster next time."

I start laughing but stop abruptly when Diogo's fist slams into the table next to us. He points at Bishop. "You know what'll happen if anyone sees those marks on her. They'll know she was bitten."

Bishop nods soberly. "Yes, they will."

I shrug, not really understanding the gravity of the conversation. "I'll wear collared shirts and scarves. What's the big deal?"

I expect Diogo to explain it, since he's the one that's so desperate to get rid of my new scar. But Bishop is the one to speak. "You weren't around during those first years after the Great Fall. Neither of you." He rubs a hand over his short dark grey hair, his expression serious. "We didn't know much about Primitives, except they were spreading fast and civilization was toppling at an alarming rate. As a species we can be reactive instead of thoughtful. Instead of studying the creatures, we just killed them. We killed anyone bitten by them, killed animals that we thought might be incubators for the virus." He falls silent for a moment, his grave eyes searching mine, reminding me once again how close to death I came, either by turning or by Diogo's knife. "But more disturbing than that, was when people started turning on people. All a person had to do was point a finger at a neighbor and they would be attacked and killed before anyone stopped to find out the truth of the accusation."

"That's terrible!" I exclaim, shuddering at the brutality of humans.

"Terrible, but not uncommon," Diogo says. "It's what humans do because they have a strong survival instinct. They destroy the weak, the competition. You can't survive in these times without it getting a little messy."

"Yes," Bishop agrees. "I saw the hysteria with my own eyes as people turned on each other, not waiting for proof of the Turn. Something as simple as a dog bite, or the common cold, would be called Necrotitis Primevil and the so-called carrier executed without a trial. Sadly, we haven't come much farther in the years since. We still react with a certain level of instinctive fear to the Death Kiss."

"Which is why I won't allow Taran to become the subject of public hysteria," Diogo growls, his hand curving protectively over my shoulder.

"I understand, son, but surgery isn't the answer," Bishop says patiently. "I can help though. If you allow me to work with Taran, find out why she survived – "

"I will not allow her to become the subject of your tests," Diogo snaps. "Don't ask me again."

"Your concern for your wife is commendable, Commander, but she is one person. Compare that to the fate of our civilization. To millions of people."

"I don't care about millions of people right now. I only care about one." Diogo's voice is so hard, so lethal, it sends a chill right through me.

I finally realize what they'd been discussing so heatedly when I came in. Doctor Bishop wants to find out why I didn't turn. Come to think of it, now that I've had sleep and perspective, I want to know too. Was this an isolated incident? And was it the Primitive who was special, or me?

"We should retrieve her body," I murmur, interrupting their argument.

Bishop smiles brightly. "Yes, we definitely should. It's been just over a day." He looks up at Diogo expectantly. "There's probably still enough of her out there that I can do a proper autopsy."

Animals tend to stay away from Primitives, alive or dead. Something about the rotting flesh turns them away from eating the remains. Still, the hot desert sun and the wind will do a number on her.

"If I deliver the body to you, then you will stop discussing Taran, she's off limits."

Bishop nods his understanding, but I notice he's careful not to verbally agree. I think Diogo notices too, but he just grunts and turns away, reaching for his military jacket. "I have to go into the station." His gaze captures mine. "You'll be okay? Grayson is on the other side of the door. He'll come in after Bishop leaves."

"I'll be fine," I tell him. He nods and leaves.

An awkward silence sits between the doctor and myself. We're both thinking the same thing, but I'm the first to speak. "I think you should examine me."

"Good girl." He grins and pats my leg. "This is more important than your husband can comprehend."

"No," I say admonishing him. "Diogo comprehends the implications just fine. What he objects to is my involvement. If there's something I've come to understand about him, it's that I will always be his priority. Over Sanctuary, over himself, over the whole damn world."

The doctor thinks about my words for a moment. "And this way of thinking suits you? I would've thought the Desert Wren would object."

I laugh. "You are a wily one Doctor, trying to appeal to my rebel side."

Despite his manipulation, I think about his question. Does Diogo's insane level of protectiveness suit me? It drives me crazy. I can't leave without him or an escort. He curtails almost all of my activities and allows me to do only those things he deems safe. Yet, we haven't had enough time to settle into a suitable routine. I think it's possible to work around Diogo's protective instincts.

"It neither suits me nor sits particularly well. It just is," I explain. "Diogo is the Warlord of Sanctuary. His job is to protect, his entire life geared toward that one thing. It's only natural that it should extend to me. And I won't argue that there's something appealing about his feelings toward me. The constant knowledge that I'm taken care of is not something I've ever really experienced. But will it make me happy in the long term? I don't know."

"You are very wise for someone so young," Bishop says, his voice gentle.

I shrug. "Is anyone in this world really young? We've all seen horrors. The difference in age is only chronological, our souls have all aged from the Great Fall."

"Too cynical, my dear."

"But true, nonetheless."

"Yes, true." He smiles sadly, before wiping the expression from his face and going to his pleasant fallback. "Now, we'll need to discuss a plan. How do we get you tested without your husband murdering me?"

ELEVEN

DIOGO

Gunther is laying on his back, almost in the same position I found him in earlier when I visited. He's in a lot worse shape now though. Which is saying something considering he narrowly survived a Primitive attack. His blond hair and short beard are caked with blood. A few of his fingers are swollen, having been broken and then reset. His clothes are torn and I can see blood seeping through several spots in the material.

"Come to see your handiwork?"

I'm surprised by the strength in his voice, and when I look at this face, the light of purpose brightening his eyes. He's been beaten severely, but he hasn't been broken yet.

"I know you gave the order to have me tortured."

I turn away and sit on a nearby chair, leaning forward to place my arms across my knees. I have the advantage of being physically above him, but I'm maintaining a deliberately relaxed pose. Almost a friendly pose. He didn't say a word to my men, despite hours of torture. He spoke once, to ask to speak to Taran.

"I don't deny it," I tell him. "Nothing happens in these walls that I haven't given my express consent for."

He snorts, and then winces and lifts a hand to gingerly hold his ribs. His fingers are too stiff and swollen to be much help so he presses the heel of his hand against the injury instead. He gives me a wry look. "All of this over a woman."

I smile coolly. "If it appeases you to think that I had you beaten out of jealousy, then you may believe that."

"Ah, insulting my intelligence. Do you think I'm stupid, that I'll spill all of my secrets in a war of words?"

"You took my wife over the wall and into a desert filled with Primitives. My opinion of your intelligence doesn't have much lower to sink." I allow a deadly chill to infiltrate my voice.

He inhales a deep breath and then winces again, letting out a painful rattling cough. It takes him a few minutes to recover and when he does he looks exhausted and winded. He runs a hand through his hair and when it gets caught in the strands dried together with his own blood, he lifts the hand, hovering it over his head for a moment, before bringing it back down to rest on the floor.

Gunther has been my enemy for decades, since I've known of his existence, known we were on opposing sides. I've alternately despised him, admired him and used him to my own ends. I have never seen him brought so low as he is in this moment. If it weren't for his role in Taran's injuries, I might be able to bring myself to feel compassion. To end his misery now, quickly. But he signed his own death warrant the moment he touched my wife.

His blue eyes seek mine and his face twists. "I'm sorry."

I stare at him perplexed.

"I'm sorry I took her over the wall. It was my fault she

was attacked. I misjudged the Primitive response to the explosion. Misjudged the distance out into the desert. I played it stupid." His gaze fixes on the ceiling above him and he frowns as if trying to decipher his own actions. "Everything I do is with careful planning, the end goal a shining point in the distance that I will eventually reach with every step forward. And somehow, I lost sight of the people around me, the reason for my mission. I lost sight of Taran. I wasn't just the cause of her injuries in the desert, I hurt her years ago."

Anger beats at me, telling me to go to him, to finish him. It doesn't matter that it won't be a fair fight. It was never going to be a fair fight. "Do you think this confession will move me?"

He laughs, the sound bitter and humourless. "Do you think this confession is about you?"

His intelligence strikes me again. He knows what to say and when to say it. He's a master manipulator. "Give me the information I require, tell me of all rebel plots and I will make your death a quick one."

He turns his head to look at me, piercing me with eyes bright with manic energy. "Let me talk to Taran and I'll give you everything."

"Names, places, plans?" I demand.

He hesitates for a split second, then seems to look into the eyes of his own death and says, "Everything. I want to talk to my wife."

I stand and walk to his side, removing my knife. I point it down, the tip less than an inch from his eye. "My wife."

He stares defiantly back.

"I will enjoy your execution."

"Good," he replies with satisfaction. "Me too."

I step back, frowning. Why would be look forward to his own execution?

Then understanding dawns. He's expecting a public spectacle, something the citizens of Sanctuary will talk about with zeal. When he's executed, news of his death will spread across the city like fire. Taran will find out and know I ordered it. She won't forgive me. No matter how much distance had grown between her and her former lover, she will see his execution for what it is, a major blow to the rebellion and the loss of a dear friend.

With those few words he changes everything.

"She doesn't know you made it out of the desert," I tell him, kneeling at his side.

"What are you talking about?" he demands, trying to lift himself up onto an elbow.

"You died in the desert, Xavier Gunther." I grip the back of his head and lift him toward me.

He cries out in pain as his ribs move. His eyes grow wide with the implication of my words. "No, you can't do this!" he cries. "You need me. You need my information."

"I doubt it." I place my knife against the edge of his ribcage, beneath his heart. "There are others within the rebellion that'll give me information. What I need now is for you to die a quiet death."

"Don't do this," he begs. "Taran will never forgive you if she finds out."

I lean closer, putting pressure on the knife. "The difference between you and me," I tell him. "Is that I care enough about her to keep the painful secrets. To put her happiness and well-being above all else, including the truth."

"Please," he begs, wrapping his broken fingers uselessly around my wrist, trying to stop the execution rushing at him much faster than he'd anticipated.

"Consider this atonement for every hurt you've ever caused her."

"But – "

I slam the knife sharply up into his ribs, burying the blade in his heart. Two beats later his wide eyes dim and, as I release him, his body collapses to the floor.

TWELVE

TARAN

"Blood."

My heart leaps into my throat as Diogo strides through the door. He ignores me and continues through to the bedroom, peeling his clothes off as he goes. Grayson tacitly leaves while I trail after Diogo, picking up the clothes off the ground and holding them gingerly, not wanting to touch the blood. I heave a sigh of relief when his magnificent, uninjured body is revealed. Not his blood.

And as always, my next thought it to wonder whose blood has soaked his uniform this time. What poor soul has died so that Sanctuary might go on?

I won't ask him though. We've had this argument, and I don't want the answer. Can't handle the answer. The death surrounding Diogo's job builds a wall between us. I understand the necessity of what he does but I still think he can do so much more to prevent individual persecution. I follow him wordlessly as he goes into the bathroom and turns the shower on. He stands, waiting for the water to heat, his magnificent body bare to me. His arms are crossed over his chest, his legs spread.

He finally lifts his eyes to mine, allowing me to read him. I see nothing. Not pain, not elation, just the constant death that is a part of his world.

"Diogo," I whisper, stepping closer to him.

He narrows his eyes. "Don't." Then he gets into the shower, shutting me out.

I debate with myself. He clearly wants space. He always wants space after a hard day. No, I'm lying to myself. He wants space after he's had to kill someone. He doesn't want to drag me into that side of his job, but he needs to know that I'm here, even if he just needs a hug after he's had to do something he'd rather not.

I drop his pile of clothes on the floor and step up to the shower and into his view. He turns his head from the spray, water droplets dripping from his hair roughened chin. He wipes a hand over his face and then pins me with his stare, the irises so dark they blend with his pupils. I reach for the buttons on my shirt. His shirt, because the collar is high enough to cover most of my bandage, and my long hair does the rest. His eyes follow the path of my fingers as I nimbly work my way through each button, parting the fabric and allowing the shirt to fall at my feet. I reach for my pants curling my fingers in the soft fabric.

"Taran." He says my name like a warning.

"Diogo," I say back, but use his name in a soft caress. I push my pants down my legs, dragging my shoes and socks off too. I straighten, standing before him completely naked except for a bandage and the hair swirling around my shoulders.

"If you get in here with me I'm going to want to fuck you, and you haven't healed enough yet."

My opinion of how much I've healed is definitely different from his. I'd climb him like a wall and jump that hard cock in a heartbeat if he let me. But even in his currently aroused state I know he won't fuck me as long as he thinks I need more time to heal.

I shrug. "Then don't fuck me, Diogo."

I step into the shower, right into the spray and up to him. He stiffens, his body growing rigid next to mine. I look up at him through the hot water pouring over my head and face, blinking the droplets from my eyes. His face is stony, set in grim lines. The careful control he always exhibits is there, but I sense how close to the edge he is. I'd expected a reaction from him, but he doesn't so much as blink as he stares down at me with those cool, bottomless eyes.

I didn't think this through. What if he rejects me? I'm about to mutter an apology, step back and flee when he reaches out, grabs my arm and drags me against him.

The move is so swift, so sudden that I stumble and grab his arms to steady myself, my fingers curling around his biceps. Water pours down my back and over my head. I try to wiggle out of the direct path of the spray, but his hands tighten around me, holding me still, holding me against him.

My heart hammers, part in fear and part arousal. Diogo is always an intense man, with forceful thoughts and actions. But when he looks at me like this, holds me like this, I feel like we're strangers. Like he's purposely distancing himself from everyone, including me and he doesn't know how to build a bridge.

I stand on my toes, leaning into him so my face it out of the water and I say, "Let me in."

His hands tighten around my waist and he drags me up his body until I'm on my toes. His hold is tight but not hurtful and I know my Diogo is still in there, despite the death he's seen. His cock is between us, standing up, pressed against my belly.

"You shouldn't be here, Taran. I need time alone."

"Why?" I demand. Despite his words, I can feel the desperation in his hold. He wants me close but doesn't know how to accept me in his darkest moment, into his darkest thoughts and memories.

"I'm a monster." The words are soft, his voice emotionless. "I kill without remorse. I'm no better than a Primitive."

I reach up and wrap my arms around his neck, tugging his head down until we're inches apart. He allows the move, his hands falling to my waist, holding me physically while still holding back emotionally. The distance is still there, but he's trying to breach it, accepting my comfort, giving me some of his thoughts.

"If you were a remorseless monster then it wouldn't bother you to kill. But I've seen your eyes when you come home, you're haunted by what you've done."

He drags a hand from my waist to my hip and then up my back, caressing each curve until he's touching my face, drawing his thumb over my lips and across my cheek. I shiver at his soft, sensual touch that contrasts with the hot water pounding against my back.

"You're beautiful to think that, but you're wrong." He pushes his fingers into the wet strands of my hair and grips it tight. "I'm not haunted by the kill, I'm haunted by my reaction to the kill."

It takes a moment for his words to sink in and then I realize what he means. He enjoys hunting, enjoys the kill.

I don't want to hear anymore. I'd rather live with my version of Diogo than the terrifying truth. A truth that I saw out in the desert when I watched him kill that Primitive. When he stood over me, her dead body at my side. I try to pull his face down to mine, try to smash his words under a kiss, but he stops me, his grip on my hair becoming painful as he forces me still.

"I enjoy killing, Taran," he tells me in a low growl his eyes lighting with a dark fever. "At first, as a child, I despised it. Hated when my father would put yet another Primitive in front of me, forcing me to stab them in the heart then take their heads off. Then, as I grew, as the kills came closer and closer together, I grew numb. Distanced myself from an action I thought necessary. And now... now, when too much time passes between kills, I grow restless. I crave the blood."

My heart is hammering so hard I'm becoming dizzy. I shouldn't have followed him in here. This isn't the Diogo I've spent weeks getting to know. This is the Warlord who took me because he wanted me. He once called me his perfect conscience and I begin to understand why. I'm the woman who worries over each death, who forces him to think about every kill. The responsibility suddenly feels crushing.

"I want out," I tell him.

"No. You wanted to be close to me, to see the monster. Well, here he is." His lips take mine in a rough kiss. A kiss meant to punish me for daring to try to understand, to soothe the monster who loves to kill. There is no desperation or even passion in this kiss. He breaks me down, forces my submission as he steals my breath, hard hands pinning me against an even harder body.

Tears gather in my eyes and any passion I might have felt flees. I'm lost in the haze of his darkness and cruelty. Memories of the Warlord I grew up fearing and hating flood through me. I'm disgusted, frightened, confused. I want my husband back and this man gone. But most of all, I want to rewind the last ten minutes. I want to go to the roof while he showers away his demons. I don't want to know what I know about him. Because loving a man like this is a terrifying responsibility.

As if reading my thoughts, he drops his head into the crook of my neck, kissing the now soaked bandage over the bite mark. "I'm sorry," he murmurs against me.

His apology snaps me back into the moment and chases away the chill his words and kiss caused. I can feel his sincerity. And though it takes a moment for me to calm my rapidly beating heart I still want to reward him for apologizing, for not carrying his punishing kiss further. I wrap both of my arms around his neck. "Don't do it again, and you have nothing to be sorry about, my darling."

He leans back, searching my face, a sad smile curving his lips. "You've never called me that before."

I shrug self-consciously, my gaze sliding away from him. "It's old-fashioned."

He taps my chin, forcing me to look up again. "From now on you will always call me 'my darling.'"

I laugh. "You can't demand an endearment, they need to come naturally."

He stares at me with a raised brow, all former darkness lost from his countenance.

I laugh again, knowing what he's waiting for. He squeezes my ribs, tickling me until I relent. "Fine! Endearments need to come natural, *my darling*."

"Then make them natural." He kisses the tip of my nose and gives me a satisfied look. He steps back, breaking the tight hold he had on me, that we had on each other. "Come, let's go to bed."

"You always want to go to bed when I'm ready to get up," I grumble, stepping out of the shower and submitting to a vigorous toweling.

"And you need more sleep than you think, my wife." He dries himself off and then walks me into the bedroom and pushes me down onto the bed.

He crawls in behind me and tucks me against his side, forcing my head to his chest. I snuggle in, finding a comfy spot. I close my eyes. As annoying as his assumption is, he's right. I do seem to need more sleep. As though I've spent years living in an adrenaline-fuelled rush, heading from one mission to the next, never getting quite enough sleep.

I'm about to drift into oblivion when his voice rouses me.

"You know I would do anything for you."

I frown and tip my head to look at his face. His expression is unreadable.

"I know," I say quietly. "What is this about?"

"Even the things you won't thank me for, might even come to despise me for." He persists, ignoring my question.

I nod solemnly. "I know, Diogo."

"We went into the desert to retrieve the Primitive that attacked you." His eyes are on me, serious and dark.

"You found her?"

"Yes. We brought her back for Doc Bishop to examine." There's something else. Something I'm missing. His eyes are roving my features searching for reaction, but I don't understand for what. "We found another body out there."

Suddenly my throat tightens, and I know what he's going to say. "Don't," I whisper, trying to roll away from him, put distance between me and the truth of what he's about to say.

"Xavier Gunther."

THIRTEEN

TARAN

I curl into myself, hiding from Diogo and the rest of the world. My only companion is a stoic bodyguard who watches expressionlessly as I struggle to cope with the death of a man that meant both nothing and everything to me. I spend my days on the roof, sitting listlessly under my birds, watching over them as they grow. Watching as my tomato plant grows. Maybe I'm trying to convince myself that fragile life is still possible. That we creatures bound to the Earth can still flourish in a hostile world.

There are so many different ways to grieve for those that pass. There is the moment of realizing someone isn't there anymore. This happens more often in the beginning, until you've trained yourself to recognize that they're gone. Then there's the ongoing constant tug at your soul as you try to live a life without the other person whose presence made an impact. And finally, there are those sharp stabbing moments when a memory assails you and you feel almost crippled by the pain of remembrance. This will dull out to something more bearable eventually. Where a smile is the dominant emotion over tears. But there will still be tears, there will always be tears. Because the living remember the dead, and we grieve.

I didn't love my ex-husband. Not in the way a wife should love her husband. No, we weren't that to each other. He was my friend. A constant in my life since coming to Sanctuary. He existed within my orbit for twelve years. He took me in when I needed a home. Even if he used me for his own private war, he was still all I knew. A mentor, a brother, a father figure. His death feels like cutting a planet loose from my private solar system. After losing my parents and my brother, then my sister, and finally my grandparents, I can't cope with the idea of losing Xavier, so I just don't.

I drift through time holding myself back from the grief, only feeling it when I'm forced to. When a memory surfaces unbidden to torture me. To remind me that I lost a friend. That yet another person lost a son, a brother, a lover.

We live in an unfair world where our fragile lives mean nothing to the greater forces. We die too easily, we're taken too soon. Too violently, too suddenly. And though he didn't have my heart, Xavier broke it nonetheless. By being one more person to abandon the world I'm left behind to live in.

FOURTEEN

DIOGO

For days my wife is a listless shell of herself. The only things that she's willing to show any interest in is her tomato plant and the baby birds. She doesn't eat more than a few bites of food and wouldn't have bothered showering if I hadn't stripped the clothes from her body and cleaned her myself. In fact, she's done very little without my direct intervention except wander to the roof and stare out at the city or watch the baby birds.

I've been more than patient, allowing her to grieve for a man that was nothing to her. Nothing to us. I tell myself she's not grieving for him, but for his memory. She's grieving for the first person in Sanctuary to take her in and show her any kind of family. For the few things that they shared in common and for the rebellion.

The fact of her grief eats me up with jealousy. I want to kill him all over again. Only this time I would erase all memory of him. I thought I'd be giving her closure by telling her we found a body. Now I think that was a mistake. I should have told her that we didn't find him, that he escaped into the mountains during the attack. Left her behind to face the Primitives and an uncertain reunion with her husband.

I stand behind her, watching her as she sits on the warm stones of the rooftop terrace. She digs her fingers into the dirt of her tomato plant but stares into the distance, her thoughts far away. Far away from me.

Is she grieving a dead love? Did I murder a man she actually loves? He didn't deserve her regard in life and he certainly doesn't deserve it in death. He was a deeply flawed man with only a few redeeming qualities that made him a good leader for a half-assed rebellion. He'd been useful to me for a while, keeping the rebels occupied. Now he is more useful to me dead, and, under different circumstances, his death wouldn't cause me a single moment's thought. Now, however, I'm forced to think of how my action might affect my wife. I can't force her to stop loving someone, can't control her emotions.

She hasn't said she loves me. She's had plenty of opportunity, yet the words haven't passed her lips. Is it because she's spent all these years pining after another? I search myself, looking for an ounce of remorse for the death of Xavier Gunther. Even if just to appease my wife. I find nothing. Given the chance, I would kill him over again. Same time, same method.

Gunther was correct when he stated that his execution would create a martyr. And martyrs can be very dangerous. Can serve to stir dangerous public sentiment if allowed to flourish. Taking Gunther out of the picture quickly and quietly was the only answer. I won't pretend that his death doesn't also serve the purpose of removing him from my wife's affections. I'm not a saint, and I will never be a martyr. I'm Sanctuary's Warlord. My love for Taran doesn't weaken me, doesn't change me. It gives me incentive to be even more vigilant than before.

My gaze drifts over her slim back, bent over her precious plant. She can have her grief. She can have her love for another man. But she won't be allowed to harm herself in the process. I step up to her and crouch at her back, hovering over her, casting a shadow on her and the plant. She doesn't react. Does she even know I'm here? I've been out here for the past half hour watching over her.

I lean forward and speak in her ear. "Enough, Taran."

She doesn't move, doesn't react in any way, telling me she knew I was there but was ignoring me. I shove the fury down. Anger is not a reaction that will help in this instance. It would be an indulgence on my part to take my wife in hand and shake the self-pity from her. She needs time with her grief and I've given her that. Now her time is up.

I reach over her shoulder and take her hand in mine, pulling it from the dirt, then I take hold of her chin and force her head sideways until she's facing me. Her grey eyes are cloudy, faraway, unfocused. She's looking at me, but she's not seeing me. I pinch the skin between my thumb and fingers until I know it must hurt. She blinks, her gaze focusing on me. A frown creases her forehead, drawing her eyebrows toward each other. She tries to move back but I hold her in place.

"Enough, Taran," I repeat.

This time I see a flare of acknowledgment in her eyes, then a flash of resentment. She jerks her chin to the side and looks back down at her plant. "I don't know what you mean," she mumbles.

"You do." I take hold of her shoulders and turn her until she's facing me. Then I indulge the jealous anger, just a little, digging my fingers into her flesh and giving her a small shake. "You're allowing the death of one man to affect your health. I can't allow this behaviour to continue."

Her eyes narrow at me and she shrugs out of my hold, scooting backward, putting a few feet of distance between us. "How do you think the death of one man should affect me? Should I just get over it, get over him? Should I move on and be happy with my life?"

"Yes," I growl impatiently, longing to grab her again, but holding back, trying to give her the space she apparently needs. "He was nothing to you in life, Taran. He should be nothing to you in death. Shouldn't affect you to this extent."

"You don't know me!" she snaps furiously, going to her knees and slapping a hand against her chest. "You didn't know what I was like before you took me and you haven't bothered to get to know me now. You just boss me around, giving me rules and expecting me to be content. I can't live this way!"

I stare at her, surprised at the outburst. "Where is this coming from?" I try to moderate my tone into something reasonable. "You've spent weeks patiently trying to get me to know you and understand your point of view, and now you tell me I can't possibly understand you? I don't believe it."

She blinks, trying to get rid of tears, but fails when one escapes trailing down her cheek. "You're the Warlord. You don't care about us, about the rebellion. You don't care about what's happened now that both rebel leaders are gone. They needed us."

Relief floods me as I realize where her despondency is coming from. She might be upset over Gunther's death, but she isn't heartbroken. She's upset that the rebellion can no longer continue without the key players.

"They still have you," I tell her.

"They don't!" she yells, blinking hard, more tears falling down her cheeks. She swipes them impatiently with a dirty hand smearing soil across her face. "How can they have a woman who's locked up in a tower?"

I don't answer. I can't. There's nothing I can say that will calm her right now and still be the truth. She glares at me, her beautiful eyes, tilted at the corners, sparkling with moisture.

"You have no answer, do you?" she demands. "You know that the rebellion can't survive. Not now, not without... without... "

"You?" I ask softly.

She stares at me for a moment then lifts her chin and says, "Yes."

I say nothing. Just watch her as she struggles with herself, finally sitting back on her heels. She tucks a lock of hair impatiently behind her ear. She stares at the ground, tears still making wet paths down her face. After a few moments she finally collapses back onto her butt and pulls her knees up, hugging them. She still refuses to look at me.

"No... I don't know. The rebellion will go on without me, and without... without... him." She swallows hard, unable to say Gunther's name. I bite back the jealousy rising up to ruin this moment. This epiphany she's about to have. "But they were my family when I had no family. The rebellion took me in, cared for me, nourished me and encouraged me. Not just him, but all of them. They embraced me and I embraced them back. They are the people that sit on the fringes of this city, that scavenge to survive. They aren't elite, and too often, they're illegal. But none of that mattered. I belonged to them."

"And I took you away." I move closer. I don't touch her, but I want to be close in case she needs me. Even if I'm the one to cause most of her grief, I'll still be the one to catch her when she falls.

She nods emphatically. "I was important, I meant something. But here..." She drifts off, looking broken and lost.

"Here you are my wife," I remind her firmly.

"I don't want to be just a wife!" she snaps, swiping the tears away with a sleeve.

She's lashing out, trying to find a place for her grief. Despite my annoyance at her attitude, the way her sharp brain picks away at a problem she's creating in her head, I am happy to see her working her way out of the cloud of despair she buried herself in. Even if I must be the target.

"Your place with me is the most important thing in your life."

"Why?" she demands with a glare. "I don't cook your meals, I don't make your bed or ask you how your day was. All I am is the woman you fuck."

Her words are like a slap to the face, harsh and irrevocable. I lunge toward her, knocking her onto her back and caging her with my body. I know she's trying to throw off the unwanted grief invading her soul, but I can't help but take exception to the path her anger has wandered toward. I grab her flailing arms and pin them over her head, against the hot stone tiles. She gasps and arches her body against mine.

"Let me go!" she yells.

"You're pushing in a way you shouldn't, Taran."

"Fuck you!" she snarls recklessly. "The big, bad deadly Warlord is going to beat his wife? Fuck her into submission? Go ahead! That's all I'm good for now."

I check the urge to slam her against the stone rooftop until I've obliterated her words. Love is making me more dangerous than I'd ever imagined. Dangerous even to my wife. I close my eyes, trying to centre myself. Trying to remind myself that she's hurting inside. That she's lashing out in any way she can to get a reaction. To alleviate her pain.

Instead of hurting her, I drive the urge back, fist my hand in her hair and force her head up toward mine. "Do you want a fight?" I demand.

She glares at me, her light eyes flaring in fury. "Yes," she hisses.

I slam my lips over hers, knocking her back. I place my hand under her head before it hits the stone slab underneath her. She gasps into my mouth as I devour her. It takes her a few seconds to understand my attack. Once she does, once she recognizes it for the outlet that it is, she grips fistfuls of my shirt and drags me first toward her, and then pushes me away.

She fights me for supremacy, alternately trying to throw me away from her and then dragging me closer. Lust explodes through me, obliterating my good intentions. Her aggression clashes with mine, and my self-control slips. I tear her shirt from her body without a second thought, filling my hand with her small breast. She shrieks and then arches into me, encouraging my exploration.

She drags me down to her, wrapping her legs around my waist and clinging desperately. She grabs my hair and pulls, forcing my head sideways until she's able to sink her small teeth viciously into my ear. I growl aggressively at her rough handling, the adrenaline rushing hard through my system. I've never wanted to fuck my wife more than I do in this moment.

Apparently she's in the same mindset. She reaches between us, yanking on the button of my jeans until it pops open. She jerks the zipper down and reaches inside, filling her hand with my hot, ready flesh. Any thought of her injury leaves my head in this moment. The only thing I know is that my wife is laying underneath me, eager and ready to fuck.

I tear her pants away, the soft material ripping easily beneath my fists. Her flesh fills my hands, warm, soft, willing. Her wildly sweet and earthy scent fills my nostrils, driving me over the edge of sanity. There is no delicate wife, no more healing, no more grieving. Just Taran, the woman who has obsessed my every thought from before I even met her.

I drive into her, sparing only a second to note my relief that she is wet enough to take me. She screams her passion and fury, digging her nails into my shoulders and then dragging my shirt up, tearing a button in the process. I reach over my head, pulling the shirt from my body, giving her access. She sinks her sharp teeth into my pectoral muscle, just over my nipple, biting me with a vengeance that both hurts and exhilarates. My gentle wife is taking her anger out on me in the best possible way.

I grip the back of her head and force her face to my flesh, encouraging her terrible little bites, revelling in the pain because she is the one causing it. I would never allow any other person to do such a thing to me. Only Taran. Only my love. She can make me vulnerable, strike me low. And I will willingly allow her the opportunity.

As I surge into her body, over and over, driving through her tight, wet passage, I realize that I could die happily at her hand. If she were to hold a knife to my throat, whisper her love and slash me open, I would allow it. I would take it and revel in her power.

She bucks against my thrusts, throwing herself back at me, fighting me for dominance. She isn't just taking my lust, she's giving in equal measure, climbing toward her own orgasm. Her face is strained in concentration while her hands are buried in my flesh her nails drawing crescent moons.

I grip her face, forcing it back until her head touches the tiles beneath her. I hover over her, my lips inches over hers. "Come with me," I instruct her.

"Fuck," she gasps, her hips surging into mine, the heels of her feet digging into my ass as she desperately claws for the upper hand in our skirmish.

"Now, baby!" I snarl into her face and then swoop down to kiss her.

She has no choice but to accept my brutal kiss, the slam of my body into hers and the bruising grip of my hands on her flesh. Despite her bid for power, for dominance, I will never allow it. She will always take the submissive position. Behind me, beneath me. Protected.

The walls of her vagina tighten around me, holding me captive. Squeezing, milking. I surge deep within her, unable to hold back. "Now!" I yell, my lips touching hers, my voice swallowed by her mouth.

We come together, exploding in a height we've not previously reached before, her nails sinking deep into my arms, my cock buried as far into her body as it can get. I jerk back, pumping into her again, bathing her with my come. An image of her pregnant body blazing through my mind. Chained to me by flesh and blood. Not discontent as she is now because a child will fill her mind and her time.

Still caging her in my arms, I hold her as she relaxes beneath me. She releases her sharp grip and drops her hands. I regret the loss of connection right away. I don't care if she draws blood, I'll always want her hands on me any way I can get them.

"I'm sorry, Diogo," she whispers, touching her own cheek her voice awash in sorrow. "I've been terrible, I know I have. I don't know why I'm feeling this way."

I know what she's feeling and why, but I don't voice my thoughts. Instead I gather her against me, holding her tighter. "Talk to me, baby."

The words come in a rush now, like she's been holding onto them for days, trying to find the right way to express herself, express the grief and pain that's been haunting her for a lifetime.

"I feel useless. Like I'm settling into this life that I used to despise and disparage without a second thought or single complaint. Like my friends are dying and being arrested but I'm seduced by hot water, sleeping with... " She cuts herself off, glancing sideways at me guiltily.

"Sleeping with the enemy," I finish for her.

"Yes," she agrees softly, lifting her hand to trace my lips. "I'm sorry, Diogo. It sounds bad, but it's true. I used to stand for something. I was the Desert Wren, the woman that flouted authority and brought illegals into the city. Now what am I?"

"You are everything," I tell her.

She shakes her head. "I'm the wife of the Warlord. My power lies through you. I can't even leave our apartment without an escort."

I grip her chin and force her face to mine, chasing away her despair with a look. "You are my everything," I say again. "You are the future of Sanctuary, and that future needs protecting."

"I don't understand," she whispers, her voice catching. "How can I be the future of Sanctuary when I'm forced to abandon my people?"

I touch her head and run my knuckles over her cheek.

"You're young, Taran, you don't need to rush toward understanding. Accept your life as it unfolds, and understanding will come. You are more important than you can imagine."

"As your wife?" she says stubbornly.

"As my wife," I acknowledge. "And so much more."

FIFTEEN

TARAN

"No, Mrs. Fuentes."

I narrow my eyes at the man in front of me, Grayson, my bodyguard turned jailor. He's blocking the door I'm trying to exit through. "Why?" I demand, hands on hips, trying to bury my annoyance. I knew leaving the apartment wasn't going to fly, but I'm over being cooped up. "Am I a prisoner?"

He clears his throat and shifts, looking distinctly uncomfortable, which is a funny look on a guy his size and scariness. He actually reaches for his gun and rests his hand on top of it. Probably a habit when he feels threatened. I swallow a grin at the possibility that I'm making this huge military man deeply uncomfortable. It's only going to get worse.

"Did my husband tell you to block me from leaving our apartment?" I demand stepping closer into his space.

"Commander Fuentes gave orders that you can't leave without permission and an escort. I don't have any excursions outside the apartment cleared with him."

"Then," I say with an edge to my voice, "Get. His. Permission."

He shuffles back a step, probably so I won't accidentally touch him and risk loss of limb due to the angry and possessive Warlord. "The Commander doesn't like to be interrupted at work unless it's an emergency."

"Consider this an emergency then."

"What exactly is the emergency, Mrs. Fuentes?"

"I'm about to set this apartment on fire," I snap. "Does that work for an emergency?"

The edge of his lip twitches and I wonder if he's amused or annoyed. The stiffness in his shoulders seems to ease slightly, so I'd guess amused. "I'd have to stop you from setting a fire ma'am."

Damn it, this one is sharp. Next time I won't announce my arsonist intentions before I set the fire. I turn away from him and pace around the table, thinking. Then I stop in front of him again. "Grayson?"

"Mrs. Fuentes."

"I assume you have a way of contacting my husband in case of emergency?" There's no way Diogo would leave me alone if he didn't have a way to check in.

Grayson drops a hand to the radio on his belt. "I can call the Commander with this."

"Excellent." I give him a bright smile that immediately brings the stiffness back to his body. He gives me a suspicious look. For some reason he doesn't enjoy verbally sparring with me. "Did my husband say I need permission to use the radio?"

His Adam's apple bobs and his eyes widen as he realizes what I want. His brain is whirring for a way out, but there's none. Diogo wouldn't think to forbid me from using the radio to contact him. Still smiling I hold my hand out to Grayson.

Still desperately trying to think of a loophole where he can deny my request he slowly hands it over. "What do I need to do?" Without actually touching me he shows me what button to press when I'm ready to speak.

I hold it up to my mouth. "Commander Fuentes?"

Nothing happens for a minute and I begin to wonder if my message got through when his voice comes on, loud, clear and deeply concerned. "Taran? Where's Lieutenant Truss? Are you hurt?"

I wink at Grayson who's beginning to look a little green. "I'm not hurt, thank you for your concern. And your lieutenant is standing right here next to me."

A long pause, and then, "Why are you using his radio, Taran?" Impatience replaces the concern in his voice.

"Grayson very clearly told me that I need permission to leave our apartment. I'm attempting to get your permission."

"This is an emergency line, we'll talk about this later."

Apparently Diogo wants me to set a fire too. "If you don't grant permission immediately, there won't be a later to talk about. I will create an emergency that you'll have to respond to."

"Mrs. Fuentes, this isn't a private channel," Grayson whispers urgently. "You shouldn't be threatening the Commander."

Then Diogo's chuckle comes through on the radio and I grin my relief. "You will pay for that comment later, wife, and for torturing my man with your antics. Where do you want to go? I can meet you."

I sigh impatiently over his protectiveness. "I want to go see Doctor Bishop."

I really should've worded my request better. As soon as the Doctor's name leaves my mouth, Grayson seizes the radio while Diogo bursts through with. "What's happened, you said you were fine!"

"Are you hurt?" Grayson demands. I roll my eyes and wave a hand down my body showing him that I'm clearly not hurt. He sighs his relief and speaks into the radio, "She's in perfect condition, Commander."

"I'll be home in five minutes. Do not leave the apartment," Diogo's voice is harsh and rushed. I'm certain that he's already heading out the door.

I grab Grayson's hand and drag the radio back down to my face. I push Grayson's finger which pushes the button. "I'm bored, Diogo. I consider the doctor a friend and would like to go and visit him. There's absolutely nothing wrong with me except that I'm bored out of my mind. Stop over-reacting."

"I would be happy to have a visit from the lovely Mrs. Fuentes." Doctor Bishop's amused voice breaks into our conversation. I smile in delight and glance up at Grayson. He pushes the button for me.

"There, you see. Now you can grant me permission to leave and I'll head over for a visit."

"He can come visit you in the apartment," Diogo interrupts.

"No, Diogo," I say as patiently as I can. "I promise you, if I'm forced to spend another minute in this apartment you won't have a home to come home to. I want to go see the Doctor, wherever he is. Doctor Bishop?"

"At my office, dear."

"In his office, Diogo."

"I can hear just fine, Taran," he growls. "And so can all of my men, this is a public channel."

I grin at Grayson. "So I've been told."

A long pause, and then, "Very well. You have two hours. If you aren't home by the time I get there, you will not enjoy the consequences."

"Wonder where I've heard that before?" I release Grayson's radio and give the poor man some space.

The call is ended and I wait impatiently for Grayson to get us prepared to leave. He buckles a small arsenal onto his belt before waving me out the door. He insists on taking the lead, treating each corner as though a Primitive is going to jump out and attack us. A week ago his hyper-vigilance would've amused me. Now, I can only feel grateful.

I get a nasty jolt as we approach the car and Grayson holds the door open for me. "This was Garrett's car."

His eyes flash bleak fire for a moment and then he nods. "Yes, it belonged to him. Now it's been assigned to me. I was his roommate and closest friend so most of his property fell to me."

This makes sense. Garrett hadn't any family in the city and I've often thought that most of the military is the same, Outsiders ready for Sanctuary and orphans with size and brutal tendencies on their side. I slide into the passenger seat and he closes the door behind me.

As he drops into the passenger seat I say, "I'm sorry for what happened to Garrett. I considered him a friend."

Grayson sets his hands on the wheel, the dark skin of his knuckles shining white as he grips it. "He spoke highly of you too, Mrs. Fuentes. Said you had honesty and integrity. That you were good for our Warlord." He turns his head toward me, the accusation he's managed to hide over the last few days now shining bright again. "That's why I can't figure out what happened. If you really were his friend, as good a person as he thought, then why would you lead him to his death?"

I have no answer and I don't think Grayson wants one either. I wasn't responsible for Garrett's death, yet I was there and part of me wonders if I could've done more. Could've maybe reasoned with Xavier. I know better, and so did Garrett right before he died, but survivor's guilt is something we all live with in a society riddled by death. Without another word Grayson starts the car and pulls away from the Tower.

Doctor Bishop's office is located near the police station in Sanctuary's commercial sector. It looks like a small house that's been converted into an office. He greets us at the car, opening my door and reaching in to help me out. I smile at his old-fashioned manners, but they suit him.

"Come on inside, my dear, and don't mind the mess." His deep voice belies his pleasure in having some company and I'm happy I made the decision to come.

"I'll be out here." Grayson stations himself at the door, his rifle within easy reach and his hand resting on his sidearm.

I follow Bishop inside and am surprised to see a familiar face. "Dee!" I haven't seen her since the botched dinner party.

She lifts her head from where she was sitting at a desk writing something down. "Bishop told me you'd be coming, and um..." she glances sideways at a radio sitting next to her and shrugs. "We have it for emergencies. Those commandos are always getting themselves hurt."

"I didn't know you worked with the doctor."

"I have some medical training so I'm able to assist the doctor whenever he needs an extra set of hands. After my husband died, working here gave me something to do while my kids are in school."

Once again it strikes me how much I don't know about the elites. We have jobs and schools in the slums, but nothing as organized as what I'm seeing here. Definitely no doctor offices with helpful receptionists. I must talk to Diogo about this lack of medical resources in the other sectors of the city.

"If you'd like to step into the back with me." Bishop opens a door and waves me toward the interior.

I smile at Dee. "It was nice seeing you again."

"Oh, you too," she agrees enthusiastically. "Think about coming to our women's volunteer group. We'd love to have you speak."

At first I think to refuse, not wanting to be part of a group of over-privileged women talking about the bright shiny aspects of Sanctuary. But the more time I spend with elites, the more I see of their sectors, the more I'm convinced we have a real possibility of bridging the gaps in this city. Plus, meeting with the elite women will get me out of the apartment for a few hours and I wasn't kidding when I said I was going stir crazy being cooped up all the time. Diogo can't possibly object to my spending time with Dee, Milla and some of the other women.

"I'd like that," I tell her and then follow Bishop through to his back office.

"Have a seat right here," he instructs me, patting a medical bed.

I hop up on it, looking around to take in the small but homey office. There's a desk with some paperwork on top, the medical bed and some instruments and jars. He catches my eye and nods toward the back of the building.

"I have a small surgery and a make-shift morgue in the

back." He comes to stand next to me, reaching for the bandage on my neck. He peels it back gently and probes the healing wound. "If I need more space then there's a section of the police station that I can use as a hospital."

"Why would you need more room?" I ask.

"Multiple casualties," he says matter of fact.

"Oh." That makes sense but 'multiple casualties' isn't something I want to think about, especially because my husband would likely be in the line of fire if an emergency situation arose. "Does that happen often?"

He drops the bandage from my neck into a garbage can and steps back to look at me. "More than I like, but not as often as life under most Warlords. Even the food riots produced minimal casualties. Just broken bones and bumped heads." He pats my leg. "You won't need another bandage for this. Just keep it covered up with a scarf and let it heal naturally."

A scarf. The reminder is chilling. I can't let anyone see the wound yet. Maybe not ever. It finally hits me that the wound I sustained has life-altering consequences. Which reminds me of my real reason for coming to Bishop's office.

"Did you get a chance to have a look at the Primitive that attacked me?"

His gaze turns serious. "I did."

"And?" I ask, eager for news.

Bishop steps back and drops into the chair behind him, rubbing his knee absently. "She wasn't in good condition when she was brought in. Your husband and the elements did number on her, but I managed to get enough for a proper autopsy."

I shudder imagining Xavier out there in the desert, alone. Even though he'd died during the attack, I hate the idea that his body could've been disturbed. In life, he was such a handsome man. I can't imagine the vibrancy he had in life being drained from him, just a lifeless shell decomposing in the harsh desert. I force the gruesome image away.

"Did you find anything?"

He shakes his head. "I've seen my share of dead Primitives, even done some research on them. This one was no different from the others. Same blood type, same skin, same organs, same everything."

The Death Kiss alters humans right down to their blood type, creating a new type categorized as Type N for Necrotitis Primeval. Only Primitives or humans infected by the disease have Type N blood.

"What about her teeth, did you examine them?" I badly want to know why I didn't turn. "Could there have been something different about her bite?"

"Her teeth were typical for a Primitive. I'm sorry, Taran but I can't find a reason why you wouldn't have turned. Given her condition prior to her death I'd say she was an older Primitive, possibly as much as five years. That she had survived that long suggests she'd killed or bitten her fair share of prey. If she was an ineffective Primitive, she would've been killed off years earlier, either by her prey or by her own kind. It's my opinion that her bite is no different from every other Primitive."

Most Primitives don't live beyond a few years. Their total disregard for their own safety kills them quickly. While in pursuit of sustenance they will leap off buildings, in front of cars, into water where they quickly drown with no memory or ability to swim. If their bite wasn't so deadly, they probably would've died out years ago. I'd even heard a story once about a horde of Primitives leaping off a cliff while chasing a bird over the edge. The Death Kiss eradicates the thinking centers of the brain until there's nothing left but violent instinct.

"But if there wasn't something wrong with her…" I trail off trying to follow the path of logic. I touch the wound on my neck, my fingers drifting over the tiny ridges where her teeth burrowed into my skin.

"Then there's something right with you," Bishop confirms. He watches me carefully, then says, "Years ago, when you would've been just a child, there was a rumour circulating around the Sanctuaries of a woman who was immune to the bite."

I gasp, "Really? Who was she?"

He shrugs. "No one knows, the rumour died along with the hopes of an antidote. In all the years since the Great Fall no one has even come close to creating an anti-virus. Civilization has never seen anything as virulent and effective a disease as the Death Kiss. As far as we know, there are no known survivors. If you're bitten you either die or turn. No alternative."

"Until me," I murmur.

"Until you."

I straighten on the bed and give him a stern look. "The we'd better get to work and find out why I'm different."

He smiles and stands. "I was hoping you'd say that."

DIOGO

I'm trying to read over a report on the wall progress, but I find my mind drifting back to my wife over and over. I can't help but smile over the way she manipulated her outing to the doctor. Her feistiness is one of her best qualities and I can't seem to find it in me to squash it. Especially after days of watching her grow progressively more listless, obsessing over Gunther's death and the fate of the rebellion without her.

Finally, I give up on the report and drop it on my desk. I'll get Stryker to give me a verbal report when he comes in from wall duty. I'm about to pack up and head back to the apartment to meet Taran after her appointment with the doctor when I'm interrupted.

"Commander?" Boss sticks his head in the office. "You're wanted in interrogation."

I frown, straightening from my desk. "Whose request?"

"Uh, mine," he says sheepishly.

I raise an eyebrow, waiting for him to explain. I'm not wanted in any interrogation room unless I decide to be there myself.

"It's one of those Outsider prisoners, he's spent the week refusing to tell us anything beyond asking to be released. Now he wants to talk, only he's saying some strange things."

"I don't understand why this requires my personal attention, lieutenant," I say impatiently.

"He's been talking about your wife."

I leave the office so abruptly that Boss is forced to whirl around and run to catch up. "What exactly is he saying?"

"He's refusing to speak to anyone except you, Commander."

I grunt my acknowledgement and allow the lieutenant to show me to the interrogation room. The Outsider is chained to the table, his hands in front of him. He's worse for wear, his face and neck bruised, dried blood on his knuckles and under his nails. A full beard covers half his face and thick eyebrows are drawn low over sharp blue eyes. His stench hits me in a wave, and I make the decision to allow the prisoners picked up in the Primitive attack to bathe. When certain primary comforts, such as basic cleanliness, is taken away, it can often chip away at the morality of a prisoner, making them more likely to talk.

Given the attitude pouring off the mercenary, I would say he doesn't give a shit about the state of his personal hygiene. He's decided to talk for another reason. Before I can ask him for answers, he tells me.

"Been listening to the rumours gadding about this place." He snorts his derision. "Never come across such a lack of security in my life. Within a day I knew who was running this city. Two days I knew all the players. Three, I knew who the woman in the desert was." I growl a warning, but he ignores me. "Wife of the Warlord."

His eyes drift up my body, his gaze impersonal, uncaring. "Saw her leave the attack site at your side. Saw the way you took care of her."

"You're going to want to tread very carefully when speaking of my wife." I step closer to the table, pinning him with a stare. "I don't tolerate much when it comes to her."

He shrugs off my threat. "We're all the walking dead, Commander. It's just a matter of when and where. If my information can make life a little more bearable until death, then I'll speak my piece."

I drop into the chair opposite him. "Then speak. Tell me why your life is valuable to me."

"I recognised your wife out there in the desert. Something about the way she looks, a sort of familiarity."

"You've met my wife before?" I demand.

"No," he says firmly. "Not her."

"Then how do you know her?" I'm confused but there's something about this guy that draws me. I suspect he's telling the truth. He has motivation to lie, but my gut tells me he's not.

"I don't know your wife, your Desert Wren." He speaks her rebel name like he's familiar with the concept. I want to show him in no uncertain terms that he has no idea who my wife is. But I'm also deeply curious, needing to hear what he has to say. "I've met her sister."

"Impossible." I lean back in my chair and cross my arms over my chest, staring at him coldly. "Her sister is dead."

"That what your girl told you?" He leans back in his seat too, the chains on his wrists rattling. "She lied. Her sister is alive and well, or she was four years ago when I last saw her."

"Assuming I'm willing to believe that you aren't mistaken, where did you meet her? How did you get close enough to be sure in your assessment that she's Taran's sister?"

"She was my bounty, and I never forget a face," he says carelessly. "Her hair's a little darker than your girl's and she's taller. Maybe a little older, but definitely related. If not sisters, then cousins. Their faces are identical."

"Did you get a name?"

"Skye."

Fuck. I believe him. The details he's giving are too certain, too close to Taran's history to be wrong. Her name is the same too. It's too much of a coincidence that this woman isn't Taran's sister.

"How was she your bounty?" I demand.

"Was sent out to retrieve women of birthing age not affiliated with a Sanctuary and bring them in. She brought a good price. Young, pretty, feisty. The Warlord was eager to get his hands on that one, break that beautiful spirit. Rumour has it, she held out for months before he finally broke her down, integrated her into his harem."

I slam my fist down on the table, unable to hold my temper back. It could have just as easily been Taran at the mercy of a brutal Warlord.

Then the uncomfortable truth strikes me and I sit back down. Taran is at the mercy of a brutal Warlord. I don't know that Skye has it any better than Taran. I don't know anything about the girl and her Warlord. They could be happily married.

"What Sanctuary?" I demand.

He stares hard at me letting the silence hang between us. He held off, feeding me enough information that I would bite. Now he's withholding the last piece unless I bow to his demands. He's a smart one, this Outsider.

"You'll release me," he finally says.

"Done." I agree without hesitation. I'd expected this and it's an easy boon. Means nothing to me to turn an Outsider away from my city.

"I want my men released too."

"No." I can't have him rebuilding his army. They may be few in number, but they're filled with a brutal strength that could be a potential threat to the city.

He searches my face, as if trying to determine how far to push me. Then he shrugs. "Wasn't too fond of them anyway. I'll go it alone."

A true Outsider.

"I want my supplies back and a few new ones."

"You tell me where you sold Skye."

"Got nothing else I need or want," he tells me with a shrug.

"Fine, done. Now give me the Sanctuary."

"She's in Santa Fe." He rattles the cuffs again. "Now take these fucking things off. I need a shower and a meal and then I want the fuck out of here."

"Good." I sigh my relief as I breeze through the apartment door, with Grayson behind me. Diogo isn't waiting to tear a strip off me as I was halfway expecting. "He's not home yet."

Grayson clears his throat and nods toward the table, or more specifically the chair at the table with Diogo's jacket folded across the top, his Commander insignia facing up.

"Well, I didn't do anything wrong, so he shouldn't be upset with me," I argue with no one in particular.

"He said two hours, Mrs. Fuentes."

I turn around and glare at my bodyguard. I'm getting the distinct feeling that he doesn't care if Diogo punishes me for my relatively minor transgression. "He suggested two hours and I'm barely over."

"By an hour."

I narrow my eyes at him. "You were counting."

He shrugs and points to the door going up to the roof. There's no sign of my husband in the apartment so I'm also thinking he's on the roof. Still... I point to the main door and raise an eyebrow. Grayson snorts and shakes his head before leaving. I like to think I'm making inroads into the big guy's affections.

I run up the steps to the rooftop, eager to see my husband, despite his possible annoyance at my being late. When I push the door open, I see him standing next to the ledge, surveying his city. I join him, stepping up to his side and gazing out across Sanctuary. Diogo is looking toward the Southeast, toward the ruins of our old city. Only about half of Tucson was saved and rolled into New Tucson. The wall cuts off the other half of Old Tucson on the South-eastern part of the city. I've only been in the ruins a couple of times, when I was required to meet with refugees coming in from that direction. I try to stay away though, as easy as it is to hide among the dilapidated crumbling buildings it's also dangerous. Lots of places for Primitives and Outsiders to hide too.

"Hi." My voice is quiet, I feel almost shy around Diogo when he's not asserting his dominance. He's larger than life, both physically and mentally. I'd be lying if I didn't admit that I'm a little in awe of my intimidating husband.

"You're late."

I can tell by the tone of his voice that he isn't really angry. He knew where I was, had a bodyguard tailing my every move. I was perfectly safe every moment I was out of the apartment. I ignore his accusation and say, "I'm hungry."

He looks down at me, his dark eyes sparkling in the early evening sunlight. "I knew you would be."

"Then feed me," I say cheekily, wrapping my arm around his and leaning into him.

The look he gives me is intense, as always, devouring me in one glance. He takes in every inch of me, his eyes lingering on my neck where Bishop removed the bandage.

I reach up self-consciously and tug at the collar of my shirt. He takes my hand in his and pulls it away, then pushes the collar back and leans down to look at the wound.

"It's healing well," he observes.

"Bishop said I don't need a bandage anymore." I'm hoping the good news will deflect his obsessive need to keep me safe.

"I should've been there."

I sigh heavily and lean my head on his arm. "You don't need to watch over me constantly, Diogo. Bishop took excellent care of me, made sure I was completely comfortable and then fed me tea and cookies until I was ready to leave. Grayson stood guard over the clinic with I was inside. There was no reason for you to be there."

"No?" he asks, pulling my arm out in front of us and pushing up my sleeve. The tiny bruise left behind where the Doctor had pulled my blood glows like an accusing beacon.

I try to tug my arm away, but Diogo holds tight, running his thumb over the needle prick. "You went against my express orders, didn't you? He's experimenting on you to find out why you didn't turn."

I yank my arm more forcefully, pulling it from his grip. "You make it sound so sinister! All he did was take a little blood and give me an exam, which I might add, was long overdue. There are no decent doctors like him in the slums."

"Don't change the topic," Diogo says coolly. "We aren't talking about the lack of resources in your precious slums right now. We're discussing your blatant disobedience."

"Oh, come on." I step back and cross my arms over my chest in a defensive position. "You knew as soon as I said I was going to Bishop's office that we'd be looking into my possible immunity to the Death Kiss. Let's not pretend you're stupid."

He stares at me until I drop my eyes. Okay, maybe I didn't need to suggest he was being stupid. But still!

"I knew," he admits. "But knowing what you were up to and being able to do anything about it are different things."

"You could've told Grayson to stop me from leaving the apartment," I point out.

"And you would've done what if I'd tried to stop you?"

"Set a fire." I instantly admit my nefarious plan.

He grunts a laugh and replies, "I like my belongings."

"What belongings?' I ask poking him in the ribs. "This place is as empty as an abandoned town."

"You, baby, I like you. Don't go setting fires. I don't want you to get hurt."

How am I supposed to resist this man? A fierce Warlord one minute, and a simple husband the next, begging me not to do anything that might bring me harm. We haven't been married long, but already I know he's different from most men. He has a core of steel that dictates his actions. He believes that he doesn't understand morality, but he's wrong. The way he treats me is testament to his ability to care. I just need to get him to extend that beyond our insulated relationship.

"Diogo," I say his name in my most reasonable tone of voice. "You know that Bishop needs to run his experiments. If there's any possibility..." I trail off, not wanting to dare suggest such a thing.

"If there's any possibility of creating a vaccine," Diogo finishes for me.

"I know that the likelihood of creating a vaccine using my immunity to the Death Kiss is astronomical, but if there's even the glimmer of a chance we have to take it."

"I know," Diogo says quietly, his dark eyes searching mine.

"You do?" I'd expected more of an argument. His quiet agreement is taking the wind out of my sails.

"As much as I despise the idea of you being poked and experimented on, ultimately if a vaccine can be created, you'll be safer. The zombie that bit you was trying to tear your throat out. You would've died regardless of your immunity. They run on adrenaline. They're stronger, faster and driven by pure instinct. You won't be safe from the Primitives unless we eradicate them entirely."

My jaw drops at his logic. Despite knowing how obsessed he is with me, living with it firsthand for weeks, I'm still stunned by the depth of his need to protect me. It's an awe-inspiring prospect, being the object of such deep obsessive focus.

He takes my hand in his and pulls me away from the edge of the rooftop toward the greenhouse. "Come, let's get you fed."

I'm okay with the change in subject. Diogo's fascination with me, while flattering, can also be uncomfortable.

"In the greenhouse?" I ask curiously when I realize where he's leading me.

"Wherever I want to feed you is where you'll eat."

I smile at his highhandedness and follow him into the greenhouse. I gasp in delight when I see the surprise he's set up for me. He pushed the shelves of plants to the side and set up a small table with two chairs. Candles light the shelves, casting a lovely glow across the indoor garden. I'm grinning by the time I reach the table. I pick up a rose, set between our two plates, and press it to my nose, inhaling the delicious fragrance. I can count on one hand the amount of times I've had the opportunity to smell as rose.

"Wow, Diogo, this is..." I try to come up with the right word, "romantic."

He chuckles and holds a chair out for me. As I sit, he pushes it in and leans forward. "Wait until you've seen the meal. I had our top chef in Sanctuary cook for us this evening."

"We have a chef in Sanctuary?" Another glimpse into elite privilege. The very idea of a chef in the slums would be laughable.

Diogo picks a plate up off a shelf and sets it down in front of me, lifting the napkin from on top. I grin at the spread underneath, my fingers twitching to dig in. Somehow I find the willpower not to touch it until Diogo is seated across from me. He lifts the napkin from his plate and inhales the fragrant aroma drifting from our plates.

"Eat, baby, have your fill," he says.

I need no more invitation. I dive into my plate piled high with buttery, flaky biscuits, roast beef, shelled peas, potatoes and gravy. I want to ask him a dozen questions about the meal, but I'd choke on the mouthfuls of food I'm stuffing down my throat. Then something hits me, a question more important than the possibility of choking.

"Is there more?" The question comes out garbled and I have to take a swallow of the wine he kindly sets next to my plate as I lose any and all table manners in my bid to get as much of the delicious food in as possible before it disappears.

He smiles indulgently and retakes his seat, picking up his fork. "There's plenty left over. You may indulge yourself without fear."

Without fear.

Yes, I fear the lack of food on a visceral primitive level. I've known food shortage my entire life. The surplus I'm experiencing now is new to me. It's triggering something in me, a response to horde, to eat while the supplies last. This sobering thought slows me down. There are still plenty of people in this city that don't get enough to eat. Several families that I know personally who are getting less than usual since I've been removed from the rebellion.

"How is this food possible?" I ask him, forking another delicious bite into my mouth and savouring it despite the guilt I feel at not being able to share. "The beef, the cream for the gravy? Even the peas are new to me. Not part of the rations given out in the slums."

He sets his fork down and studies me, his dark eyes troubled. He knows where I'm headed with my line of questioning. Knows how I feel about the inequality in Sanctuary.

"You are aware that we have greenhouses in the city."

"Yes," I say patiently, also setting my fork down. "But you don't grow cows on vines, Warlord. I want to know where the beef came from. The only meat we received in the slums was either canned or freshly caught game, which was rare as we needed hunting passes to leave the city and your administration is notoriously stingy with the passes."

He's told me on multiple occasions that he wants my opinions, that he values my way of thinking. Well, this exact issue is one of the main things the rebels and the Authority disagree on.

"There is a small farm within the city. It raises different types of livestock." he admits, though I can tell this is not something he intended for me to discover. How did he think the beef roast was going to pass me by without an explanation?

"Where is this farm?" I ask, frowning. I've been all over this city. I would've noticed.

"Hidden."

"Because the elites don't want to share their precious meat with the rest of us." I glare at him accusingly.

"Is that really what you think, Taran?" he asks, an edge to his voice. I don't heed the warning though.

"You've always segregated yourselves, sitting over here in Sector One, taking the best of everything, doctors, food, shelter, while people die of starvation and sickness in the slums." I push myself away from the table, completely done with my food.

"I take a lot of argument from you, Taran, for the single reason that I respect your opinion. But I will not be treated disrespectfully. You will think about what you're saying instead of hurling childish rationale at me because you feel guilty."

"Excuse me?" I yell furiously. "I'm not guilty, you're the one in the wrong here! In all the years I've lived in Sector Thirteen I never once received beef in my rations."

"Why might that be?" he asks, his voice deadly quiet. "I have reasons for everything I do. Why was there a lack of meat in the slums? Or am I wrong about you, are you just a mouthpiece for the resistance with no real thoughts of your own? I'd thought better of you."

His insult stings but he's not entirely wrong. I'd jumped on my assumptions without a single thought toward the man I've spent weeks getting to know.

"I don't know what you're trying to say," I admit.

"I'm saying that I have reasons for everything I do, and that I want you to trust me. You don't have to agree or believe in my way of doing things, but you need to trust that I have my reasons."

"But I don't understand the rationale behind food shortages, behind the elites taking the best of everything and giving us the leftovers." I stomp away from the table, away from him, before I do something I'll regret, like hurl a plateful of food at his head. "Unless you're purposely trying to keep morale down."

"There are no food shortages," he says coldly.

"There are!" I can't contain the angry passion rising in my voice. "How can you not see your citizens starving to death right under your nose?"

"My citizens have no reason to starve because there is just as much food given to Sector Thirteen as there is to Sector One. The elites get the same food as everyone else."

"You're lying!" I snap.

"You know better, Taran. Why are there food shortages in the slums? Use your fucking head and then come find me. I'm done with this conversation." He strides past me and slams out of the greenhouse, an angry chirp following him out. I'd forgotten about Skye and her babies.

Tears fill my eyes and I slump back into my chair staring listlessly at the food in front of me. My appetite feels as though it'll never return.

"He's right," I whisper to no one in particular.

The food shortages are my fault. There would be plenty of food for all the people of Sector Thirteen if it wasn't overloaded with illegal refugees.

EIGHTEEN
DIOGO

I give her time to come to the correct conclusion, to release her guilt and then reform her opinion. My Taran is as intelligent as they come, but sometimes her passion gets in the way of her logic. I trust that she'll find her own truth and that it'll be the optimistic, shining opposite of mine.

She finds me in the bedroom, sitting on the edge of the bed, looking over some reports. Her face is pale and drawn, and though she isn't crying there are tear marks down her cheeks. My chest aches at her misery and I can't find it in me to continue my lecture. I set the papers down and beckon her over.

"Diogo..." she whispers, walking toward me.

I catch her arm and tug her down into my lap, cradling her against me. I press her head under my chin and wrap my arms securely around her small, quivering body. A sob escapes and, though I can't see her face, I suspect the tears have started again.

"It's my fault – " she begins, but I cut her off.

"It's not your fault, baby. The food shortages would've

happened with or without your presence. Yes, you exacerbated already strained resources, but you aren't to blame."

"I helped bring people into the city, lots of people!" she argues, hiccupping and accidentally banging the top of her head against my chin as she twists to look up at me. "I added more people to an already crowded system. I'm the reason for everything, the shortages, the riots. I deserved the Judge's sentence."

I swallow my laughter at her dramatic pronouncement. "You're giving yourself a lot of credit, sweetheart. You didn't do it all by yourself. Many of the illegals would've found their way into the city without your help."

"Maybe, but not nearly as many."

I tip her chin and look into her stormy eyes. "I knew about you for years, and though I had my men chasing after you, had I been serious about capturing the Desert Wren, I would've done it. Yes, you contributed to the problem, but you were doing me a favour by assuaging some of my own guilt for turning these people away."

It's a small lie, meant to appease my upset wife. The truth is, I feel no guilt over turning people away from Sanctuary. It's my job to protect the city and make the hard decisions. I am good at my job.

"What made you finally decide to come after me?" she asks curiously, wiping her tears on my sleeve.

The truth is I wanted her. Wanted to finally meet the woman who had slowly, over the course of years obsessed my thoughts. I wanted to discover how a person could be so selfless in a time where survival is the most important motivator. She has far exceeded my wildest hopes.

"It was time for us to meet," I tell her. "For someone to take care of you instead of you taking care of everyone else."

She laughs and gives me a sceptical look. "That's not really the reason."

"It is now." I kiss her lips, lingering over the salty taste of her tears, trailing them up her cheeks and then kissing each eye, essentially telling her it's time for her moment of sadness to be over.

She sighs happily as I explore her face and then drop my lips to her neck, gently tracing the contours of her healing scar. She accepts the caress, tipping her head back to allow my exploration and wrapping her arms around my shoulders to keep herself steady.

"I want to go see the farm, Diogo," she says firmly.

I smile against her throat. She wants more than to see the farm, she wants to figure out how to stretch the resources within to encompass her whole precious city.

"Of course," I tell her. "I will arrange an escort for you tomorrow if you like."

"Thank you." She takes my face in her hands and presses a kiss to my lips.

"Just keep in mind that the entire production is experimental. That's why we haven't been spreading the produce across the city. We're trying to decide if this farm can be sustainable in the long run and expand to feed more than just a few sectors."

She nods, but I can see her enthusiasm for the idea, the bright hope lighting her eyes. The expression is so lovely that I decide to find a way to join her tomorrow if I can get away from my duties long enough.

She turns on my lap and presses her lips fully against mine, surprising me with the dart of her tongue. I grip her waist in a tight hold and open my mouth to her, allowing her to explore further. At first her licks are shy, hesitant, but gradually she gains confidence, wrapping her arms completely around me, anchoring herself and deepening the kiss.

When she rocks her hips against me, grinding herself on my lap, I lose what little sanity I had left when she started touching me. One day I'll find the self-control to let my woman explore her fill, but today is not that day. My need for her is still too strong, too all-consuming and driving. It outweighs my ability to let her have control.

Without breaking our kiss I turn us around, taking her down to the bed and pinning her beneath me. She moans into my mouth, her arms tight around my neck, anchoring me against her. She's strong for such a small woman. Instead of breaking her hold and our kiss, I lift my hips, reach between us and start tugging clothes away. She lifts her own hips allowing me to tug the soft material of her pants down her thighs. I don't bother with her shirt. There's no time. I need to be in her now. Her scent, the feel of her, it's driving me insane.

I position myself and drive into her warm welcoming heat. She wraps her legs more firmly around me, drawing me deeper into her snug passage. I could die happily in this moment, wrapped up tightly in my wife. She squeezes me from the inside out, holding my cock deep inside while her arms cling as though she'll never let go.

"Diogo," she moans into my ear. "Feels so good."

Her softly spoken words, laced with passion is the catalyst I need to start fucking her in earnest. Her moans increase as my movements get rougher, harder, as I slam into her trying to fuse us together. She moves with me, lifting herself, pressing herself to me. Her nails dig into my back where she clings. The bite of pain is enough to drive me close to the edge.

"Come with me," I demand, leaning back, finally breaking her hold.

I reach between us to rub her clit, rubbing it as gently as I can, knowing I'm probably not as gentle as I should be. My balls are full and tight, ready to release within her. She grabs my hand and guides my finger, slowing down my caresses, controlling the rhythm of my strokes. Her moans are sweet music to my ears. The way she sprawls on the bed, widening her legs, touching me and herself at the same time is a feast for my senses.

Nothing has ever been, or will ever be, as beautiful as my wife lost in the abandon of her impending orgasm. And though I'm close to coming myself, I refuse to take the leap before she does. The need to see her face twisting in the heat of orgasm is worth the agony of delaying my release.

"I'm coming!" she shouts, arching her neck back and frantically rubbing our combined fingers over her smooth, sensitive clit. The sight of her, lost to the world, completely taken by pleasure is enough to drive me to my own orgasm. I slam into her again and again, driving her higher as I bathe her in my semen.

I collapse on top of her, then remember that she's a solid half person less than me and roll to the side, breaking our connection. I tug her arm, trying to get her to roll against my side, but she groans and remains sprawled.

"I think I died," she announces.

"There is no circumstance where I will allow you to die." I grip her arm and haul her against me, sprawling her on top of my chest. I hold her in place, kissing her nose as she tips her face up to me.

"Nothing?" she asks.

"Nothing," I confirm. "If something were to happen to you I would destroy what's left of this miserable planet and follow you into death. Not even the devil himself could prevent me from spending eternity at your side."

She considers me, her long red-brown lashes sweeping down and then up. Her lips part on a sigh that stirs the hair on my chest. "I think I feel the same."

I flip her over, holding her underneath me. Framing her face with my hands, I say, "Tell me, Taran. I need to hear it."

Her solemn eyes hold mine. "I love you."

NINETEEN
TALON

Sanctuary New Tucson is not an easy city to slip into and out of. The wall is ridiculously high and solid, the security personnel sharp, but I'm resourceful, tough and determined. I was ejected from the city several days ago with just a few of my supplies and a dozen bruises as souvenirs of my visit. The Warlord must expect me to die in the desert. No vehicle, few supplies, and badly beaten. I've seen worse conditions though. A little adversity is incentive to rise up stronger.

I found my way around the city and into old Tucson, a hazardous place I'd been warned about in prison. The perfect place to find shelter and recover. The few starving Primitives I came across were easy kills, hardly worth the time to stop. But one had still been wearing the shoes he'd died in, or been turned, as some prefer to call it. My personal belief is that a bitten human is a dead human. The heart may still beat, but no one's home upstairs.

Wearing my new shoes, I built a bunker for myself in an old elementary school in the crumbling ruins of the former city. The school is one of the few buildings left standing that can provide half decent shelter. A place to hide out, gather my strength and heal while I formulated my plan to get back into the city.

The wall had been a daunting prospect. I had to watch the security rotations over the course of a week. After I figured them out, I attempted the wall, only to fail, slipping and falling a dozen feet and landing on my back. I took a time out after that, reassessed. I'd assumed the wall would be easy considering the rumours I'd heard of the Desert Wren climbing it repeatedly. If that tiny woman I'd seen during the Primitive attack could climb it, so could I. After my first botched attempt, I'd been forced to set aside my ego and attack the wall with more caution, testing a few different sites to find an easier way over.

I tried and failed a few more times, learning what worked and didn't work until finally, I succeeded. I'd made it over and into some kind of industrial section of the city. Most of the buildings were unused shells, but a few were still in operation, enabling me to steal supplies and take them back over into my hideout in Old Tucson. Now, after almost two weeks of preparation I'm just about ready to get the fuck out of Fuentes' territory. Something tells me the man isn't into giving second chances. He'll have me executed on sight if he finds me within the city limits.

But before I go, I need to take something of his.

And, as luck would have it, I manage to find her without even searching. She's been making regular trips into the industrial sector of Sanctuary, exploring the barns and greenhouses with only minimal protection in tow. She's going to make this capture very much easier than I'd expected.

If the Santa Fe Warlord was willing to pay as much as

he did for one fiery beauty, how much will he pay for the set? A sister, the exact replica except this one is smaller, feistier and younger. Warlord Silas will pay top dollar if he wants the opportunity of breaking the Desert Wren and adding her to his harem.

TWENTY

TARAN

"The smell!" I exclaim, covering my nose and mouth.

Diogo chuckles and places his broad hand on my back, guiding me out of the barn and back into the fresh air. I'd known livestock would have a smell, but I wasn't expecting it to be so horrendous. I suck in mouthfuls of fresh air and wave a hand in front of my face.

"This is why we keep the stables to this side of the city where there are fewer residents. But honestly baby, it's really not that bad. They're much worse in the summer."

"How long have you had these barns?" I wave toward the four rows of buildings housing Sanctuary's livestock.

"I organized the farm and food supplies when I became Warlord. We've been expanding slowly over the past two decades."

I frown toward the barns my mind racing at the possibilities. "If you've been doing this for so long, I don't understand why you haven't expanded faster. Created a more plentiful food source for all the sectors."

"It doesn't work that way." Diogo takes my hand and leads me toward another barn. I cringe in his grip, not wanting to be treated to more of the awful manure smell. "Livestock can't be our main food source. We can't keep up with supply and demand on the scale it would require to feed this entire city. These barns can only take up a small portion of Sanctuary or they become a health hazard. The animals themselves have to eat too and grass and feed are scarce in this part of the world."

"Can you feed them something else?" I reluctantly follow him into the next barn. This one stinks but not nearly as bad as the cow barn. But the noise in this barn is something I wasn't expecting. I stare open-mouthed at the sea of chickens clucking their way around, pecking at bits of seed on the floor.

Diogo leads me down the rows, past the chickens who are studiously ignoring our arrival. Row after row of hen houses line the side walls where the chickens can lay their eggs. Two people are going down the rows, pulling eggs from the houses and putting them into baskets. The chickens go about their business, completely ignoring the humans. I'd had no idea chickens would allow us to get so close.

"We tried feeding the cows ground up corn to supplement their grass diet but many of them got sick. We don't have enough antibiotics in this city to cover the civilian population. I can't spare any for the animals. As a result, we've had to keep about half the population and half of those again are strictly used for milk, which is a far more renewable resource."

I'd never really thought of the mass production of meat before. This experience has been eye-opening, as I'm sure Diogo is aware. He's showing me these barns for a reason. In fact, I'm beginning to think our entire meal was planned for a reason, to get me thinking about food resources for our city. Especially since food shortages is the biggest issue facing the slums.

"Why are we here?" I ask him.

"To see this." He guides me through the next door and a blast of heat hits me.

Tiny little cheeps sound all around us, though they're mostly drowned out by the overwhelming clucks from next door. I drop to my knees next to a big wooden box with a heat lamp placed over top. Tiny fluffy little chicks lurch around the box and huddle together in groups.

"Can I touch them?" I ask eagerly, reaching into the box without waiting for an answer. I stroke my finger down the silky fluff and sigh happily. "They're so beautiful."

He chuckles and drops to his knees beside me. His big hand brushes mine as he reaches into the box and scoops up a chick. "Here," he says, dropping it into my outstretched hands. I laugh as it pecks at my fingers and tries to leap out of my hand. I bring it up to my face and rub it against my cheek.

"He's so soft," I whisper.

Diogo watches indulgently as I spend the next twenty minutes petting baby chickens and going around to each box, scooping them up and cuddling them. Finally, he announces his need to get back to work. I sigh my disappointment and gently drop my baby chick back in its box. As I stand Diogo brushes bits of straw from my clothes and hair.

"You enjoyed yourself?"

"I did." I smile, feeling utterly content as we walk away from the barns. "I don't think I'm going to be able to eat chicken again though."

"You'll get over it. You need a variety of food to keep healthy, and meat is your main source of protein here.

There's a period of adjustment once you get a closer acquaintance with your food. But I think it's important to know where our meals are coming from."

He has a point. Beyond accepting my food rations, I hadn't thought of where the food was coming from or why we couldn't produce more. This experience has been eye-opening. "I'd like to see the greenhouses too."

His eyes sparkle with pleasure when he glances down at me. He holds the door to his car open for me. As I slide in, he says, "I'll have Grayson take you tomorrow."

"Thank you," I tell him, meaning it.

He climbs into the other side of the car and turns the engine over, revving it, before leaving the farm community. I glance around as we drive taking in the tidy little community surrounding the farm. There are several houses within walking distance, each one with a private garden. They don't look like the same type of housing in the rest of the city, they look newer, as though they were created specifically for the farm.

"Who lives there?"

"The farm workers and their families. This is an industrial sector, there were no living spaces when we installed the farm. It's much easier for them to live in close proximity than to try to commute in every day from residential sectors."

I think about this concept as we drive. Though the work looks hard, the idea of this type of living is very appealing. They get up in the morning and go to work creating food for themselves and the rest of us. The ability to produce must be very satisfying.

"Why isn't this part of the city, the animals and food production widely known?" I look around as we pass through the sector gates. Security is definitely heavier here than at most of the other gates.

"I can't take the risk that our food production resources become a target. It took years to set this up and it's delicate at best, too easy to destroy through carelessness. Disease could wipe out the animals. If anything were to happen to the pipes bringing in water from the dam, our food supply would take a serious hit."

"Why are you showing me, then?" I turn in my seat to watch him as he drives. He's concentrating on the road, avoiding the roots and debris littering our path. "I'm part of the rebellion. I could easily tell my compatriots about this hidden sector."

"You aren't stupid, Taran, so let's not pretend you would do something that stupid." His voice is harsh with scorn, not the same as he'd used when he was showing me the area. "You aren't a rebel anymore. You're my wife and your loyalty is with me."

His answer stings, even if he's right. I wouldn't do something so stupid as set the farm up as a target. He's wrong about one thing, my loyalty is torn. Not so long ago I wouldn't have hesitated in telling my fellow rebels all about what I'd seen and trusted them to make the appropriate decision on what to do with that information. I would've trusted Xavier. But he's gone now, and I don't have access to the rebellion. Without knowing who, if anyone, is making the big decisions, I can't trust this information to get out.

Taran is quieter than usual for the rest of the evening, less smiley, less chatty. I don't like it, but I understand. She's struggling with her transition from rebel to Commander's wife. She's beating herself up in ways she shouldn't. She had no choice in her situation. I would've married her regardless of the ease of our relationship. I couldn't be happier with how it's developed, but I do wish it weren't at the expense of her conscience.

"Do you want to talk about it?" I invite, watching her pick at her dinner.

This is how I know she's definitely struggling with something. An array of delicious courses, including baked carrots, mashed potatoes and sausage are in front of her. I even managed to get my hands on fresh baked bread with honey, a rare commodity. I'd thought the mouth-watering food would perk her up after the somewhat contentious end to our greenhouse visit.

"No," she says shortly.

I wait a moment. I've come to know my wife over the past six weeks. She might be feisty, occasionally hot-headed, but she is, in the end, always thoughtful. Experience has taught her to use her head to work through problems. This is something I admire about her. She may have had the rebellion chosen for her, but she came up with her own reasons for staying. Now she's been removed from the rebellion and is forced to reside on the opposite side. Instead of fighting the transition every step of the way, she's working through her philosophies and moral dilemmas, coming up with solutions to merge the two worlds. I'm proud of this wife I've managed to acquire.

"Yes," she says with a sigh. "I don't know what there is to talk about though."

"Start with how you're feeling and let's go from there."

She nods and lifts her eyes to mine. The anguished look in them is gut wrenching. If I could wipe that expression from her face and never see it again I would die a happy man.

"I'm sad... I think. I miss Garrett."

I quickly smother the anger rising up over her feelings toward another man. A dead man. Jealousy won't heal what's bothering Taran.

"He was with me all the time, and we'd just become friends. I... I tried to save him, but I don't think Xavier was ever planning to let him live."

"Xavier needed the head start," I agree with her. "He couldn't allow your bodyguard to radio that you'd been taken."

She swallows hard and continues to move the food around on her plate. "I hate that he ended that way. He was like me, no family."

"There's nothing you could've done, baby." I try to reassure her.

She lifts stormy grey eyes to mine. "I have no family,

Diogo. And it's beginning to feel like I don't have any friends left either. Xavier is dead, and I don't know what's happened to Emery."

"You have me."

She stares at me, not saying anything to that. A combination of guilt and annoyance rises up within me. I'm not enough. She might love me, but she wants more. More people, more purpose. I can't force her happiness, as much as I want to, so I give her something else. "Your friend, Emery, was arrested in the rebel sweep after the wall explosion."

She gasps and sits up straighter. "Why didn't you tell me?" she demands, accusingly.

"You didn't need to know," I tell her bluntly.

"Because I'm a rebel security risk."

"I'm going to say this once more and then never again, Taran. You are no longer a rebel, you are my wife." The wounded look she give me is a jab to the heart. I relent. "You weren't told about her arrest because there was nothing you could do for her. You would have worried and, despite your anger now, I don't regret saving you that concern. Emery was released two days after her arrest. I determined that she had nothing to do with the explosion and didn't constitute a risk to the city."

She bites her lip and nods but stops short of thanking me for my action. We both know I did it for her. Most of the other rebels picked up in our sweep are still languishing in cells, two of them scheduled for execution. Only a few were released. Emery is high up enough in the rebellion that she would still be imprisoned if I wasn't married to Taran. Emery's genuine and selfless care of the young Taran has created a soft spot for the other woman in my almost non-existent affections.

It's time to change the subject. Unfortunately, I need to address another uncomfortable topic. "I need to ask you some questions, about your family."

A look of surprise crosses her features and then she gives me a strange look. "You know what happened to my grandparents. I don't really think that's a topic we should discuss. Especially after you've just told me you had a woman I considered a second mother arrested."

My feisty girl, always in there with a jab to keep me on my toes.

"I'm not asking about your grandparents. I want you to tell me about your sister."

"Skye?" she asks, her confusion growing.

"Yes, tell me about Skye."

She picks up her fork and shoves a mouthful of potato into her mouth, chews and then swallows. "I don't know what you're looking for. She was a lot like me, except taller, prettier, more determined. She was part of the reason we survived as long as we did when we were travelling south. Her stubborn tenacity went a long way toward saving us. She wouldn't let anything get us, not starvation, not Primitives or illness. And never despair. She was the rock in our family. I think my grandparents might've given up long before we reached Sanctuary if it weren't for her."

"You looked up to her."

"She was a complete asshole." She laughs, remembering her sister fondly. "But yes, I loved her dearly, and looked up to her. Losing her was like losing a limb. I didn't know how I would survive. How any of us would survive. Honestly, Diogo, it was a miracle we made it here without her."

"Tell me what happened to her," I urge.

"She died," Taran says shortly.

I push my chair back from the table and lean forward,

taking her hand in mine. "I know it's hard to think and talk about, but I'd really like to know about your family."

"Really?" she asks, her eyes shining bright with tears.

"Yes." I give her fingers a squeeze and bring them up to my mouth, kissing them. "Please tell me. I'd like to hear, and I think it'll be good for you to talk about it."

I feel like a complete dick, using her love and feelings of nostalgia toward her dead family to get her talking about her sister. But I need to know what happened to the girl, need to find out if Talon told me the truth about Skye. I'm not ready to tell Taran about the possibility that her sister still lives though, she's been through enough without raising her hopes and then crushing them again.

She gives me a watery smile. "Okay, I'll tell you." Then the smile disappears, and the haunted look comes back. "We'd barely arrived in the Las Vegas Sanctuary when the illness hit, the same type of flu that killed my parents and brother back in old Canada."

The reminder of the amount of loss Taran has seen in her short years is difficult to hear. If I could go back and save her every second of pain, I would do it in a heartbeat. Even if it changed our future. Even if we never met. It would be worth it, knowing she was happy.

"The sickness swept through the city faster than the Death Kiss spreads. It was terrifying to watch people fall sick one at a time and never get back up again. My grandparents were already in the process of packing us up to leave the Sanctuary, fearful that we'd get sick too, when the city guard weakened to the point that Primitive's were able to penetrate the defences. There weren't enough people left to defend the city. The Primitive's swept through, killing and turning everything in their path."

She pauses here in her story, reaching for her glass with

a shaking hand and taking a big gulp of water. A tear escapes, dripping down her cheek, where she impatiently brushes it aside. Taran often lets her emotions have free reign. She laughs when she sees something funny, she cries when she's sad. I love this about her. Her ability to take life as it comes and simply react. In a world where we are suppressed by the constant grim truth of our impending demise, Taran's emotions are entirely human and entirely welcome.

"We were lucky. The place we were staying in was located near the edge of the city, near a side gate, and we were already packed and set to go. We grabbed as much as we could and we ran as fast as we could, joining another group of survivors. We were just about to go through the gate and escape into the desert when a horde caught up to us. They began picking us off one at a time. The slow and the sick went down fast."

She stops again, gulping in deep breaths and blinking away more tears.

"Did Skye fall behind?" I ask softly.

She shakes her head and takes another moment before she's able to speak. "No, she was faster than everyone else. I was the one falling behind. I was only thirteen and small to begin with. I couldn't keep up with the adults. I was about to be attacked."

"She saw and intervened," I guessed, finishing for her.

Taran nods and gives me a watery smile. "She was such an idiot. She turned around and launched herself at the zombie, attacking it with her bare hands and screaming like a banshee. I swear, if a zombie can look surprised, that one didn't know what the fuck was coming at him."

"Brave girl." Yet another person I'm grateful to for giving my wife the opportunity to live.

"She sacrificed herself to save me. I would've gone back for her, but my grandfather grabbed my arm and forced me through the city gates. The last I saw of her, the Primitive was dragging her down onto the road, his teeth buried in her neck."

This is what I was waiting for, what I'd begun to suspect. Skye was bitten, probably left for dead right there in the road. But the same blood that runs through Taran's veins also runs through Skye's. If I'm right, the sister didn't turn. She survived the Primitive attack and somehow managed to survive the fall of Las Vegas. A few years later, as she was making her way south, toward her sister, she was taken. Intercepted by Talon and sold.

I watch Taran for a moment as she struggles to contain her emotions. I grip the back of her neck and drag her forward, off her chair and onto my lap where I tip her face up to mine. "Thank you for telling me, baby."

TWENTY-TWO

TARAN

"Stunning," I whisper, more to myself than the man dogging my steps through the massive greenhouse.

Stunning is truly the only word that encompasses what I'm seeing. Row after row of beautiful greenery of all kinds. I recognize some but not all. "What are these?" I ask, reaching out to touch the tips of one row of plants. The even rows are neat and attractive, the tips green and almost fuzzy instead of leafy.

Manuel, the man in charge of the greenhouses, snatches my wrist and pulls my hand away. "Carrots," he says disdainfully, as though I should've known.

Grayson steps between us, breaking Manuel's hold. "Don't touch her again."

His voice is so cold and mean sounding, his stance so aggressive, that even I want to take a step back like Manuel is hastily doing. I place my hand on Grayson's arm and step around him. "Thank you, Grayson. Let's continue the tour."

We explore the rows of greenery and I ask more questions, penetrating the inner workings of the greenhouses. I find out that this one is for hardier vegetables while the other holds a variety of fruit and a few of the more difficult to grow vegetables.

"Depending on the variety, fruit tends to be more delicate. We need to adjust the warmth in the house, which requires an extra generator. It's an expensive process."

"I'm sure it is." I stop walking and turn to him. "I'll need a breakdown of the exact materials you'll need to make a third greenhouse, including building supplies, planting supplies, everything."

"But your husband knows everything we used to build these first two greenhouses, Mrs. Fuentes. You can just ask him if you're curious. There aren't enough resources for a third greenhouse."

Grayson opens his mouth to put Manuel in his place again for arguing with the Warlord's wife. I raise a hand, halting him. I haven't needed anyone to fight my battles since I was a child. I certainly don't need anyone's help dealing with this snobbish man, though I appreciate Grayson's willingness to defend me.

"How many people does this greenhouse serve?" I ask sharply.

He hesitates for a moment side-eyeing my bodyguard, clearly not wanting to continue this conversation, but not wanting to annoy Grayson either. "It serves the entire city, Mrs. Fuentes."

"No, it doesn't," I contradict him.

He looks offended by my assertion. "I beg your pardon? These greenhouses were built to supplement the entire city. Our top advisors took part in their construction. I must insist that the produce coming out of here is more than enough for Sanctuary."

"I'm going to have to disagree with you, Manuel," I say sharply, and when it looks like he intends to argue again, I continue, "You've clearly never spent any time in the slums, trying to make food rations stretch, running on an empty belly more often than not. If you had, you'd be doing everything in your power to extend your food supplies and help me get another greenhouse built instead of standing here arguing with me."

He gapes at me for a moment before opening his mouth. Grayson steps closer to my back, his arms crossed over his chest. Manuel takes a step away and nods, "Of course, I'll get your list together. I'll have to run it by Commander Fuentes though."

"You are welcome to waste his time," I tell him, turning away and walking toward the entrance leaving him to follow or not. "I have the Warlord's complete approval for this project." I glance back and give Manuel a stern look. "I would suggest you readjust your attitude before I come back tomorrow. You're much better off working with me than against me."

"I HEARD you were torturing my head of food manufacturing." Diogo's voice sounds from behind me and I twist around to look at him.

I sigh deeply and wave my hand over the strawberry plant. After spending time in the lush greenhouses, I immediately came home and immersed myself in our lovely little greenhouse shed. As wonderful as the industrial greenhouses are, I prefer our tiny sanctuary inside of Sanctuary. The fragrant aroma of flowering plants soothes my agitation with Manuel and helps me think.

"Skye has been pecking away at the strawberries before we even get a chance to eat them." I cluck my tongue over the holes eaten away in the plump red fruit, though I'm amused by the plucky little bird. I'll be forced to pick the fruit and throw them out. I glance up at the nest where the baby birds have fallen silent and the wren is giving me her beady-eyed stare, watching as I handle her treats with barely concealed hostility.

"I'm not surprised." Diogo steps up beside me and touches the leaf of one of the strawberry plants. I lean into the heat of his big body, inhaling his familiar masculine aroma. "Food is scarce, her easiest source close to her hatchlings is right in here."

He turns me to face him, taking my hands and placing them on his chest before pressing me tight against his body in a hug. His hands curve over my hips and then my ass, squeezing the cheeks. A spark of pleasure ignites, sending cascades of awareness through my body.

"You are so fucking perfect," he mumbles, lifting me up and dropping his head into my neck.

I laugh and hold him just as tight as he's holding me. "I'm too small."

"Blasphemy," he growls. "You might be small, but you have a big heart and big ideas. I wouldn't want you any other way."

"Thank you." I lift my head and mould my lips to his.

"You have nothing to thank me for, baby. I mean what I say. There is no other person in this world that will hold my heart the way you do."

We stand that way for a few minutes, deep in each other's embrace, the world around us fading to nothing as we enjoy our newfound love. Finally, we break apart and Diogo sets me back on my feet. I turn back to my strawberries and start gathering the ruined half eaten ones.

"Your production manager is an arrogant jerk." I finally

address Diogo's earlier observation. "He needs to go spend some time starving in the slums."

Diogo chuckles indulgently. "He may be obnoxious but he's good at his job and he's a trained agriculturalist. He knows what he's doing better than anyone in Sanctuary. We're lucky to have him."

"So you want me to stop arguing with him then?"

"You can argue all you want, baby. I'd have enjoyed watching you put him in his place. Perhaps I should come out to the site and help supervise."

"You wouldn't have watched. You'd have done something terrible to him for daring to talk to me the way he did." I'm only part joking. Diogo doesn't tolerate insults toward his wife. I hadn't even known him a day when he threatened to cut off the Judge's tongue for being disrespectful. "If you expect me to work with the man then you'd better stay clear of the greenhouses for a while."

"If you wish." He tugs the tips of my hair and then runs his fingers down my back, drawing a shiver from me. This is something I've noticed about Diogo. When we're in a room together, he's always touching me.

"It's for the best," I assure him. "By tomorrow evening we should have a comprehensive list of all the supplies we'll need to start construction on another greenhouse. I'll run everything by you before we get started."

"No need." He leans down and runs his lips over the shell of my ear. "You have my permission to go ahead with whatever you want on the farm. I'm putting you in charge of food production and distribution. Hire who you need, build what you need. My resources are at your disposal."

The responsibility he just placed on my shoulders is massive. But it's also exactly what I want, and I'm definitely up for the challenge. I know what he's doing. He's giving me a project near and dear to my heart to help soothe my restlessness at abandoning the rebellion. Even if his intervention is manipulative, his methods are sound. I can do so much more to help the slums on this side of the fence than I could as the Desert Wren.

I twist in his arms and tip my face up to his. "Thank you, Diogo. You have no idea how much this means."

His dark eyes narrow on my lips and the heat that always simmers close to the surface when we get within a few feet of each other, bursts into flames, igniting between us. "Then thank me," he says huskily and drops his head to mine, taking my lips in a stinging kiss.

And though I try my best to thank him the way he wants to be thanked, he takes over, pressing me down on the bench and proceeding to take what he wants anyway.

Despite Manuel's bad attitude, he can't quite contain his excitement over the new greenhouse, though he makes it quite clear he still disapproves of me and my involvement in what he considers his project. I try to thaw his reticence by deferring to him almost entirely, only making suggestions here and there when I see something that can be improved. And even then, I stop and ask questions first, working out the logistics of everything before making any changes.

True to his word, Diogo made sure we have every resource readily available at our fingertips. Manuel snorts his derision. "If I was prettier and a woman I might've gotten this done a lot sooner."

I turn to look at him, giving him my best death stare, which is quite effective when backed by a stony-faced Grayson. "My husband is a busy man, Mr. Sharp. Security is his number one concern in this city. And by that, I mean making sure we aren't overrun by Primitives, taken over by competing Sanctuaries or blown up from the inside by rebel forces."

"I might point out that you belonged to the exact group

your husband fights." Manuel's dislike is palatable, and I wonder why his attitude has taken such a personal turn.

"There is nothing wrong with my memory, Mr. Sharp. But I am forced to wonder why you've taken such an interest in my background."

"I don't trust you." His face flushes with ire as he judges me harshly. "You were a rebel and now our lovestruck Warlord has seen fit to give you access to our precious food resources. You could easily poison us all."

"Don't be stupid. There is absolutely no political or moral reason to poison a food supply. The rebels don't go in for such extremist behaviour," I snap scathingly.

"You blew up the wall," he points out.

He's right about the wall, but wrong in his logic. "One man was responsible for the wall destruction and he's dead now. The rebels don't want to hurt people, they want to promote fairness and equality. Building an extra green-house, expanding our food production is a big step toward easing those tensions."

"I still don't trust you," he says stubbornly.

I'm done with coddling this man. "And I think you're a narrow-minded disagreeable man, but I'm still willing to bow to your expertise and work with you."

He doesn't say anything for a moment, seething his annoyance and then he jerks his head in a short nod. "Fine." He turns on his heel and strides away. I sigh and rub my forehead wondering if I've taken a step forward, or back-ward with the man. I should've held my tongue, not told him what I thought.

"You have me convinced."

I jump at the sound of Grayson's voice and turn around to look at him. His expression is more thoughtful and less stern than usual. "About what?"

When he speaks, his words are slow, as though he's thinking out loud. "I used to think of the rebellion as a nuisance at best, and a dangerous cult at worst. I think when you're not in the heart of a thing, you miss the philosophy and see only the actions. I saw the riots, the illegal activities. I didn't understand the reasoning behind it."

"Are you turning into a rebel?" I tease, smiling at him as I pick up my notepad and continue toward the site of the new greenhouse.

He smiles tightly and falls into step beside me. "No, something more important I think. A rebel's bodyguard, protection for the Desert Wren. So she can help our Warlord fix the issues in this city and raise it up stronger and more united than ever."

I look at him, shocked. His words are surprisingly passionate. Grayson has always been aloof and stoic with me. I'd begun to suspect he'd forgiven me for Garrett's death, but I hadn't realized his regard had risen to this point.

"That's a big responsibility for one person."

"You aren't alone," he assures me.

I stop and take a good look at him. Though I try to see all people as individuals, I'm guilty of writing Grayson Truss off as just another annoying security measure trailing after me. But he's definitely more. And he's correct. In order to end the rebellion without bloodshed we all need to work together.

"Thank you," I say and turn back to my task.

We work for the better part of the day, measuring space and going over the list of supplies Manuel gave us. We make several amendments and then head toward the first greenhouse in search of the Production Manager. I'm hot, sweaty and tired. Ready to go home for a meal and a shower. Ready to see my husband and thank him once more for this incredible gift.

"Manuel... Mr. Sharp?" I call out into the space. I glance toward Grayson, my constant shadow. "He said he'd be in here."

"Check the office," Grayson points the way and we head toward the back, to Manuel's office.

"Manuel?" I call as we enter the cluttered space. I don't see him at first and I'm about to turn away when something odd strikes me. His office, though stuffed full of supplies, is usually tidy and neat. Now there's a stack of papers on the floor in front of his desk as though they were swept off the top.

I go toward his desk and that's when I finally see him, or his shoes, sticking out from underneath. "Oh no!" I yell and drop to my knees, crawling around the side. Manuel is laying on his side, his eyes open and staring at nothing. Even though I know he's dead, I still press my fingers to his throat, still shake him, trying to get a response.

"He's gone, Mrs. Fuentes, and we need to get the fuck out of here." Grayson grabs my arm and drags me away from Manuel. "Get behind me, hold onto my shirt and don't let go until we reach the car. Got me?"

"Yes, I understand." I blink away tears and grab his shirt as Grayson starts moving. "Do you think someone attacked him?"

"Yes," Grayson says shortly, holding his sidearm out in front of him and scanning the corridor before moving forward.

I don't understand, it looks like Manuel fell and hit his head on the edge of the desk, but I guess Grayson knows what to look for. I'm about to ask him if we should call for help, when I'm knocked to the side so hard I slam into a row of plants, rocking the wooden platform. I try to catch myself but end up on the ground. I look over, completely dazed in time to see a man standing over Grayson's prone body, a pipe in his hand. He lifts his foot to stomp on Grayson's head.

"Hey!" I yell, drawing his attention. He looks up and I gasp.

Talon!

The Outsider Xavier took me to meet. His big, bushy beard and tattooed skin are immediately recognizable. Somehow he's gotten out of police custody. But why would he attack me and my bodyguard? He throws the pipe away and strides toward me, bending down to grab me.

I roll over onto my stomach and scramble under the rows of plants, crawling as fast as I can. He tries to come after me, but this is one time my smaller size gives me an edge. His big body doesn't fit under the tables. He shoves the one behind me, knocking it over. Plants crash to the ground, but I continue to scramble forward, glancing quickly over my shoulder. Just as he reaches under my table, I roll to the side and crawl across the aisle underneath another row.

"Get the fuck out of there!" he snarls angrily, throwing a table to the side and coming after me. I'm about to roll again, zigzagging under the tables toward the exit when he shoves the table I'm under. It crashes to the side, barely missing me. Plants and dirt smash to the ground all around me.

I look up at his massive form, hulking over top of me. He reaches down and grips me by the throat lifting me from the dirty remains. I yelp and grab hold if his arm, trying to pull myself out of his grip.

"Stop it!" he snarls, giving me a shake. "Or I'll snap your neck."

Though it goes against instinct I force my body to go limp. As soon as I do he lowers me to the ground until my feet touch and eases his grip on my neck.

"Let me go!" I gasp.

"Not happening," he says and starts dragging me back toward Grayson. "You're my ticket out of here."

"Please, what are you going to do?" I stumble against him, caught in the net of his fingers wrapped around my neck.

"Car keys," he grunts.

Shit, I don't want him anywhere near Grayson. I've already lost one bodyguard, I don't want to lose this one too. Not when he's just starting to like me. "I'll get them, they're in his pocket."

Talon raises an eyebrow and then hurls me toward Grayson's prone body. I hit the ground hard and grab hold of Grayson's arm, dragging myself up his body to look at his face. There's blood soaking the side of his head and his eyes are closed. I have just enough time to put my hand over his mouth and check that he's still breathing when Talon reaches for me again.

"The keys, girl."

"I'm sorry," I whisper and start searching pockets until I come up with the car keys. I turn toward Talon and toss the keys. "Here, take them. Just go!"

"Told you," he says, grabbing my arm and dragging me to my feet again. "Not without you."

He reaches down and picks up the gun Grayson dropped and points it at Grayson's head. I try to jump in front of the gun, but he pulls me back. I slap him repeatedly, everywhere I can reach but he ignores me.

"Why?" I yell. "Why kill him? You have the car, you have me!"

"Can't call for help if he's dead."

"He already called for help," I lie desperately.

He looks down at me, his blue eyes sceptical. "Any good bodyguard will secure the package and then call for help. He wouldn't have taken the extra time and distraction to call for help."

"It's true." Instead of slapping him I switch tactics and try to pull him backward, away from Grayson, using my entire weight. He shifts, my pulling dragging him slightly off balance. "He called back in the office before we left. And... and there's lots of other people in the area, workers in the other greenhouses. They'll come searching any minute."

I'm not lying, there are other people working the green-houses, but the houses are huge and noisy, there's no telling when someone might stumble on this scene. Apparently, I've managed to convince Talon though. He readjusts his grip on my arm, turns away from Grayson and drags me toward the entrance.

As we walk, he presses the gun into my side. "You call for help when we're outside I shoot you somewhere incred-ibly painful but non-lethal and then I start killing anyone and everyone that responds."

"I understand," I say faintly. I'm just grateful I'd managed to stop him from killing Grayson. Of course, it might've been for naught if he doesn't recover from the head wound. Manuel certainly isn't going to be recovering.

As we leave the greenhouse I look around, desperately searching for another person. There's no one close by and even if there was, I couldn't get their attention and risk us both getting shot. We walk rapidly toward Grayson's car. Talon opens the passenger door and climbs in, dragging me with him. He manages to maneuver his big body over the console while keeping his gun pointed at me.

He starts the engine and then turns to me, pressing the gun against my cheek. "I need you to get me out of the city. If I can't get out, then you are of no use to me. Understand?"

If I don't get him out, he'll kill me. He's probably figured out that if he's recaptured, Diogo will have him killed. Probably swift and extremely brutal.

I close my eyes for a second and then open them, giving him a blazing look. "I'll get you out, but then you let me go."

He laughs grimly and shakes his head as he grips my chin, squeezing painfully, the barrel of the gun pressed hard under my jaw. "No princess, I came here to collect you. I'm not leaving without my prize."

He lets go of my face and straightens in his seat. Resting his hand on top of the steering wheel, he pulls out of the farmyard.

"I don't understand, why did you come back for me? It's suicide if Diogo finds us."

He floors the gas, heading toward the nearest checkpoint. "I'm an Outsider, suicide is my favourite game." He throws a tight smile my way. "Let's go for a ride, princess."

TWENTY-FOUR
DIOGO

"How long ago?" I demand furiously, trying not to let my anger override my need for answers. If I wasn't desperate for the answer I'd kill this guy where he stands. He let my wife's abductor take her out of the sector. He saw Grayson's car, thought it was Taran's bodyguard driving and waved them through without a pause.

"Twenty minutes, Commander. We realized our mistake as soon as lieutenant Truss alerted the checkpoints to the security breach."

This is my fault. I should've thought to tighten checkpoint security where my wife is concerned. I hadn't imagined this scenario. Why would someone take her? The only people I can think who might have an agenda involving the Desert Wren are in the rebellion.

"Shut down the checkpoints. Only necessary personnel can go through and they must show paperwork. If anyone catches so much as a hint of my wife, they detain and call me."

I'm about to turn away, about to go to the slums to question the one person who both cares about Taran and has a reason to abduct her, Emery, when a call comes through on the radio.

Cruz informs me, "We have confirmation that a vehicle matching the description given to all checkpoints passed through the main gates five minutes ago."

My heart pounds at the implication. Taran was taken outside the wall and I have no idea who took her. I would suspect her ex-husband if I hadn't killed him myself. The fear rising up inside me freezes my ability to think. The only thing I want in this moment is to race outside the walls and find my wife.

Cruz must sense my state of mind because he immediately steps in with a solid plan, rapidly shooting out instructions. "Stryker is our best tracker. We'll have him meet you at the city gates. I'll collect several of our best men and vehicles to follow behind in case you need the backup. I'll keep the city standing while you go hunting."

Before I have time to acknowledge his orders, others pipe in with their assent and positions.

"I'll be at the gate in five," Stryker grunts.

"I'll take over wall duty from Stryker," Boss chimes in. "I'll pull in some of my best men and send them out to assist."

"Someone needs to pick me up at checkpoint 12," Grayson's strained voice interrupts. "I'm coming."

I want to tell him to stay behind. From the account I was given, he'd taken a solid hit to the head. A similar blow had killed the greenhouse manager. But in Grayson's place I would feel the same way. I'd need to hunt down the person that took my charge, redeem myself.

"Boss, have one of your men pick up Grayson," I grunt. "Grayson, no driving. We don't need you killing yourself before we find the bastard that took her."

A small hesitation then Grayson says, "Commander, there's something you should know. She put up a hell of a fight. Half the greenhouse is in ruins."

I grin savagely. That's my girl. Taking charge of her own destiny when faced with adversity. I hope that she wasn't injured in the struggle. She might be feisty, but she's small. Smaller than most. If a large man got his hands on her, he could easily kill her. My smile falls away and I stride toward my car.

Five minutes later I meet Stryker at the main gate. He gets wordlessly into the car while the men at the gate go through the elaborate process of opening the doors. I'm pissed off all over again that she could have made it through so many checkpoints without being questioned. Why the fuck would she go outside the wall with her bodyguard? There's no good reason she shouldn't have been detained.

But then, there's no reason she should've been detained. As the trust between us grows I've given her access to several city sectors. Why not outside the city? As far as the guards knew she could leave whenever she wanted to with my blessing.

"Stop the car a minute," Stryker says once we clear the gates. "Need to talk this through before we can start tracking." He gives me a sharp look. "Who would benefit from taking her? The ex is out of the picture, correct?"

"Correct," I grunt, not bothering with details. I'd allowed Xavier to quietly disappear. Only Cruz and a few others know what happened, but I'm sure there's speculation on the rebel leader's fate.

"Anyone else from the rebellion have reason to grab her?"

"Yes, but I don't think it went down like that. Grayson says there was an obvious struggle where she could've been hurt. The rebels revere their Desert Wren, I don't think any of them are capable of this." I stare out into the desert, toward the Catalina mountains. "They have no reason to bring her out into the desert either. She'd have been safer in the city, hiding out in the slums."

"If that's true, then who else would have reason to grab the girl?" Stryker's brow furrows as he tries to piece the abduction together. "Enemies?"

"No. As I said, the rebels love her, and the elites are fascinated by her. I can't think of anyone who would want to do this to her."

"I didn't mean her enemies, I meant yours, Commander."

I give Stryker a hard look and raise an eyebrow. "First rule of war, lieutenant."

"Don't leave behind an enemy capable of coming after you."

"Indeed," I confirm. "Yes, I've made my share of enemies, but they don't live long. I'm smarter than that."

Stryker nods his understanding and continues to think through the possibilities. I try not to get in his face, let my frustration show. I want to rip out of there and head after my girl, not sit and talk things through logically. But Stryker is my best tracker, part of the reason he's so good on the wall. Sharp eyes, sharper reaction time.

"What about prisoners? Someone in the city thinking they got an unfair shake, using your girl to strike back at you?"

I shake my head. "No, again I don't leave enemies behind."

"But you do allow the release of some prisoners."

"Only the ones that won't come back to bite me. For the most part I stay out of the criminal justice system. I can see someone going after the Judge, or their arresting officer, but few would dare to come after me personally. Besides, why leave the city? They'd be safer abducting Taran and keeping her inside Sanctuary."

"What about someone outside of Sanctuary?"

I open my mouth to deny the existence of Outsiders, only to trip over my own thoughts. "Motherfucker," I snarl. "He took her." I turn to Stryker. "That Outsider I set free a few weeks ago. Talon. He told me Taran has a sister. Seemed to take an interest in Taran."

Stryker absorbs the information and then nods slowly. "Two sisters would be worth a lot. Especially if the other looks anything like your bird. Where's the sister at?"

"Santa Fe Sanctuary."

"Then we're going Northeast, Commander. He probably intends to sell her. But even if that's not his plan, he'll need supplies."

"You sure?" I ask impatiently, cranking the wheel and heading around the wall toward the East.

He shrugs. "We'll know soon enough when we start seeing fresh tracks. Let's hope he intends to sell her and wants her intact."

The alternative doesn't bear thinking. I can't cope with the idea that we'll find her beaten, raped body in the desert, picked to the bone by Primitive scavengers.

"We'll stop here."

I don't respond to Talon's comment. Just continue to stare out the side window of Grayson's car. I haven't spoken a word to Talon for over a day, since I realized he wasn't going to give me anything. No information to help me figure out where we're going or what's going to happen when we get there. He doesn't seem to care about my lack of conversation. Talks regardless of my response.

"I know a place we can grab some fuel here. We'll stop for the night too, I need to get some sleep."

I'm not surprised by this revelation. We've been driving for more than twenty-four hours and he hasn't had any opportunity to rest. Though he looks tired, he doesn't look much worse for the wear for staying awake that long. Unable to stay awake, I'd drifted in and out of a light slumber while he continued to drive through the night, only stopping long enough to use the fuel reserves in Grayson's trunk before pushing on.

Finally, I unbend enough to ask, "Where is *here*?"

Talon glances over at me, before turning his gaze back to the road. "She speaks."

I glare straight ahead. "Fine, don't tell me. It's not like it makes a difference anyway."

"True enough," he says. "But to assuage your curiosity, we're heading out to an old pre-Great Fall farmstead. It's out of the way, not easily accessible unless a person knows where it is and the zombies don't bother with it, since it's deserted."

"How do you know where it is, if it's so out of the way?"

He doesn't speak for a long moment and I think he's going to ignore the question, then, "It belonged to my grandfather. Belonged to my family for generations before the Fall."

He had a family. Of course, he did. This shouldn't be shocking, everyone has origins. But somehow, this guy, this Outsider feels like a lone maverick. Like nothing shaped him but the world we live in and his disdain for it.

"What happened to the farm?" I ask, curiosity getting the better of my desire to stay silent around this deadly man. Before leaving old Canada my family had lived off the land, avoiding the worst of the Great Fall by moving constantly. My family had been farmers for generations, giving them an edge in survival. Or that's what I like to I think, anyway.

"My grandfather and his kin tried to hold out, continue to produce, but irrigation was one of the first things to go, and farmers in this region need water to survive. It was a pointless cause anyway, the Primitives were making their way across the country, toppling cities, infrastructure, farms, everything. A few years after the Fall, most of my family was attacked and driven out of the area, forced to abandon the homestead."

I want to feel nothing, want to continue treating him with disdain, but his story is similar to so many others, similar to mine, it makes him more human. I remind myself that he killed Manuel and fully intended to murder Grayson too. And I'm far from safe. But still, his story should be told, it probably shaped him into the remorseless killer he's become.

"Most of your family?" I ask, picking up on his careful wording. "But not all."

"No," he says shortly.

I can read between the lines. The family members that stayed behind would've died or turned. "I'm sorry."

He gives me a sharp look as we turn off what used to be a major highway and head down a dirt road. Most of the gravel is still intact, shaping a road that's almost better than the cracked and abandoned highways.

"I don't want your sympathy," he says, his voice bland.

"You'll get it anyway," I persist stubbornly. "We all come from somewhere and there's tragedy in all of our backgrounds. You are no better than anyone else, but you are also no less. You're a survivor and that means something."

He watches me, his startling blue eyes tracing over my face, as if really seeing me for the first time. For a moment, I think he'll relent, allow his human side to reach out and touch mine in a moment of shared understanding. Instead, he says, "You're special little Wren. You'll make me a rich man."

TWENTY-SIX
TARAN

He's going to sell me. I guess I should've known. He's made no move to touch me, hasn't treated me as anything more than a commodity. His attitude is coolly distant.

We arrived at his old family homestead a few hours ago. I'm wandering the property, stretching my legs. I was a little surprised he let me go anywhere without him, but all he said was, "You have no place to run away to. Even if you managed to drive the car by yourself, you don't know how we got here and you have no way to take care of yourself. Just don't go too far out, I can't help you if I don't hear you scream."

I shudder at the implication as I walk further from the house, into a nearby grove of trees. Maybe I shouldn't be walking by myself, should worry more about being attacked by a Primitive while out on my own, but I need some air and some distance from my captor. The trees surrounding me are all dead, dried up and skeletal. I reach over my head snapping a twig off one as I pass underneath it. Dead foliage crunches under my feet and the sun blazes overhead. I won't be able to stay out for long without burning.

The rows of trees are evenly spaced, though some have fallen to the earth and either dried out or decomposed. I step over one such fallen tree, the dead branches crunching with each footstep. I begin to feel vulnerable as I realize how much noise I'm making. Talon's warning echoes in my head and I'm about to turn back when something catches my eye. Something bright and pink, waving in the air like a banner.

Drawn to the small splash of colour on an otherwise empty horizon, I push through my unease and walk toward the object. As I get closer revulsion rises up inside me and my heart starts to pound hard against the walls of my chest. My steps slow but I don't stop. Something inside me feels like I owe these people at least an acknowledgment of their existence. An acknowledgment of their passing. No one else will do it. In our battle against the disease that wiped out a once thriving civilization, these are the forgotten.

The pink splash that'd drawn me toward this horrific discovery belonged to a girl. I sink down next to her, studying her small body. She can't have been older than ten when she was turned. Who knows how long she survived after that. The thing that differentiates her from a regular human corpse is the desecration of her bones. Holes had been jabbed through parts of her face, sticks and bolts of metal embedded in her skull. Surrounding her are the bodies of her horde, maybe fifteen dead Primitives.

There are several odd things about this child; her age, her placement slightly away from the rest of the horde and the teddy bear clutched tightly in her arm. She was young, the youngest Primitive I've ever seen. Children usually die under the brutality of a turn. Another strange detail about the girl is that she's been placed separate from the others. While their bodies are strewn carelessly about, this one was placed purposefully, her limbs arranged and the teddy bear tucked against her little chest; as though she'd died peacefully with the toy in her arms. But she hadn't. She'd died the same violent death as the others. Someone had destroyed this horde as it crossed the farmstead.

Whoever had killed them must've separated and arranged the child. Tears prick my eyes as I imagine the care and grief involved. He probably hadn't wanted to kill a child, probably hadn't any choice.

I sniff the tears back and get to my feet, moving quickly away from the grave. A wave of dizziness hits me and I'm forced to stand still for a moment, sucking in deep breaths. I must've been kneeling for longer than I thought. I shake it off and head back toward the house. I've been outside long enough, put some space between me and my captor. Now it's time to face the man who wants to sell me and convince him to turn around and take me home.

I look longingly at the car as I pass it on my way to the house. It's really my only hope for getting out of here, but there are so many obstacles. I have no idea how to start it, no idea how to drive it and no idea what direction to drive in once I got it going. Talon is right, I'm better off, safer, with him.

"Thought you'd try taking off," he grunts when I open the door.

He's sitting at a table with an impressive array of weapons laid out in front of him. While they should make me nervous, the thought of that dead horde up on the hill makes me feel grateful that I've been kidnapped by a guy who knows what he's doing. I saw him in action, killing Primitives with ease when we were attacked in the desert.

"Thought about it," I admit, approaching the table and tentatively taking a seat.

"You wouldn't have made it far."

"You'd come after me?" I'm genuinely curious. This man seems like such a contradiction. He's capable of hurting people, yet he hasn't touched me. I suspect he's the one that killed that horde, but then arranged the girl in an almost ceremonial way.

"Wouldn't have to," he says, not looking up as he unsheathes a knife and looks closely at the blade. "You'd have come back on your own. It's pretty dry out there. No food and water for miles. All kinds of predators."

"Like you?"

He smiles at my comment. "Sure, predators like me."

"I don't think you're as bad as you pretend."

The smile melts from his face and he lifts cold blue eyes to me. He's not really looking at me though, but through me. Like I'm not a person to him. "It would be a mistake for you to think that."

"You haven't hurt me and you've had plenty of opportunity," I say defiantly. "I saw the grave up on the hill, past the orchard."

He frowns. "I don't know what you're talking about."

"The little girl," I prod, and when he continues to look confused and annoyed, I add, "With the teddy bear. Primitives don't carry things, especially toys. Someone gave that to her after she died."

"Wasn't me," he says dismissively.

"I still don't think you're as bad as you try to make yourself out to be."

He sits back in his chair and crosses his arms over his chest. "How do you figure that?"

"You saved me during the horde attack, told Xavier to put me in your car." It's weak reasoning since he didn't actually check to see that I was okay during the attack, but I'm willing to grasp at straws. I need this guy to not be as evil as he seems. "And I don't care what you say, someone arranged that little girl, gave her a bear and treated her like a human instead of just another Primitive. No one else knows about this place, it must've been you."

"So what if it was," he snaps, his words cold. "I don't like seeing kids die. Doesn't make me a good person."

"You have a heart, Talon. You've had every opportunity to hurt me and you haven't," I insist.

He stares at me now, his eyes finally seeing me, finally showing emotion. But not the kind I was looking for. A new fire has lit in those icy depths. "You want to see my bad side, princess?"

I swallow hard and lift my chin, staring back at him. It's a stupid thing to do. Prod a man like Talon, but I'm out of options. I can't escape. He's essentially forced my reliance on his survival skills. The only thing I have left is to reason with him, reason with the man that tenderly arranged the dead girl.

He erupts out of his seat so fast, I barely have time to blink and he's around the table reaching for me. I hurl myself sideways out of my chair, scrambling to get away from his explosive advance. He grabs me by the hair and drags me backward into his chest. Then he lifts me off the ground, an arm around my waist, my kicking legs barely fazing him.

"Stop!" I shout, trying to drag his arm away.

"You wanted to see the monster, you got him." His words are terrifyingly similar to Diogo's when he dragged me into the shower.

Talon drags me through the house, toward a set of stairs. He takes them two at a time until we're on the second level. He strides down the hall and shoves a door open. I barely have time to glance around, taking in an old dresser with a smashed mirror, a wooden chest and a four-poster bed. He hurls me face down on the bed grips my hips and drags me back until I'm standing on the floor with my upper body pressed into the bed.

I realize in that moment that he intends to rape me.

I try to crawl backwards, but he grips my neck from behind and pins me to the bed. His hands seem to be everywhere at once, holding me down and reaching under me to unzip my pants and then drag them back over my ass. My screams of terror turn to sobs as he reaches back to unbuckle his own pants.

"Please don't," I beg through the tears, trying to twist around, to look at him. He forces my face back into the bed refusing to let me turn or look behind me.

Then I realize, he can't look at me while he does it.

I turn my head to the side and yell, "Look at me, you coward!"

He takes a fistful of my hair and drags my head back, arching my neck. He leans down and says, "What?" his voice chillingly devoid of emotion.

It would probably be safer to shut my mouth, to just take the punishment and tread more carefully in the future. Still, this is my only chance to avoid being brutalized by a man just trying to prove a point. I twist my head to look at him. "Look me in the eyes, asshole. Or are you incapable of that?"

He whips me around hard enough that I think my neck will snap, then he picks me up and throws me on the bed. I land on my back, a puff of dust flying up from the blankets. "You have a fucking death wish!" he roars, climbing on top of me and pinning me down.

"Maybe I do," I snarl back, "but at least my life means something."

He stares at me, tension flowing between us. Gradually I can feel his intent shift, and though I'm terrified of pushing him too far, I need to take advantage of this moment. "You don't want to do this, Talon." God, I hope I'm right. He might be a murderer, might be a mercenary. But I don't think he's a rapist. "Please, don't."

"Why are you so fucking invested in making me out to be some kind of good guy?" he demands, punching the pillow next to my head. A cloud of dust flies up and then settles over both of us.

I gasp in a lungful of the dusty air between my sobs and say, "Because if you're good then you won't sell me. You won't make me some stranger's slave. Because if you care, even a little, you might take me back to Sanctuary, back to Diogo."

He sits back on his haunches, looking down at me, his expression pitying. That look is enough to bring the tears back. Maybe I've touched him, maybe he does think of me as more than another payday. But nothing I've said has changed his mind.

He confirms my thoughts when he says, "The world don't work that way anymore, princess. Good or bad, doesn't matter. Only survival."

His words are like a knife to the heart. Brutal. Unkind. Sort of true.

They're also an echo of the same thing Diogo has said to me.

"You need to slow down, friend."

"I'm not your fucking friend," I snarl at Stryker, hitting the gas even harder. "I'm your boss, and that's my wife out there in the hands of an Outsider."

"Yeah, I know, but you ain't gonna make it far if you tear up the vehicle on this shit cracked road. We'll blow a tire or run out of gas before we can get to the next fueling station. We won't be worth anything to your girl if we're stuck out in the desert." He says calmly, scanning the horizon in front of us, looking for any signs of other cars or predators. "Besides, you've left your backup in the dust, *boss*."

The desire to punch Stryker in the face is nearly overwhelming.

"Fuck." I hit the brakes and we skid, the vehicle sliding on the broken pavement. He's right. If I keep abusing the jeep, I'm going to blow a tire. Once we're stopped, I reach for my door handle. "You drive."

Without another word we switch spots. It's not easy for me to give over control when I'm desperate to get to Taran as fast as we can, but I know my man, he'll get us there almost as fast and in one piece. He understands the stakes. Stryker speeds over the broken highway, his sharp eyes catching problem spots where he takes us through at a slower pace. We don't talk during most of the trip. Nothing to say. He just drives, taking us across the desert. Most of the truly impassable sections of highway, fallen bridges and such have been mapped out. Although we don't usually go this far out from Sanctuary, we're well versed in the topography. Unfortunately, a few sections slow us down, sections of road that have become too deteriorated to pass over. We end up having to go around, tracking across the naked desert.

As we pass over one such section, Stryker comments, "Someone's been here recently."

"How do you know?" I peer through the window trying to see what he's seeing. After a moment of scanning I see faint track marks, heading the same direction as us.

"Mother nature likes to erase our tracks as we make them. Wind and water in this area are quick to take out human activity." He squints into the setting sun, taking the jeep carefully over the rougher terrain. "Bet a month's rations these tracks belong to our guy. Not many people would come out this way. No good reason and it's dangerous. Think we're on the right path."

"You'd better be right," I grunt. "We don't have the time to turn around and look somewhere else."

The thought of never seeing Taran again turns my guts to acid. It would be too easy to lose her out here. If we're wrong and Talon wasn't the one that grabbed her, or if he went in another direction, they could disappear and I'd have no way of finding her again. In a world without people, it's surprisingly easy to lose a person.

After we cross the broken section of pavement, the tracks lead back onto the main highway and disappear. There's not enough dirt to see where he's gone. As if sensing my unease, Stryker speeds us up until we're flying down the road, everything around us a blur.

"We'll have to hit up the nearest fuel station," he comments.

I nod, but don't say anything. We scanned a map shortly after leaving Sanctuary, noting the important stops. Fuel stations, safe places to rest and towns to avoid. The fuel station is off the highway and dangerous to reach. Dangerous to linger at. Somehow, despite their limited capabilities, Primitive's have figured out that there are several things humans can't survive without; food, water and fuel. Unfortunately, they like to gather around fueling stations, waiting for their prey to show up.

I might not like it, but we have no choice, we need gas. I reach into the back seat, grab my rifle, check the chamber and say, "You fuel, I'll cover us."

He jerks his head in a nod and hits the gas harder. "We'll have five minutes to do this. I've been here before, this place is popular."

It's popular because anyone driving through here has to stop for fuel. In a barren land, with very few humans to feed on, the Primitive's know exactly where to hang out.

"Let's hope there's still fuel in the pumps."

He doesn't acknowledge my concern. He doesn't need to. On a normal day, if the pumps were damaged or empty, we'd be completely fucked. Luckily, today, we have an army following close behind us. A few of the guys would have enough fuel left to get us to the next station.

"Head up, Fuentes, we're coming in hot."

My head snaps up and I immediately see what he's

talking about. Two Primitives, currently dots on the horizon, are running toward us, following our dust trail to their next meal. If this is any indication, then this town is for damn sure overrun. I prime the rifle and check that I have my sidearm and knife. While Stryker hurtles toward the fuel pumps, I check his weapons, making sure his holster is easily accessible.

Neither of us say a word as he skids to a halt, the jeep sliding into position next to the first pump. I leap out of the car and take aim at the first Primitive headed our way. I don't shoot though. I'm a damn good shot, but I won't risk wasting a bullet. God only knows how many Primitives will converge and bullets are a premium in a society where pretty much all resources, including weapons, are hard to come by. Stryker grabs the pump and slams it into the fuel tank. Instead of the familiar gush it should make as the tank fills, the handle clicks in his hand. He checks the tank, checks the pump and tries again. Nothing.

"Motherfucker!" he growls, checking the next one, it clicks empty too. Someone's been here, fueled up some big tanks or something and emptied a ground reservoir that's been working since the Great Fall. I've done the same. Sent trucks out from Sanctuary in search of large amounts of gasoline. "Gotta move to the other side, boss."

"Do it!" I shout. "I've got us covered."

He leaps into the jeep and pulls it around the gas bar to the other pumps. The advancing Primitives come within range. "I'm about to bring the fucking town down on top of us. Be ready."

I don't have time to see if the new fuel pump works, I aim at the first Primitive and take its head clean off its shoulders. The body hits the dirt, rolling hard from the momentum. His partner doesn't even slow, doesn't look back, just continues its mindless advance into the path of my slugs. I take the second one's head off, the boom of the shot echoing through the buildings around us.

I back toward the fuel pumps, reloading my rifle. The sidearm has more shots in it, but the rifle is more effective and works better for long distance. All is quiet, the only sound is the gentle rushing of fuel as it fills our tank. I scan the buildings. It doesn't take long, seconds later they look like they're moving as a crawling mass of bodies bursts through broken windows and doors, hurtling toward the sounds of the gunshots, the sounds of humans.

"Hurry the fuck up!" I yell, moving back toward the car as I empty the rifle taking down the first few. I shove the rifle back into the holster on my back, pull my sidearm and my knife.

"Get in the car," Stryker shouts as the horde converges. I take out as many as I can as I back slowly toward the car.

Shooting from behind me draws my attention and I turn. Stryker and the car are covered in them now. He's killing as many as he can as fast as he can, but more and more come at us. I'm used to dealing with Primitives at fueling stations, but this is a whole other level.

A Primitive lands on my back, it's claw-like hands digging into my shoulders as it tries to find a grip. I reach over my shoulder, wrap my arm around its neck and drag it to the ground, my knife following closely behind, slamming deep into the creature's neck. I don't have time to make sure it's dead, to cut off its head. I yank the knife out and twist around to take the next one, its strong arms reaching for me, preparing to tear the flesh from my bones.

I'm completely overwhelmed by Primitives, I don't even

see Stryker anymore. I can't worry about what's happening to him. He can take care of himself. There's a reason he's part of my team. Minutes later, or maybe seconds, he proves my confidence correct as he slams the vehicle into the group of Primitives lining up to take me down. Several of them go under the jeep while a few roll over the top. He barely misses hitting me. Although at this point I would welcome the distraction.

He slams on the brakes sliding to a halt several feet in front of me. I maim and kill as I work my way to the passenger door. I'm about to reach for the handle when the window next to my head shatters, a bullet lodging into the head of a Primitive trying to bury its teeth in my shoulder. I dive through the now open window, twisting onto my back as Stryker hands me a loaded gun. Taking it, I shoot everything that tries to climb in the window behind me.

Stryker hits the gas and peels away from the fueling station. A Primitive thumps against the back of the jeep as it rolls off the top and hits the ground. I continue to kill anything that pops up in the window, the sound of gunfire in such close confines ringing in my ears.

Except for the ones clinging to the frame I can't see any more Primitives, but I know they're chasing us. They'll continue to do so until they collapse, unable to run any longer. Gradually the ones on the vehicle fall away until I'm relatively certain we're alone. I pull myself up in the seat, reload the gun and point it at the window, preparing for another attack if it comes.

We continue that way for several miles, Stryker driving the jeep hell-bent across the desert, back toward the main highway while I maintain cover on the window. Finally, I begin to relax, setting the gun down on the seat. I send a signal out on the all-communications channel that the Oasis fuel station is no longer viable. The entire area has been overrun by Primitives. I put the radio back and eye Stryker.

"You shot my fucking window out, you bastard."

He laughs, the sound a short, rusty bark. "You're welcome, *boss*."

I wake up feeling disoriented and a little sick. I haven't had anything to eat in over a day. I've become used to eating since Diogo took me and forced me to eat regular meals. The thought of my husband brings a lump to my throat. I shake off the feeling and sit up, pushing a blanket away. It had been tucked tightly around me. Weird, I don't remember covering up after going to bed.

I don't hear anything. No movement, no sign of my captor. I creep through the door, making my way downstairs on silent feet. I'm not afraid of him discovering me wandering around the house. Far from it since he knows exactly where to find me. But something about the silent still morning has me moving cautiously.

Last night, after Talon punched the pillow next to me, he left the room, slamming the door shut. I'd stayed in that room for several hours, not wanting to prod the beast with my presence. I didn't needed to worry though. When I finally left the room, my growling belly and parched throat forcing me out, he wasn't there. He stayed away all night. If the car hadn't been parked in front of the house I would've worried that he'd abandoned me there to die. He must've spent the entire night outside somewhere.

As I creep down the stairs I smell something different. Smoke. I peek around the corner and spot a wood-burning stove, smoking away, filling the room with the pleasant scent of fire. I step off the bottom step and into the room, looking around curiously. A skinned rabbit sits on the counter near the stove. My belly rumbles in gratitude that Talon is talented enough to catch such a creature.

Though certainly wary of my captor after his near-rape of me last night, I'm not as frightened as I maybe should be. I got the feeling rape isn't something he's ever resorted to. He tried to scare me and control me through physical violence. And, while I'm definitely not fond of him, his attack had the opposite effect. Or rather, the fact that he stopped.

He's determined to prove how bad he is, how little he cares about his fellow humans, but I sense something different than what he projects, a deep need to connect. Something inside him wants to reach out and feel what it's like to live an existence free of the constant spectre of death. Unfortunately, that's not an option, not since the Great Fall. But if he wanted to, he could find a place in society, integrate himself and his talents into a Sanctuary community. Much the same way Diogo's men are accepted, their violent and extreme tendencies turned towards making themselves productive members of the community.

I'm not going to try to convince him though. I don't want a repeat of the last night. Instead I'll show him how helpful I can be, show him my human nurturing side as often as I can, as subtle as I can. Maybe gain his trust before we arrive at our destination. At the very least I'm going to make it hard for him to sell me.

I look around the kitchen, going through cupboards, searching. I find all the ingredients I need to make a batch of basic biscuits to go with the cooked rabbit meat. Everything looks fresh enough, confirming my belief that Talon comes back to this place often. It's like his escape when he needs to call a place home, or the life of a nomad gets too lonely. Maybe being close to his family home gives him comfort.

A scraping sound near the doorway has me turning on the spot. I open my mouth to ask Talon where I can find a baking pan. The words freeze in my throat. Instead of the giant Outsider, a stooped, starved looking Primitive fills the doorway. I resist the urge to scream or run. It's facing away from me, slowly shuffling on the spot. It must've been attracted by the smoke. For some stupid reason I hadn't believed there would be any in the area. Not after seeing all those dead Primitives up on the hill.

I back slowly toward the stairs, my intent to run up them and lock myself in a room if I can. As far as I know, Primitives react completely off instinct. No logic, no ability to work through a problem. The memories of their human lives seem to have died. If I can somehow disappear from his sight, he might move on. If he's not part of a horde I might actually stand a chance, though he's still extremely dangerous on his own.

I don't quite make it to the stairway when my shoe catches on a loose board. It lifts and thumps back down, a sharp cracking sound echoing through the room. I look up in terror as the Primitive spins in the doorway facing me, its hands curling into claws, digging into the dark skin of its palms. I stand frozen, doing my best to hold my breath as it sniffs the air. A man, I think. An elderly man, which maybe explains why it's not in great shape. His head is bald, the signature dark splotches from the necrosis, the skin rot, creeping up his neck and over his head. A giant railroad spike is embedded in the socket where his eye used to be and the other is milky blue. I doubt he can actually see, which is probably how he lost his horde. The stench of decomposition is nearly overwhelming as it permeates the room. I try not to gag as a wave of dizziness hits me.

I try to comfort myself with the reminder that a bite probably won't turn me. Though he can certainly kill me another way. Primitives are strong enough to crush a person's bones into nothing but splinters. If he gets his hands on me, I'm most likely dead, despite my apparent immunity to the bite.

He tenses, his lower jaw dropping. He pulls his lips back and pushes his teeth out, preparing to bite. Oh god, I need to run and hide. But if I run I'll draw his attention for sure. He brings his hands up in an attack position and I watch mesmerized as he launches himself forward. I stumble back, slamming into the wall behind me. I prepare to spin around and run up the stairs, when the Primitive is snatched from behind, yanked backward into the chest of a huge man, a beefy arm around his neck.

Talon brings his knife up and cuts the Primitive's neck, severing his head in one stroke. I jump, my hands pressed against the wall behind me as the head hits the ground and bounces under the table. Talon wipes his blade on the Primitive's shirt and then shoves the body to the floor where it hits with an audible thump.

Talon's eyes hold mine as he sheathes the knife.

He strides toward the oven, grunting, "I'm hungry."

We eat and then head out, Talon driving the car out of the homestead without a backward glance. We drive all day, stopping once for fuel, filling the tank and the reserves in the back of the car. Talon explains that stopping in a town is a dangerous prospect, and at the station he makes me pump the gas while he covers us, but we don't run into any problems.

The town has an eerie abandoned feel to it, the only movement a flock of birds flying low over the ruined buildings as we disturb their nesting spot for a few minutes. I hold the strange looking pump in my hands, pressing the handle the way Talon had explained. I jolt as I feel a gush of liquid pass through the line and into the car, but I continue to hold steady. I fill until something clicks and then stops.

After we fill the reserve cannisters, Talon pushes me back into the car, slides into the driver seat and gets out the town as fast as we entered it. I can tell from the tension in his shoulders that fueling isn't his favourite thing to do. I wonder if he's ever been attacked in a town before and that's why he's so leery.

We drive through the night, me dosing fitfully in the passenger side. I wake slowly to Talon's voice. "We're here."

My eyes pop open and I sit up abruptly, reaching for the window frame and gripping it tightly. The light of sunrise shines bright in my eyes, forcing me to squint and lift a hand. I glance over at Talon and he nods ahead of us and to the right. My gaze drifts across the horizon. The sun is slowly rising over a city, lighting it up as though on fire.

TWENTY-NINE
SKYE

"Visitors at the gate, ma'am."

I look up sharply at the man standing in front of me. Wolfe, the Warlord's personal bodyguard, and by extension, mine as well. He's my guard, my captor, my enforcer, but never my friend. He watches me with longing, but not the hopeless wistful kind. No, like he wants to eat me up, he watches like the wolf he is. Steady, piercing, planning. His look has always made my heart stutter in trepidation. There's a clock between us, slowly ticking down to the zero hour. But does he want me for me, or does he want the power at my back?

"Why are you telling me?" I ask scathingly.

From the day I was brought into Sanctuary against my will, Wolfe has been a contentious bane to my existence. Always there, always questioning, ready to pounce when the time is right. He might be a handsome man if he wasn't so beat to hell and back. His muscles are defined and mouth-watering and his darkly tanned skin is smooth where it ripples over those muscles. A deep scar sections half his face, cutting through one thick eyebrow, crossing the socket where an eye used to be and ending just below his lips, half of which now droop. His hair is a wild tangle to his shoulders and his long, fluid limbs are covered in dark tattoos and littered with more scars.

The Warlord chose Wolfe not because he is loyal, or a good man. He chose his personal guard and second-in-command because he's fierce and deadly. He kills without thought at a single command. A perfect guard dog. He obeys... for now, though I'm convinced there's something lurking beneath his rugged, terrifying exterior that this Sanctuary should be wary of. A sort of intelligence that he keeps hidden under layers of ferocity. His actions, though brutal and feral are always calculated, even when he's following an order. He thinks through the best way to achieve his ends and acts on that analysis with such rapidity that his actions appear fluid, natural.

I wonder what will happen when he's finally let off his leash, and sadly, I think that day will come sooner rather than later.

Yes, I've spent time studying him. As the second most powerful man in Sanctuary he spends a lot of time with my husband, and therefore me. We hardly speak, but we've known each other for years. Those strange green, almost yellow eyes follow me everywhere I go. Watching, judging, never giving anything away.

After a long pause, he says, "One of the visitors, an Outsider, asked for you directly." He says the word Outsider with a little sneer. I'm surprised. Wolfe rarely allows any kind of inflection into his voice. He either doesn't like Outsiders or doesn't like the one who is requesting a meeting with me.

"Not my husband?" I've never had a visitor ask for me specifically. Though I am the Warlord's favourite, I try to keep my head down, appear calm, mild and obedient to everyone outside the harem.

"Show them in," I tell him after a moment's thought. There's little an outsider or anyone else can do to me in the Warlord's fortress. Any threat to my safety will come from inside. "Take proper security measures, please."

Wolfe nods sharply, turns and leaves without another word. The man rarely speaks. I've become used to his abrupt entrances and exits. I glance toward the Warlord's throne as I wait for our guests. It sits empty, the same as it has for months. The chair should be mine, I make all the decisions on behalf of my husband. Unfortunately, no one can know that I'm the power behind the Warlord, or there will be threats to our lives, our leadership. Women aren't respected or given any kind of authority. Not unless they take it, like I have.

I climb the dais and sink onto the smaller chair, to the right and slightly lower than the Warlord's seat. I fold my hands in my lap and wait, knowing that I look the picture of perfect wifely obedience. Hair perfectly arranged, loose and around my shoulders, just the way he likes it. A feminine dress, light and flowing paired with a pretty flower-pattered scarf, my habitual accessory. The outfit is demure with just a hint of sexy so others might see what they are missing in his lordship's harem. I used to hate the way he dresses his wives, but I have since grown accustomed to and even appreciative of the feminine clothes. Few people would consider the predator that lurks beneath them. The woman who thirsts for the kill, for revenge.

My husband has many faults, vanity included. But ultimately, he is harmless. I smirk at the thought. I am to appear less dangerous than I am, and my husband is to appear far more powerful than he is. What a strange world we live in.

I straighten in my seat and drop my eyes to the hands folded in my lap as the door opens and a group of people enter. From beneath my lashes I see a guard of six including Wolfe. He must really think the outsiders being escorted into my presence constitute a risk, six guards seem overboard.

I stand and delicately make my way down the steps, to stand in front of Wolfe. Tension rises between us, and I itch to push him out of my way. He knows that he is to step aside so I can greet my guests. Instead, he takes a long pause, telling me without words exactly who is in charge if he wants to be.

I swallow a scathing snarl and wait him out. Yelling at my guard will only serve to diminish me in the eyes of the newcomers. Until I know who they are and why they're here, they don't need a first-hand view to the contentious dynamics within our Sanctuary.

Finally, Wolfe steps aside, brushing his bicep against my shoulder as he passes. I hold my breath and then release it slowly. He means to disconcert me. I can't fall for his tricks.

"Welcome to the Santa Fe Sanctuary." I keep my eyes lowered and my posture meek.

A pause, and then a quiet voice. "Skye?"

My head snaps up and recognition slams into me like a truck. I feel hot and cold at once, my gut clenching in hopeful fear as I take a hesitant step forward, staring at an apparition. A woman I'd thought dead, or at the very least completely lost to me. My younger sister. We haven't seen each other in fifteen years. She was small then and she hasn't grown much. I'm several inches taller, my frame more robust. But otherwise, we could be twins. Our faces are nearly identical, except for a tiny mole just below my lip. My hair is also somewhat darker without the shining red that has always been her signature. We both share the same stormy grey eyes.

From the look on her face she is almost as shocked as I am. Like she didn't believe she would find me here, though our meeting can't be a coincidence. She looks like she's been travelling hard for days, without much rest or opportunity to clean herself up. Her hair is a tangled mess around her shoulders and her clothes are rumpled and dusty. Unlike my tidy dress she is wearing pants, a shirt that buttons all the way up her front and a scarf around her throat.

"Taran," I manage to choke out from a throat rapidly constricting with emotion. My gaze swings to the side and I look at Wolfe, directly in the eye. He must have realized. We look too much alike for him to have shrugged off the resemblance. His gaze remains distant and cool. Did the bastard hope to disconcert me by showing them in without warning me?

"Skye!" Taran says again and steps toward me, reaching out. The man next to her grabs her arm and drags her back.

I look toward the other person, the Outsider, and I get my second shock for the evening. Standing next to my sister is my kidnapper, the man that snatched me from the safety of my travelling companions seven years ago and sold me to the Warlord. Before I can stop myself, I stumble back a step.

Talon's hard gaze is on me. I expect malevolence or a leer, but his expression remains bland, waiting for me to pull myself together. I remember that he was always that way, quiet, stoic. I've turned him into a monster in my head. I take a steadying breath and straighten my shoulders. Stepping forward I reach for Taran and gather her into my arms, jerking her from his hold. She wraps her arms tightly around me, pressing us together as hard as she can. A tiny sob shakes her frame.

"I'm here, honey." I call her the same thing our grandmother used to call her. Then it occurs to me that Taran must know what happened to grandma and grandpa. All these years of wondering and the answers are standing right in front of me in the shape of my only kin. My heart swells. I finally have a piece of my past.

Taran leans back far enough to look at me while still clinging. "I can't believe it's really you!" she exclaims. "All these years, I thought you were dead."

"I know." I can't stop looking at her, at my beautiful little sister. I hold her hand tight, unwilling to let her go, for even a second. I turn back to Talon. "Thank you for bringing my sister to me."

He nods slowly, his gaze thoughtful. "Thought the Warlord would appreciate a matching set."

The reminder of my husband brings home the precarious position I'm in. Someone like Talon can't know that the Warlord is incapacitated. He'll use the information to his advantage, selling it to anyone looking to challenge our authority.

"Of course," I murmur.

"If he wants her, she's going to cost him."

My hand tightens around Taran's and she takes a small step closer to me. Now that we're together we won't be separated again. I'll fight until my dying breath for her.

"Of course he'll want her," I say sharply. "He'll pay what you ask."

He smirks at me. "The price is high."

A wave of cold revulsion rolls through me. The price the warlord paid for me was high. He'd given Talon a new car, gasoline, supplies, and access to his fortress for the duration of his stay.

"I also have information he'll want," Talon continues. "For an additional cost."

"We don't trade in information," I snap. "You can keep whatever you think you know to yourself. You will be fairly compensated for producing my sister and then you will leave Sanctuary."

Sliding my arm through Taran's I turn with her, preparing to leave. I need to be alone with my sister, figure out how she got here, what happened to her, what happened to our grandparents, everything. But before we can leave the room, Talon's gravelly voice halts me.

"Fair enough," he says, his voice deceptively nonchalant. "I would like to speak to the Warlord personally though."

I release my sister and turn to look at him, all the feigned demureness fading away as I square my shoulders, lift my chin and give him the chilliest, most queenly stare in my repertoire. "I'm afraid that will be impossible."

"Is he incapacitated somehow, is that why you're now speaking on his behalf?" He scratches his bristly beard. "Have to admit, when I dropped you off here, a pathetic, sobbing mess of a scrap, I hadn't thought to come back and find you running the place. Thought they had better standards around here."

His words are like icy daggers as he knowingly plays to all my fears. The bastard is too smart to believe a lie and I can't have word get out that my husband isn't the one running Sanctuary anymore. I automatically glance toward Wolfe who is studying me with a calculating expression. I can't tell what he's thinking. I can never tell what he's thinking, but I usually know I can use him as backup if I need. In this moment, I don't know what he'll do if Talon calls me out.

"I'm afraid that you misunderstand," I say as regally as possible. "The Warlord is not incapacitated. He simply doesn't want to be bothered with petty Sanctuary business and has entrusted me as his wife to take command while he attends to more important business."

Talon nods thoughtfully, his expression deceptively bland. "I see, well that does explain it." The sarcasm in his voice is clear and I see the guards exchange a quick glance. Fuck, I can't have them questioning a system that has worked for more than a year.

"If that's all, I'd very much like to retire with my sister and get her some proper care. She looks as though she's been through a horde attack." The jab that he didn't properly care for her seems to hit home as his glance slides quickly over her, assessing for damage. Interesting. The Outsider seems to have developed feelings for Taran.

I reach out for her arm and turn to leave again. Again, he speaks. "Tell the warlord I want to talk to him about a cure."

I whip around, tired of this sick fucker playing games with me and my family. "I don't know what you're talking about." I turn my scathing stare to Wolfe. "Please escort this man from the building. Pay him appropriately and escort him beyond the city walls. I don't want to see him again."

The men close in around Talon and I'm satisfied that my problem is taken care of. But, of course the Outsider has more to say and he plans his jabs perfectly. "I'm talking about the cure to the Death Kiss. Humans with immunity to the bite."

I freeze in place my heart pounding so hard in my chest that my ears beat with the blood rushing through my veins. A gasp draws my attention. Taran reaches up to clutch at her neck, terror brightening her eyes.

My gaze clashes with Wolfe's and his hand falls to the hilt of his dagger. I hope that I'm understanding him correctly. This is a critical moment in the future of our Sanctuary. If Talon knows of my immunity and he divulges the information in front of all these men, he'll destroy everything I've worked so hard to achieve.

I give him one warning. "You need to stop talking."

He doesn't heed my words.

"I think your husband will be very interested in his new acquisition." His eyes flit to Taran and every person in the room looks at her. She stares back at him with a stubborn tilt to her chin, but she's gone completely pale. I look to where her fingers play with the edge of her scarf, sliding beneath, touching the skin. Could it be? Is it possible that she was bitten too?

If she was, I can't allow Talon to divulge her secret.

I glance at Wolfe again. He tenses in preparation.

"And what makes you presume to know what my husband will be interested in?" I ask, staring at him. I release my grip on Taran and step closer to my adversary, getting directly into his space. The same spark that I felt ten years ago ignites between me and Talon. The sexual tension that nature instilled in us, clashing with my need to escape captivity and his desire for a payday. He hadn't fucked me all those years ago, but he'd wanted to.

He takes the final step separating us until my chest brushes against his with each breath. Out of the corner of my eye I can see the tension vibrating through Wolfe. He hates my proximity to the Outsider, hates the heat stirring between us. He so badly wants to kill the man standing in front of me. I lift my lashes, turning what I know is a soul-sucking grey gaze up to my enemy.

"What makes you think you can leave this room alive if you breath so much as a word of what you think you know?"

He bends his head to mine. I turn my face to the side so his lips brush my cheek instead of my lips. He moves his mouth to my ear, speaking in a low voice, the deep rumble sending shivers down my spine. "I'm a gambler, darling Skye. Life has taught me to take risks."

I back up a step. "This is a risk you shouldn't have taken, Talon." I flick a look toward my guard.

Wolfe pulls his dagger and, in one fluid motion, swings it up in an attempt to drive it into Talon's ribcage. Talon twists to the side, blocking the thrust and reaching for his own weapon. His weapons would've been confiscated before he was escorted into my presence though, so he has no recourse as Wolfe swings on him again.

Before Talon can properly protect himself, Wolfe throws a jab to the solar plexus, which Talon blocks and then slams the knife into Talon's neck. I'm sure Talon is a good and skilled fighter. He'd have to be, to have reached this age as an Outsider, to battle not only Primitives but humans with ill intent, deals gone wrong, any threat that comes his way.

"No!"

I'm startled by the scream from behind me. I twist around to look at Taran's white, stricken face, the hand hovering over her shaking lips. Have I done the right thing? Was there something between the two? I hadn't stopped to think, just instinctively tried to protect my sister, and by extension, myself.

As I turn away from him, Talon lunges forward, taking my arm in an unbreakable hold. As he struggles for breath, choking on his own blood, we crash to the floor together. He lands on top of me, the blood from his wound dripping onto my white dress. I bring my hands up to protect myself, but his grip is already loosening. I stare into his eyes as the light slowly fades, leaving the icy blue orbs lifeless.

Men lurch all around me, reaching for us, belatedly trying to protect the Warlord's wife from being attacked by a dead man. Wolfe reaches us first. He kicks Talon off me and reaches down to grip my arms, dragging me back to my feet. I'm startled by his touch. I can count on one hand the amount of times he's touched me over the past seven years. Today makes four. He holds me slightly longer than necessary, his green gaze assessing as he sweeps me, looking for injuries. Then he abruptly lets go, giving me a small push back toward my sister. His gaze lingers on my breasts, on the blood.

He steps next to Talon's body and reaches down to drag the knife from his throat. It slides easily from the flesh. Wolfe kneels to wipe his blade on Talon's shirt, dragging it over his chest, cleaning it in an insulting gesture.

The other five guards straighten back into position and stand stiff, facing forward, as though they hadn't even noticed the death that'd just happened right between them, or my involvement. They are a well-trained group.

I slide my arm around Taran and lift my eyes to Wolfe, who has turned back to me. He gives me a slight nod to indicate that I should leave. Everything about him seems to have relaxed, shifted somehow. I'm not sure why. He's a born killer. The hired gun of each Warlord inhabiting the Santa Fe Sanctuary from the moment he could lift a weapon. He should be a mindless puppet, but he's not. He's my protection, and he's my greatest enemy within the city walls. I shiver as an image of him slamming that big, lethal knife into my throat blurs my vision. What happens when he wants Sanctuary and I'm standing in his way? I'm under no illusion that he won't take me out just as quick as he killed the Outsider.

"Come," I whisper and turn away, my arm around Taran as much for her support as it is for mine. "Let's get you cleaned up."

THIRTY

TARAN

"I think I'm going to be sick," I manage to whisper before clamping a hand over my mouth.

Skye graciously leads me directly to a private wash-room, where I immediately fall to the floor in front of the toilet and heave my guts out. I can barely catch my breath as another wave of nausea slams into me, stealing my ability to breathe and bringing tears to my eyes. The tears manage to sneak out, trailing down my cheeks as I throw up everything I've eaten today.

Skye's cool hand pulls the hair away from my sweaty forehead and holds it back while I'm sick. She doesn't speak, doesn't do anything other than pin my hair back. When I'm finished, she helps me lean against the nearest wall and hands me a wet cloth. As I press it to my hot face I wonder where she got it from. Do they have running water in their fortress, the same as we do in the Tower? This Sanctuary does seem very organized.

When I'm finally capable of focusing on something other than my own discomfort, I search out my sister. She's leaning against a sink, her arms crossed over her chest. Her eyes are narrowed in concern and speculation.

"I'm sorry," I offer pathetically.

She waves her hand in the air between us. "You have nothing to be sorry about. You just watched a man die horrifically right in front of you. It's not an easy sight."

"No," I agree grimly. "But it's not my first time either. I've seen death."

"This one is different," she observes. Then she asks matter of fact, "You loved him?"

"God no!" I give her such a look of disgust that she laughs. "He was a pig. He fucking sold me."

"Glad to hear it," she says, still laughing. "He sold me too. There was no love lost on that man."

It would seem not. I don't know why Talon's death is so gut-wrenching. I suppose I'd learned something about him as a person, and humans in general while I was travelling with him. Despite his missing morality, his brutality, his terrible manners, there was more to him. A depth that took me by surprise. Much like my time with Diogo, I'd learned that not all people can be typecast, can be written off as one thing or another. Good and bad don't exist in our world. Just survival. Something both Talon and Diogo taught me.

I suppose, in a way, seeing Talon die so suddenly has reminded me of the fragility of life. I'd been bitten by a fucking zombie and somehow survived. Yet he'd survived for years on his own, outside the walls of a Sanctuary, only to have his life brought to an abrupt end once he stepped foot inside one.

Finally, I look at Skye, and say, "He had a family once, a farm, land of his own. He took me there, showed me a piece of himself. He liked children. Maybe it was that one saving grace that's making his death harder than it should be for me."

She nods, her gaze searching mine. "Then, for your sake, I'm sorry we killed him."

"I'm not," I shrug. "He was about to out us."

Her hand flies up to her neck. I nod in shared understanding, reaching up to tug my own scarf away. She drops to her knees beside me, her fingers grazing the deep scars in my neck, before creeping up to cover her mouth. "Dear god," she whispers. "It's a miracle you survived."

"I almost didn't," I confess. "I don't know how Talon knew about it. He was there when I was attacked but I didn't know he saw anything. He didn't give any indication that he knew I'd been bitten."

"He saw my bite marks when we were travelling here together, before he sold me to my husband. Maybe he put two and two together, assumed you had the same immunity I do." She pulls her own scarf down and tilts her chin up, allowing me to examine the marks on her neck. Though obvious, they are much fainter than mine. White teeth marks surrounding slightly raised flesh.

"I thought you'd died." Tears spark in my eyes again and I have to swallow hard to stop them from falling.

"I know." She pulls back a little, tugging her scarf back up and then settling beside me on the floor. She takes my hand in hers and holds it in her lap. "I never blamed you, or our grandparents, for leaving me behind. When I was bitten, I thought I was as good as dead too. I just wanted to give you the chance to live."

I choke back a sob. "I didn't want to live after that. I missed you so much."

She nods sympathetically and then tips her head back against the wall. "But the point is that you did live, despite your pain. When I was recovering, when I realized I would likely never see my family again, that was the one thought that kept me sane."

I pull in a deep breath and dash the tears away. I've been through the emotional wringer lately, it's a miracle I don't just break down and cry all the damn time.

"Just tell me you've managed to build a life for yourself," she says suddenly, her grey eyes piercing as she turns to me. I know what she wants. She wants me to tell her that her sacrifice was worth it, that she gave me the opportunity to live a happy life.

"I did," I tell her truthfully, thinking of my time in the rebellion as the Desert Wren, my place in Emery's home, my friends, and finally, my husband.

"Then it was worth it," she whispers.

I have my own opinion about that. I will never believe that Skye should sacrifice herself for me, but I also understand that she will continue to do so at every opportunity. Her actions today have proven that. When Talon threatened to out me and my immunity, she stepped in and silenced him. At the time, I'd been too distraught to pay attention. Now, I remember the looks that passed between her and the man who killed Talon. There had been some kind of intimacy there, some unspoken message. As though her protection of me had been a major step in some kind of political game she was playing.

"Taran, can you please...?" She starts to speak and then her voice trails off.

I interpret her thoughts from her hesitant words, knowing they would be mine as well if our situations had been reversed. "You want to know about our grandparents?" She loved them as much as I did. She must have suffered over the years, not knowing what became of us. The same way I suffered when they were left outside the walls of Tucson Sanctuary.

She nods. "Yes, please tell me. Don't hold anything back."

I swallow hard and grip her hand tightly, but I don't look at her as I speak. I can't. If she wants to know the story, then I need to tell it as unemotionally as possible.

"When you were... after you were..."

"Attacked in Las Vegas Sanctuary," she supplies.

I nod quickly, reaching up to brush away a tear. This is a hard thing to talk about. "We were devastated to lose you. Grandfather had to literally pick me up and carry me or I would've run back into the city to find you. I didn't care that you were probably turned, I wanted to turn too if it meant being with you."

"Oh Taran..." she whispers.

"I was too young to realize at the time that our grandparents were also devastated. It wasn't until later, when we joined a group of Sanctuary seekers headed South that I realized how devastated they were. Grandfather blamed himself. He turned into an old man almost overnight. Grandma became hyper-vigilant, wouldn't let me out of her sight. Up until Las Vegas the four of us managed to stick together for years after our parents died. Your loss completely broke us."

She nods and swallows hard. I suspect she can't speak from the tears clogging her throat, so I continue. "We travelled South. It was a hard road, but relatively boring. We didn't run into very many obstacles along the way and managed to avoid a horde by hiding in a warehouse basement until they passed us by. It only took us a few months to get to the Tucson Sanctuary."

My throat starts to clog with tears again and I have to

swallow hard past the obstruction. Skye remains silent, giving me a minute to collect myself and my thoughts. She seems to have matured. She's more thoughtful and poised, less impetuous than she used to be. Though her actions toward Talon tells me her experiences have hardened her. She doesn't weigh human life the way I do.

"When we arrived at the gates of Sanctuary we were taken right in as refugees and sent to processing. Only when they tried to sperate us did I realize there was a problem. Grandma told me to go with them, to listen and not worry. It didn't take me long to figure out what was happening, that I was being granted Sanctuary, but they weren't. You see, there's a law within our city that all refugees must be fully capable of contributing. Our grandparents were considered too old to contribute. They were turned away. I screamed, cried and begged. I'd run after them, but they left me, insisting to the guards that I still be granted Sanctuary. I haven't seen them since that day."

I expect Skye to react in outrage, to show some of the emotion I'd shown when I was torn from the only people in the world left to love me. Instead, she nods thoughtfully and sighs with regret. "We have a similar law here."

"It's wrong," I say bluntly, catching my stray tears with the edge of my hand.

She looks at me, really taking me in, and once more I'm struck by the differences between us. So many more than there used to be. Something has happened to change the Skye I knew, to harden her.

"There's a reason the most successful Sanctuaries only take in refugees capable of contributing to society. We aren't capable of stretching resources to people who can't pull their weight or add to the community in a positive way. Without birth and regrowth, we will fail. If left on our own, we'll die out. Our birth rates aren't high enough. The rate of death is always higher if we allow the population to stagnate or overcrowd with the sick and elderly."

"There has to be a way." My argument is an old and unpopular one. It's based on my own experiences. "I simply can't agree that life no longer holds value if there's no chance of reproduction. My friend Milla is infertile, yet she contributes more to the city than many of the people producing mouths that need feeding. Experience is an immeasurable resource, yet completely discounted in Sanctuaries."

"That's not true," she says gently, smiling slightly. "You don't need to see everything in such blacks and whites. It isn't one or the other, but somewhere in between. Yes, we've probably turned away people of great value because they don't contribute a working womb or a strong back, but we've also taken in people of great value. Here in our Sanctuary we have a man, a historian, who is a constant flow of much needed information. Without him we wouldn't function near as well as we do."

I sigh heavily and lean my head back the way she does. "I do understand. It's just..."

"You wish our grandparents hadn't been turned away."

"They were left to die in the desert, Skye," I whisper. "We should've been together. All of us. Even if it meant dying together."

She holds my hand and we sit silently, working through our own thoughts. Finally, she turns to me and says, "I refuse to be sorry for whatever events have brought us back together. You're right, we belong together, and we won't be parted again."

"I've missed you," I murmur.

She gathers me against her and we hug.

"I've thought of you every single day since Las Vegas," she says fervently. "I knew you were alive and I never lost hope that we would find each other again."

We rise together. Just as she reaches for the door a knock startles us. She opens it. The man with the missing eye, the one who killed Talon, is standing on the other side. His gaze flits between us and then lands on Skye. The thoughtful weight of that look is telling. There's something going on between them. Or perhaps he wishes something were going on.

"There's another visitor at the gates requesting an audience with the Warlord."

Skye frowns, her hand tightening around mine. "Tell him to come back tomorrow, I've had enough visitors for the day. The Warlord will need to be made aware of Taran's presence."

"He's insisting, and he says he has an army at his back."

"Did he give you a name?"

"Diogo Fuentes, Warlord of Tucson Sanctuary."

Skye turns to look at me, an eyebrow raised. "Exactly what have you gotten yourself into that the Warlord himself would come searching for you?"

I give her a sheepish look and shrug. "If you want your Sanctuary to remain standing, you'd better let my husband in. He's not a patient man."

THIRTY-ONE
DIOGO

"You will produce my wife in the next two minutes or I will be forced to make a move against the Warlord of this Sanctuary." Though I am a cauldron of raging emotion, I manage to keep my voice low and even. Facing off with me is the second-in-command of Santa Fe Sanctuary. His broad shoulders are stiff, and like a good soldier, he gives nothing away in his expression.

"He's unwilling to grant an audience at the moment." The soldier, Wolfe, glances past me toward Stryker who's standing silently, his arms over his chest. I know my man well. If I choose to attack, choose to cut Wolfe down and force my way into the fortress, Stryker would have my back.

I pace, forcing my brain to work through the problem. The fact that my wife is on the other side of the gates is twisting all of my thoughts, making me reckless. I want to cut a bloody path to her side, fling her over my shoulder and leave without a backward glance. I don't give a fuck about actually meeting with the Warlord, but I'm trying diplomacy first. But first, I need to calm down so I can plan and negotiate.

I stop pacing and turn to Wolfe. "If you do not produce my wife within the next few minutes, I will leave, and I promise that you do not want this. Because when I return, I'll have an army. Men skilled in the art of war. Men with nothing and no one to lose. They'll take this city apart, brick by brick until they find my woman and then they'll burn the rest."

He twitches, his chin moving as though he wants to say something.

"Have you heard of me?" I demand.

"Yes." He nods and stiffens his posture. "Everyone has heard of Warlord Fuentes. You held the border during the Mexican horde war."

"That is only one of my achievements," I snarl. "I took my own father's Sanctuary apart and burned the rubble, giving him no recourse. He was the most brutal, most awe-inspiring opponent I've ever stood against. He invited me to take his city. I did, and then I left, not wanting a dead, burned out shell. I moved West until I found a Sanctuary I wanted and then I took it."

Nothing passes through his stoic green gaze, not surprise, not fear or respect. Just brooding acceptance.

"If you know of me, then you know how serious I am right now. You either find and present my wife or prepare your city for death."

I turn on my heel and walk away from the man, Stryker following.

"Was that a smart choice?" Stryker grunts as we make our way beyond the city walls and back to the vehicle. "You didn't give them anything to bargain with and, at the moment, you hold the vulnerable position. It'll be a different story when the men show up, but they ain't here yet."

"They won't take me out. I hold too much territory, too much loyalty." I jerk the door open and slide into the jeep. "Striking out at me would be suicide."

If Stryker disagrees, he doesn't say anything. He just gets in the car and leans back in his seat, closing his eyes. We don't have long to wait. The huge city gates swing back open at the same time as the dust cloud of my backup rises on the horizon behind us, filling the landscape with my promise of retribution of the coming negotiation doesn't go my way.

I want my wife. There will be no other outcome.

THIRTY-TWO

SKYE

Ushering my sister to the harem feels both proper and shameful at the same time. I've become a different person since we last met, accepting things into my life that didn't seem real when I was a sixteen-year-old girl searching for Sanctuary with my family. Now, the women of the harem have become my family.

The residents, particularly Hannah, took care of me when I first arrived. Taught me how to fit in, but also how to preserve my individualism in a society taken over by the base instinct to survive. They showed me that there is no shame in belonging to a group of people whose only job is to serve the Warlord. I learned that sex is just another weapon. A more subtle weapon than the weapons of men, but just as potent. Sometimes just as deadly.

I took their teachings and applied them to my Warlord, weaving him into the spell of my love as quickly and effortlessly as if I'd been born to the role. Much like my sister, I'm a survivor. Unlike my sister, I'm also practical. I don't see the world in the blacks and whites that she sees. I believe that there is nothing wrong with taking the law into your own hands when living in a lawless world. I've climbed to the top of my particular world and this is where I want to stay.

"You'll be comfortable in here," I try to reassure Taran, stepping away from her. "Hannah and the others will take care of you."

"Where are you going?" she asks sharply, eyeing the other women with suspicion. "I want to see my husband."

"I understand," I tell her calmly. "But we have certain protocols we need to go through before we allow guests into the fortress. Especially guests of Warlord Fuentes' power. I need to go and see my husband, update him on the situation and your presence here. I'll be back very soon."

She shakes her head and looks around again, her gaze sweeping the women who are watching her curiously. Their revealing flowy dresses clash with Taran's travel worn masculine outfit. The women in this room have become a status symbol. The property of a powerful figurehead. Where once I would have dismissed their power as I can see my sister doing now, I no longer underestimate its worth.

I turn to Hannah. "Please take good care of Taran. She's very special and is to be treated with the utmost respect."

"I understand," Hannah says softly, her kind amber eyes promising that she will do as I've asked.

I step closer to the other woman, bending my lips toward her ear. "Don't let her leave the room."

"I heard that," Taran says sharply, if a little sarcastically. "I'll leave the room if I want to. In fact, I'm leaving right now." She heads toward the door only to stop short when a big, mean-looking harem guard steps into her path. She turns back and glares at me.

I sigh. Same old Taran. Headstrong, stubborn and a bit

of a brat. "You need to remain in the harem, Taran. It's for your own safety."

She shakes her head and balls her fists at her side, the frustration within her visibly rising. "I want to see Diogo. Right now!" I can understand her feelings. She's been through hell, kidnapped from her Sanctuary, taken from her husband and dragged into an emotional meeting with a sister she thought long-dead. In her place, nothing would stop me from going to my husband.

I go to her, taking her fisted hands in mine and rubbing them. I talk to her in a low voice so the others can't hear. "Please trust me, Taran. I promise you, no one wants to hurt you here. In fact, everyone in this room has reason to care for the plight of a fellow woman in need. Allow them to take care of you and I'll be back before your husband can set fire to our wall."

Hannah walks slowly toward Taran, as if approaching a wild animal in desperate need of care. "Are you hungry?" she asks kindly, waving her hand in the direction of a hallway that leads to a kitchen. "We have many succulent choices. We're lucky here in the fortress, we have access to the best and freshest foods."

Taran looks as though she's going to refuse but then her hand drifts to her stomach and, despite her pique, she says, "Okay, I am a little hungry, but only because I threw up my breakfast."

Hannah laughs softly and links her arm with Taran's. "Let's take care of that and then we'll discuss what you'd like to do next. Perhaps a bath or a change of clothes. We can do whatever you please."

"I'll be back before you even know I'm gone," I assure Taran and walk swiftly to the main door before she can argue some more. I rap on it and seconds later it swings open revealing another big, burly harem guard.

Wolfe falls into step beside me as I walk. Tension flows between us until I feel like I'm going to start screaming just to crack his eternally expressionless look. Before we arrive at the Warlord's chambers, he speaks.

"What went on between you and the Outsider?" he demands.

I frown at him. "Nothing."

"Something," he snaps. Still, his expression doesn't move. When he looks at me, the only indication I get that he's annoyed is the twitch of the badly patched skin over his empty eye.

I stop walking and spin toward him. He stops too, taking a step toward me until we're standing in each other's space. I dart a glance down the empty hallway before I hiss, "What exactly do you want to know? Do you want to know if I fucked him, is that it? Do you want details?"

His fingers curve as though he wants to grab me. He doesn't touch me though. Maybe he knows the Warlord will punish him, but I don't think that's it. Wolfe has far more power that our current leader. He also commands the respect of the military and the fear of the residents within our Sanctuary. If he made a bid for power, he might actually win. The question is, would I become a casualty in his war, or would I pass from one man to another?

I have power too and could put up a fight if he tried to take over. The harem holds its own when it comes to loyalty within the city. Unlike other Sanctuaries we don't have a lot of strife or unrest among the citizens. While our Warlord and his men take care of security, the harem manages the people. We take care of medical needs and supplies, food production and distribution, clothing, water, education.

Now, if that same harem decided to rebel, decided to seize power, we'd have an entire city of loyal followers. They would burn the fortress to the ground rather than see their precious saviours harmed. And I stand at the head of the harem, proudly taking my place next to the Warlord as his favoured wife.

Does Wolfe see all this? Does he understand the implications, the potential war? I think he must. He's not a stupid man. His quiet reserve masks the constant watching and plotting that goes on behind that strange-coloured eye.

Rather than answer my question, he waves me toward the Warlord's chamber, his gaze fixed on the wall over my head. I clench my hand into a fist, resisting the urge to strike him. I turn and stride away from him, my soft slippers managing a satisfying tap, tap, tap as I walk. One day we'll be forced to deal with the tension that vibrates through every meeting. Today is not that day. My mind is elsewhere.

The doors to the Warlord's chamber are opened for me, allowing me to walk through without pause. The guards stand on the outside, rarely allowed into his private sanctum. Everything in the fortress has become a well-oiled machine. The Warlord set it all up and I smoothed out the kinks, with a harem of women at my back.

I look around and spot my husband sitting in his chair next to the indoor herb garden, a blanket over his knees. The scent of nature fills my nostrils as I approach, a myriad of smells from flowers to strong herbs like basil, lavender and rosemary. Though not a green thumb myself, I have spent many enjoyable hours in the garden watching Silas dig and muck about.

I sink to my knees next to his chair and wait eagerly for his attention. It used to come quickly, sharp and almost desperate as he realized his love for me. Now he's slower, disease having ravaged his senses. Glioblastoma, or brain cancer, is the diagnosis our doctor came up with. We were told that, without intervention, this condition would become fatal after a few years. Not trusting his assessment, believing there had to be an available cure, I'd sent away for another doctor, another opinion. At great peril and expense a doctor arrived from the East coast only to second the opinion of the first.

Ultimately, the diagnosis means that my husband will die at a relatively young age for a Warlord who was top of his game when we met. 50 or so years ago we would have been able to get him medications and treatments to either cure or slow the ravaging effects, but now, we are left to simply make him as comfortable as possible.

"Silas," I whisper when it appears he isn't paying attention. He must be having a bad day. Though slow, he's normally sharp enough to know what's happening around him. Headaches and fatigue are a constant nowadays.

He turns his gaze slowly down and looks confused for a moment. I fear we've finally reached the point where his memory can no long hold up under the pressure of the disease. Then he smiles, his special smile, just for me. It lights his face in a way nothing else can do, stretching those thin lips and showing a hint of the crooked teeth behind.

"My love," he says and reaches a shaking hand, placing it on top of my head and stroking. I close my eyes at the caress, soaking in his adoration.

When I first came to Sanctuary I fought every rule, every interaction, every command. I hated that I'd been sold into slavery to some debauched Warlord. I was determined to hate him and everything around us. But instead of crushing my resistance, as he so easily could have, he'd bowed to my fearful anger and allowed me time. Almost a year of uninterrupted time to get used to the harem, to watch and process everything around me. Silas didn't make a single demand. The only thing he asked was that I have protection and not permanently leave the harem.

Gradually I got to know and love the women. I was baffled by their acceptance of the sexual side of their job. But then I began to understand that the binary, monogamous way in which I was raised isn't the only way. That the women of the harem felt fulfilled in their relationship with the Warlord and the children that relationship produced. It helped my concerns that the women were treated fairly and with respect. They are well taken care of and as happy as a person could be given the world we live in. If they don't wish to be summoned, they have only to say.

After a few months in the Sanctuary, I began to relax around the Warlord. We developed an intellectual relationship first. He appreciated my argumentative fierceness and my uninhibited and unabashed response to everything around me. I would dive headfirst into solving a city problem, then proactively make suggestions on how to prevent future flareups. I was also just as uninhibited in his bed, once I finally consented to his touch.

For his part, I have always loved the deep sense of honour and integrity of our Warlord. His unflinching realism combined with a deep-seated optimism that allowed him to make necessary changes despite the occasional failure.

We had a few good years before his health issues began to show, and even then, I was determined to preserve our perfect paradise. Me at his side, both with a power of our own, the harem surrounding us and the guard at our backs.

Then his illness reached the point that we had to start hiding it. We couldn't allow many people to know how bad it'd gotten, only Silas' most trusted advisors and closest friends. Sadly, as time has passed, it's become more and more clear that my husband doesn't have much time left. The past months have been hard, his deterioration rate speeding up. The last few weeks have been even worse. The hands that sift through my hair are claw-like and jerky.

"Can I get anything for you?" I whisper fighting the tears that seem so close to the surface whenever I'm in his presence these days.

"No, Skye." He savours my name as he says it, his voice a quiet caress. "You are already too good to me, pulling Hannah from her duties to tend me."

I smile and swallow the ache in my throat. "Hannah wants nothing more than to ease your..." I stop, unable to continue.

"My final days," he finishes. He cups the back of my head, holding me with his gentle possessive touch. Showing me his love even as life fades from his body. "Yes, she is a balm to me right now. Very soothing to have around."

I laugh and lean into his chair, huddling against his emaciated legs where they lay unmoving beneath the blanket. "Unlike your wild and impetuous head wife."

He buries his fingers in my hair and tugs it until I'm forced to look up. "My favourite wife. I've had eyes for no one else since the day you walked into my world, spitting fire and promising hell and damnation to anyone that touched you."

Again I laugh, the sound bright and oddly fitting in the moment, tinkling through the herb garden and flowing over the Warlord. This is my husband. Wonderful, calm, patient. A better leader doesn't exist. The unfairness of his coming death is sharp. I despise the inevitable. Nothing should be set in stone. We should have choice in all things. Yet, here I sit at the feet of my dying husband, a man not yet fifty.

"How will I survive, Silas?" I gaze up at his dear ravaged face. My heart feels as though it's splintering into pieces, nothing and no one will ever be able to glue those pieces together again. This man, this moment will forever break me.

It wasn't supposed to be like this. I was supposed to seduce the Warlord into falling for me. Seduce him into trusting me and accepting my counsel. Into doing the things I command without question. And while most of those things did happen, something else happened as well. I fell as deeply in love with the Warlord as he fell for me. Since the moment we have declared that love we've been a united force. Inseparable, incorruptible, indominable. The thought of continuing a life without him feels impossible.

"You'll manage," he says in his positive, realistic way. "Now tell me, lovely wife, what brings you to my side? I'm hearing gossip among our staff that we have guests."

I tip my head down and quickly brush the tears away. Silas has no patience for them and I will respect his wishes. When I look back up at him there is no trace of tears to be found.

"My sister has arrived, she was brought here by the same man who sold me into your harem."

"Taran," he says, surprise tinging his voice. "She's alive?"

He knows about my family. Every detail. From Grandma's ingrown toenail to Grandfather's habit of gambling for cigarettes when we were on the road. He knows that Taran would often drift away in a world of her own thoughts and fantasies. That Taran is the more optimistic, passionate sister, while I am the calculating hard-ass, never willing to give an inch. He has encouraged me often to speak of them, to unload my feelings so he could hug away my negative emotions and replace them with positivity and hope.

"Yes." I reach up to grip his hand. "And she's even more beautiful than I could have imagined. She's still small, like a little wild animal, but she's incredible. Beautiful red hair and an attitude to go with it. You would like her."

"I'm sure I would." He gives my hand a reassuring squeeze. "And the Outsider?"

He clearly remembers Talon. Though it was a fortunate turn of fate that landed me in the Warlord's harem, he's never liked the men that trade in the sale of women. I've pointed out the hypocrisy in his thinking once we'd starting meeting regularly. How he'd purchased a woman from the type of person he claimed to despise. He then pointed out the hypocrisy in life. Our struggle to survive with the inevitable spectre of death awaiting at the end. The desire to reproduce in an obviously dying world. Hypocrisy abounds in everything around us. At the time it surprised me that a Warlord, men usually known for their crass brutality, could be such a deep philosophical thinker. Now, I'm used to him.

"Dead." Blunt and to the point I tell him the truth. "He threatened to tell about my immunity to the Death Kiss, or more importantly, Taran's immunity."

"So, the aberration does run through your blood, I've always wondered." He allowed light testing once we'd built a platform of trust between us. But he hadn't wanted anyone, including a physician, to know of my peculiar disorder. "Who killed the Outsider, you or Wolfe?"

"Wolfe," I tell him. "But I gave the order."

Okay, I hadn't exactly given the order, but Wolfe knew of my desperate need to silence Talon. He acted on my thoughts, the order I silently gave in a glance. But I know my Warlord's concerns. He doesn't want Wolfe acting on his own, doesn't want him opposing my command. He trusts his second-in-command, but he wants to see me take command and flourish after his death. I don't want him to worry, so I allow him to believe that Wolfe and I are in perfect synchronicity in our thoughts.

"And what is it that brings you here, my wife?" he asks, stroking my thumb. When I open my mouth, he reads my mind and interrupts. "Yes, I know that I am enough for you. But city business keeps you busy. I get to see you when something is bothering your mind."

Guilt eats away at me, but he's right. I'm not the most attentive wife. I'm too driven, too full of life to slow to the pace my husband has reached. So, I send Hannah to him instead. I come as often as I can, but I suspect, as much as he loves me, she is more comfort in his final days.

"My sister," I admit. "Her husband, the Warlord of the Tucson Sanctuary, is here to collect her. I don't want to give her up. I've finally just found her, it doesn't seem fair."

He laughs suddenly, startling me with the surprisingly robust sound. "Sisters that manage to capture the attention of Warlords, both immune to the Death Kiss, and finally reunited. What are the odds?"

I smile at his reasoning. He's right, what are the odds?

Then he sobers, his gaze turning down to me. "He wants her back?"

I nod, tears filling my eyes again.

"And what does she want?" he asks gently.

He already knows the answer, knows that I wouldn't be here, begging an audience if the answer was different.

"She wants her husband," I say quietly.

"My little love," he says, tenderly, turning to me. I grip

his leg, not wanting him to topple out of his chair. "Give the girl what she wants."

Unbidden, a sob rips from my throat. He tenderly runs a hand over my cheek, cupping my chin in his big, scarred, shaking hand. He tilts my face up. "Do not deny her the right to love if she does love him. Find the truth and you'll know what to do." He strokes his thumb over my cheek. "I cannot advise going to war with Diogo Fuentes, especially if your desire is just to hold her here with you. Fuentes will crush our resistance and bring down the city. He is a formidable enemy." I blink rapidly and a few tears fall, trailing my cheek to land on his fingers where they cup my face. "Find a way to keep her that doesn't mean war."

I nod and he takes his hand away, falling back into his seat exhausted. I stand, towering over his bent form. I brush the dust of his herb garden from my skirt. "Thank you for your counsel, husband."

He nods and closes his eyes, taking in a sharp breath. "Please send Hannah to me when she's free."

"Touch me again and we're going to have a problem."

The sound of Taran's angry voice hastens my stride. I round the corner to the women's living quarters in time to see my sister wearing a towel and brandishing a kitchen knife at Hannah, Scarlett and the harem physician. I rush to stand between the point of the blade and the others in the room, not wanting anyone to get hurt. The young Taran that I knew as a teen had hated weapons and couldn't use them, but this Taran clearly knows what she's doing. She holds the blade with ease and balances on the balls of her feet as though prepared to strike.

"What's happening here?" I ask softly, drawing her attention.

"They took my clothes away and won't give them back. And now they want this..." Her angry gaze swings to the doctor, "... person to inspect me like some kind of cow. I don't want to be touched anymore. And I'm telling you, if my husband finds out all these people have been touching me he'll lose his shit."

"Language, Taran." I try to keep the amusement from my voice. She is exactly how'd I'd imagined she would be. Lovely, feisty, take-no-prisoners. She's my sister through and through; the thought of losing her again is gut-wrenching. I reach out a hand. "Please let me have the knife, sweetheart. The kitchen staff will want that back."

She rolls her eyes, flips it around and hands it to me hilt first. A near audible release of tension zips through the room as the harem relaxes once more. I'm certain they were more worried about Taran hurting herself than anyone else getting cut. A glance at her will tell a person that she has no business threatening anyone with a weapon. While she might be able to handle a blade, she has pacifist written all over her. I wonder how she and a warlord ended up married. A question I need answered before I hand her over to the man in question.

I hand the knife to Hannah and beckon Taran to follow me into my private room. Each member of the harem gets her own room, a private sanctum where she won't be disturbed. "Come, let's find you something to wear."

"I'd rather have my own clothes," Taran says grouchily, tightening her hand on her towel and following me.

I give her a stern look. "Don't for one minute tell me you prefer to wear those travel-stained, smelly clothes. You're in my Sanctuary now, and no sister of mine is going to appear in front of my people looking like a street urchin."

Her face softens and she smiles, dropping onto my bed as I search my wardrobe for something for her to wear. "This cop that would arrest me sometimes used to call me urchin because I wouldn't give him my name."

"Taran, you shouldn't bait men in authority, that's how you get yourself hurt!" I scold.

"I can't help it," she says with a dismissive shrug. "I was born to piss off the people in charge."

"Yes, you always were a stubborn self-righteous little thing. Why doesn't it surprise me that you've been arrested inside a Sanctuary before?"

"Hey!" she giggles and throws a pillow at me. "You don't even know the half of it."

I pull a dress from the rack, it's a little old-fashioned; light blue to complement Taran's eyes, with a high neck that'll button up over the scar on her throat. I toss it toward her and sink into the seat in front of my vanity mirror. Among the luxuries afforded to the women of the harem are the vanity desks, wardrobes filled with clothes, shoes and accessories. Beyond our bedrooms, we're treated to a kitchen with a chef, a personal trainer for exercising and guards to keep us safe.

"Tell me the half of it then," I demand. "Tell me about your life within Sanctuary."

She drops her towel and pulls the dress over her head. It fits loose on her smaller frame, but is still attractive, the colour beautiful next to her skin and hair, and her slight curves visible where the fabric flows down her body. Her fingers fly up the buttons, from her belly to her neck, ensuring each one is in place. She tests the collar, making sure it covers her neck, then she falls back onto the bed with a bounce.

"I was taken in at fourteen and given a husband," she starts bluntly.

"Fourteen!" I gasp, appalled. Most Sanctuaries have laws regarding women and marriage, and unfortunately marriage for girls of child-bearing age has become rather common. Still, I can't imagine my young sister becoming a bride at such a young age. The very thought is appalling.

She shrugs and echoes my earlier thought. "It's pretty normal in most Sanctuaries."

I don't comment that it's the norm for mine as well. My standards for a sister I love and other nameless faceless women are different I suppose. Perhaps a thought I should pick apart and examine again later. Does our need for babies outweigh individual freedoms? Should it?

"Xavier, my first husband, wasn't a bad person and our marriage wasn't real." A weight eases off my shoulders when she tells me this. Even though there's no way I could have saved her from the events that happened after we were separated, she's still my younger sibling, still my responsibility.

"So the man you married at fourteen isn't the Warlord you're married to now?"

She shakes her head. "No, I met Diogo a few months ago. I knew who he was, of course, since he's the Warlord, but I hadn't met him face-to-face. Our marriage... well, it's a little complicated and I'm not sure you'll approve all of my actions that led to it."

I laugh out loud, some of my tension easing. "When you put it that way, I'm certain I won't agree with what you did. But tell me anyway."

She sighs and leans back against my pillow, sprawling out despite, or maybe in spite of, the dress. "I guess to sum things up as quickly as I can.... I was part of a rebellion that started in our city several years before I arrived. As I grew up, my jobs became more significant until I stepped into the role of the Desert Wren, a rebel leader. My main job was to guide refugees into Sanctuary by any means necessary."

My jaw actually falls open as I listen to her story. She keeps her eyes on the hem of her dress, pressing it between her fingers nervously. She cares what I think, is worried that

I won't approve. This bad ass woman cares about my opinion. Pride, along with a tiny dose of worry over her antics, swells within me. We each took different paths with the lot we were given, but in some ways, we are so similar. I'd become a leader within the fortress, while she'd become a leader within a rebellion. Both strong, both resilient, both fighters.

"I had just climbed over the wall and was preparing to meet with a small group of refugees when Diogo arrested me and charged me with treason." Here I gasp and sit up straighter, her story catching my full attention. Treason means death in most Sanctuaries. "I guess the more he got to know me, the less able he was to hand me over to the Authority. He kept me near him and eventually we married."

She's blushing and refusing to meet my gaze. I have no choice but to ask, "Were you forced into the marriage?" Her answer will dictate my next move. Whether I break my own heart and hand her over to husband or go to war with an important and powerful Warlord. A war that could possibly end in the fall of our Sanctuary. Regardless, I won't give up my sister until I'm absolutely certain she wasn't coerced into this relationship.

She sighs deeply and finally lifts her eyes to mine. "Yes, he forced me into marriage." I can feel the muscles in my face go rigid as my mind whirls, picking up and discarding different plans on how to move against her husband. But before I can get very far in my thoughts, she says, "I may not have had a choice in my marriage, but I'm happy now. I'm happy with my husband. I love Diogo and I want to be with him."

I can tell that she's saying what I want to hear, but I can also hear the sincerity in her tone. She does love her husband. Fiercely and with an unbending loyalty. Silas is right, I needed to find the truth and my path becomes clear.

I smile, hoping it's not too watery, and speak, hoping the sound of my heart breaking isn't evident in my tone. "We've wasted enough time then, haven't we? Let's get you back to your husband."

THIRTY-FOUR
DIOGO

"Your time is up," I say coldly. "And I'm out of patience."

Wolfe takes a step forward and into my space. A brave move since it puts him beyond the safety of the wall. His men twitch nervously behind him. I sensed a death wish in this one from the start. He would make an excellent addition to my elite military if I could somehow convince him to leave his Sanctuary and join mine. If he survives the coming standoff.

"We will produce your wife in our time, not yours." His face betrays nothing as he says the words that will sign his death warrant.

I growl and reach for my knife just as he reaches for his weapon.

"That's enough." A sharp feminine voice rings out and a woman steps through the massive gates.

I'm stunned speechless for a moment as a taller and curvier replica of my wife walks toward me. A white gown simultaneously hugs her curves while managing to float lazily around her body. A neat scarf wraps around her throat to finish the look. She is like a polished version of

Taran. Every male eye in the vicinity is on her. Except mine. I'm looking past her, searching for my wife.

I don't care how beautiful this woman is, or how much she has the entire Sanctuary guard wrapped around her finger. She isn't Taran. She isn't my wild little bird.

"I'm going to ask you this only once." I try to keep the snarl from my voice, the aggression from my body language, but I know I'm failing. Wolfe takes a step forward so he's closer to Skye without physically blocking her. "Where is my wife?"

"Do you know who I am?" she asks sharply.

"At the moment, you are nothing more than the obstacle standing between me and my wife. You need to stop this, whatever it is and send my wife out. Any more delays and I will have my men attack the city."

She visibly flinches at my threat and then straightens her back and lifts her chin, giving me a sternly regal look. "You didn't bring enough men to take this city."

I don't bother to correct her. If she isn't aware that even a handful of my military elite is enough to ensure my victory, then I won't tip her off. One of my men is worth a hundred of hers. Except perhaps for Wolfe. He'd have to be the first to die if it comes down to a combat situation.

"We're done talking." I turn on my heel, signalling to Stryker. We'll meet with the rest of my team and come up with a strike plan. We won't have the element of surprise, but we have skill. The only reason I've held off on this course of action is because there will be casualties on my side and if possible I'd prefer not to harm the sister of my wife.

"Please wait," she calls, rushing toward me. I pull my knife and turn on her. She's reaching out for my arm and it takes real effort not to cut her hand off. How dare this woman hold my wife and then presume to touch me? She yanks her hand back before it can touch me.

Wolfe is directly on her heels, his look of anger directed at her. He wants to yank her back to safety, but she waves him away. Interesting. The dynamics between the two would indicate a power struggle that for all appearances she's winning, yet I suspect the other man is simply biding his time. Instead of falling back, she holds her ground and speaks in a low voice that only the two of us can hear.

"Please, I just need to know that she'll be safe," she says urgently, her voice a quiet hiss. "I need your promise that you'll take good care of her and shield her from the harsh realities of this life. From what I can see she's somehow managed to maintain her idealism, and the thought of someone or something crushing it..." Her voice catches and trails off.

I study her for a moment, trying to settle on an answer. I don't owe this woman anything but talking to her might be the more expedient method of getting Taran back. I swallow my pride and annoyance. "Taran's health and safety are my priority. She will not be harmed."

"And can you... can you..." her voice chokes up as she tries to speak. "Will you bring Taran back to me? Sometimes?"

Her question is a desperate one, and I won't be able to give her the answer she wants to hear. "You know I can't do that and keep my word that she'll be safe. Travel beyond Sanctuary is extremely dangerous."

She dashes away a stray tear and swallows hard, then nods. "You're right." Her shoulders bow a little as she realizes that she likely won't see her sister again once she releases Taran to my care.

I relent, just a little. "You will always be welcome as a

guest in our Sanctuary as long as your intentions toward Taran are honourable."

She laughs, the sound soft and bitter, then glances back toward the city. I know where her thoughts are. She'll have about as much luck being allowed to leave her Sanctuary as Taran will have leaving mine. Though she has annoyed me and taken several wrong steps by keeping my wife from me, I find myself softening toward this woman. Perhaps it's her physical similarity to Taran, or perhaps it's her earnest desire to keep Taran safe.

"We can use the long-distance radio towers to keep in touch." She perks up at my suggestion. "It's not a bad idea for our Sanctuaries to stay in touch anyway, given our relatively close proximity."

Her whole countenance brightens and she smiles widely. "Maybe one day we'll be able to form some kind of alliance. Help each other in times of crisis, that sort of thing."

"Perhaps." Any future alliance hinges on one thing; the expedient retrieval of my wife and our smooth leave-taking from the city.

She nods, understanding, and gives Wolfe a look that he seems to quickly interpret. He lifts his radio to his mouth. "Bring the woman."

My patience is wearing extremely thin. I stand stock still, arms crossed, fists clenched so I don't do something that could damage the outcome of this meeting. My eyes are fixed on the gate. Moments later a vehicle emerges. Before it even fully stops, Taran leaps out and runs toward me.

It's clear from the top of her shiny red hair to the lovely new dress and shoes that my wife has been well taken care of. When she's within reach she launches herself at me, heedless of the tensions surrounding us. I open my arms and catch her against me, holding her tight and burying my face in her hair, inhaling the fragrant aroma of wildflowers and pure, raw Taran.

I push her back a little and examine every inch. Touching her arms, wrists and fingers, her neck, hovering over the scarf, knowing I can't move it but wanting to see her scar, make sure it hasn't somehow torn open and gotten infected. I don't give a shit that all my men are watching, that the guards of this Sanctuary are watching, I take her face between the palms of my hands, tilt it up and press my lips against hers.

I don't even know if it can be called a kiss. I don't move, she doesn't move. We just stand in each other's embrace, our lips meeting, remembering, promising. I hold her face to mine, savouring the texture of her skin, breathing her in, memorizing everything about her. I'd known I wanted to keep her, to make her mine and to love her, but losing her, not knowing if I would find her again, has given me a new truth. I want this woman forever. I will become as formidable as it takes to ensure she stays alive for us to have our forever.

I separate only a hairsbreadth from her lips and ask in a low voice, "Are you ready to go home?"

"I'm ready," she whispers back, opening her eyes and staring straight into mine. The deep velvety grey depths catch and hold me.

I release her face and slip my hand down her body, reaching for her hand. I take it into mine and give her a reassuring squeeze before turning back to her sister. Skye is watching us intently, her eyes bright. Her lips are curved in a small, defeated smile. She has seen the depth of our feelings and won't try to come between us. I wouldn't allow it, but I can't simply kill Taran's sister. At least not in front of Taran.

Taran tries to break out of my grip, presumably to say goodbye to her sister. I pull her back against me, wrapping an arm around her middle and holding her in place, her back to my chest. I bend and say in her ear, "No."

She twists around and raises an eyebrow at me then stares down where my arm is barring her from moving. I'm beyond glad that her attitude hasn't changed a bit while she was out of my care. Still, she's not straying from my side for at least the next thirty years, possibly the rest of her life.

"I need to say good-bye," she says firmly and tugs on my hand. I don't release her.

"She can come to us." The words come out harsher than I'd intended, but I don't care. Taran will soon learn the depths of my protectiveness. I'd trusted her, trusted my guards, trusted the whole damn Tucson Sanctuary to take care of her, but my trust was misplaced. She'd been attacked and kidnapped in one of the most secure sectors of the city. Again. I will not be allowing my kidnap prone wife out of my sight for the rest of her natural life.

"It's okay, Taran," Skye reassures her and approaches us slowly, her eyes on me as if expecting a predator to suddenly strike.

I don't release my woman, forcing Skye to wrap her arms around Taran while I'm still holding her against me. She does it anyway, braving a possible strike to say good-bye to her sister, possibly for the last time. She buries her face in Taran's shoulder, holding her tight. I can tell by the way her back heaves that she's crying. Taran wraps her arms around Skye's back and holds her tight. She's whispering something against Skye's shoulder, but even I, with my close proximity, can't hear.

Wolfe moves to cover Skye's back while she hangs on to Taran. I glare at the other man, but oddly, he doesn't glare back. His stare is on the heaving Skye. I'm confused about their relationship. My understanding is that she's married to the Warlord and that it's a happy marriage. Yet the second-in-command clearly has feelings for the first lady of this Sanctuary. A complicated mess I have no desire to dissect further.

I drop my head to Taran's ear, the opposite side of her sister's head, and say, "Time to go, baby."

At my words she only clings tighter, hugging with every ounce of strength in her tiny body. Her sister hugs her back with equal fervor. When I hear Taran gasp for breath, I decide to extricate the two. I pull Taran away from her sister, but Skye looks to follow, tears streaming down her face. I nod toward her man and he steps toward her, taking her shaking shoulders in his hands. She thrusts him away and stumbles to the side.

Straightening her shoulders once more and swiping at her tears she says, "I'm fine, don't touch me!"

Wolfe's face hardens and he steps back, giving her more room.

"Skye..." Taran whispers.

It's becoming quickly clear that the sisters won't separate on their own. I lift Taran against my chest and carry her back to the car where Stryker holds the door open. I deposit her onto the seat and turn to my man. "Keep her here."

I stride back to Skye, who's standing by herself, looking lost and lonely, the hot wind blowing her skirt against her legs. "You've got what you came for," she says as regally as possible, but still unable to hide the edge of bitterness. "Please leave. There's only enough room for one Warlord in this city."

Funny that she invokes her husband, a man that couldn't be bothered to join us. Or perhaps a man unable to join us. If that's the case, then the future of this Sanctuary is looking grim. The fall of a Warlord destabilizes the government of the Sanctuary, causing ripples through the entire community. I wonder if Skye intends to take over, or if she'll hand the reigns to someone else, someone stronger. Perhaps the man standing at her back, watching like a sinister shadow waiting for the perfect moment to strike. There is no place for a woman at the head of a Sanctuary. Perhaps she's calling the shots for her ailing husband, if he is indeed too ill to perform his duties, but once he passes, the people will never accept a woman as their next leader.

"I want the man who brought my wife here. If you're holding him, then pass him over and we'll be on our way."

Her chin snaps up and she glares at me. The grey look is both intense and familiar, an exact replica of Taran's stare. Instead of being intimidated, as I'm sure she intends, I feel only a jolt of amusement. She's lucky she's so similar to my wife. If she wasn't, these negotiations wouldn't be going so well. She and her men would be laying in bloody pieces while I walk out with my wife.

"He's dead," she says succinctly.

"I killed him." This from Wolfe.

Rage flares at the loss. I lock my muscles so I don't attack the man that has denied my revenge. Apparently feeling the tension in the air, Skye steps closer to her guard, then interestingly, slightly in front of him, as though protecting him.

"I'm sorry we couldn't keep him for you." Her gaze flickers down and then back up, then she adds in a low voice that only the three of us can hear, "He was about to point out Taran's... scar."

Understanding dawns and another wave of fury washes over me. Talon had intended to not only sell my wife as a possible concubine to the Warlord of this Sanctuary, but as a curiosity as well. She could have been examined, experimented on, dissected. If Taran hadn't had an older and protective sister in attendance who knows what could have happened to her before my arrival.

I nod at Skye. "You have my gratitude."

She smiles slightly and relaxes. Her tears are now gone and she looks wistfully toward my car. As is the way of our reality, she is once more accepting the loss of a beloved family member. In this world our lives are made up of moments, tragic moments, happy moments, moments where we have to make split second decisions that will decide our futures, or possibly decide whether we have a future. Skye is rolling with yet another blow to her life, accepting it and moving on before the dust even settles. My respect for her rises.

"If you ever need Sanctuary, you will always be granted entry into mine."

"Thank you," she whispers. "Safe journey... Diogo. Perhaps we'll meet again."

She turns and walks away, signalling for her men to fall back. As I watch, the heavy gates of her city slam shut, locking us out.

"Taran, baby, time to wake up."

Diogo's voice pulls me from the dead sleep I was enjoying. I hadn't been able to snatch more than a few hours here and there in the days that I've been away from Sanctuary. Now that I'm back with Diogo I feel safe enough to allow myself to relax into slumber. I stretch my arms over my head and yawn widely. "I hope I didn't snore or drool."

"A little," Diogo murmurs with a laugh. "It was cute. Stryker said the noises you were making were enough to scare off a horde attack."

I hadn't actually meant to say that out loud. I send Diogo a dirty look and sit up, shoving hair out of my face and smothering a wide yawn. "How long was I out this time?"

Diogo decided to drive as far as he could without stopping, switching out the driver's seat with Stryker when he got tired. I was seated between them, resting against Diogo.

"A few hours," Diogo grunts, hefting his bag from the back.

"Why did we stop?"

"Both me and Stryker need some rest and we need to fuel up. The tank is almost empty and the reserve cannisters are out." He takes my elbow and starts leading me toward a building. "We're out in the open, baby. You'll need to stay as quiet as possible."

I want to tell him that I know what to do, that Primitives aren't new to me, but I know he's only thinking of my safety. That he hates having us out here where we can be attacked. He wouldn't have stopped unless it was important.

"Where are the rest of your men?" I would've thought they'd be right here with us, but Diogo's is the only vehicle in the deserted street.

"Two on the edge of town, keeping an eye for horde attacks. The rest of my men are heading out ahead of us to stake out our path home. They'll set up checkpoints and fall in behind us as we travel. It's safer this way, they can clear a path for us all the way home. We'll be fine, this place was abandoned a long time ago. Primitives have no reason to be here."

I look around, a shiver passing down my spine. The remains of a small-town main street is crumbling all around us. Diogo leads me up the steps of an old abandoned church, the dying sun lighting up the cross decorating the top. I hesitate, leaning back into my husband.

"Do we have to stay here?" I whisper, feeling the power of the building.

"Yes," he says shortly, pulling me up the stairs with him. "It's the sturdiest looking building here and the front doors close and lock. Stryker already scouted it out."

Still, I hesitate. I've never had any real kind of relationship with religion. There simply wasn't time or opportunity. I've been on the run my entire life. First, when I was searching for Sanctuary, and then as a rebel. But my grandmother had been a devoutly religious woman, had tried her best to tell us what Christianity was and how to follow. I always wanted to believe in a higher power, wanted something that would make the strife in our world make sense. Faith has always been a beautiful and elusive emotion to me, but I've never felt like a good enough practitioner to enter into the sacred places or clumsily pray to a God I didn't know or understand. To beg favours of a deity that I've given nothing to. The idea that we might shelter in such a sacred place feels somehow right and irreligious at the same time.

I don't have a choice though, as Diogo pulls me through the front door and turns to close and lock it. I wander toward another set of double doors, walking through, staring around in awe. It's a massive room, lit by the last of the sunset as it pours through glass windows rendered in a stunning array of different colours.

"What are they?" I murmur.

"What?" Diogo asks, coming up behind me.

I point, my hand shaking in reaction. Maybe hunger too, since my last meal was eaten many hours ago in my sister's Sanctuary.

In the glass a woman is depicted kneeling, her hands pressed together, the blues, reds and yellows around her glowing like they're somehow on fire. I've never seen anything so beautiful, and I doubt I will again.

"It's called stained glass," Stryker supplies, following the point of my finger. "This is the second time I've seen it. Glass seems to be one of the worst hit casualties of the Great Fall."

"You take first shift," Diogo says shortly, dragging me forward into the church. He looks pointedly at Stryker and jerks his head toward the entrance. "Outside."

"Fuck, man." Stryker tosses the blanket aside that he was arranging in a pew and stalks toward the entrance muttering something about desecration. "If I get eaten by a fucking Primitive, it's on you."

I giggle at Stryker's grumbling. It's impossible to imagine the big, gruff man as anything but capable. If a Primitive stumbles upon him in the dark, it's the zombie I would fear for. The doors close behind Stryker and I turn back to Diogo. The look he gives me is so intense, so filled with emotion that I take a step back, forgetting for a moment that I'm married to this man, that I love him.

He stalks me around the pew, his long legs eating up the space between us. "I want to know every detail, from the moment you were attacked in Sanctuary to the moment you were released." He catches me by the back of my head, his fingers sifting through the tangled strands of my hair. He lowers his head until his lips just barely brush mine. "You will not leave out a single detail. Understand?"

My heart pounds in both anticipation and fear. Anticipation because I can feel the sheer sexual expectation that pours from his very being. He's holding himself back because he wants to be one hundred percent certain I haven't been injured, either mentally or physically. My fear stems from his reaction to my story, because I will tell him the truth, in detail. There's been so much standing in the way of our happiness, my ex-husband, the rebellion, my zombie bite, everything. I just want to start establishing a foundation of trust, so we can move forward in our marriage. No more lies or manipulations. As difficult as the truths sometimes are, they are always better than a lie given to make the truth more palpable.

I sit down and gather my thoughts. As I speak, the words pouring out of me, I find a kind of catharsis in talking over traumatic events with someone I care about and trust. Diogo leans back against the pew behind him, his arms crossed over his chest, listening, rapt with attention, a permanent scowl marring his face.

I'd only been gone from Sanctuary for five days, but it feels like a lifetime. So much has happened. I was attacked, my bodyguard was attacked, and the greenhouse manager killed. I was forced to go on the road with a man who had no conscience, but was still relatable, perhaps even likeable in some ways. I'd explored a farm, seen a zombie graveyard and then been attacked in Talon's family home. He'd saved me as though it was nothing, an afterthought, something to do until breakfast was ready. I'd completely blind-sided my sister with my existence, a sister I thought long dead. Then given less than a day to get to know her.

This last part chokes me up and I slow down, my words coming out sluggish. "I'm sorry," I finish. "But even if I'd imagined Skye had lived through the Las Vegas massacre, I would never have even hoped to see her again. It was like a dream come true, and then..."

"Ripped away," Diogo finishes for me. He settles onto the bench seat beside me and takes my face in his broad palms. "You don't ever need to apologize for loving your sister, baby. It was a gut-wrenching decision to leave her."

"I love you, Diogo," I say, the strain of the past few days cracking my voice. "I couldn't live anywhere that you aren't. It's as simple as that."

He kisses my lips, the same way he'd kissed me outside of Santa Fe Sanctuary. Soft, slow, but still urgent. As though savouring everything about me, about us, in a single kiss. He breaths deep as his lips love mine, passionately, but without insisting on entrance. He breaks away, barely an inch and says, "Had you decided to stay, I would have dismantled that city, stone by stone until I found you."

I laugh, unable to help myself. I know that he's serious, but his fervent, over the top declaration is exactly what I expected in my husband. A rush of affection and relief pass through me. This man will protect me until his dying breath. That is an awesome power to hold in the palm of my hand, something that I will have to be careful with.

I touch his cheek with my fingertips and continue to smile. "You don't have to prove your love by dominating major cities anymore, I believe you."

His face splits into a smile, though a tight one. He won't soon release the stress of the past week from his shoulders. Time spent hunting a wife that he couldn't say with certainty was even alive.

"I knew," he murmurs, kissing me again, before running his lips up my cheek to my ear, exploring, savouring, loving.

"How do you always know what I'm thinking?" My voice sounds breathless. I grip his shoulders and hold him against me, enjoying his touch, even if his fingers are a little too hard, a little too desperate as they run down my back, wrap around my waist and hold me like he's never letting go.

"Your every expression gives you away." He kisses my neck and along my collarbone, moving the neckline of my dress as far as he can to get at the flesh beneath. It's an unyielding dress so he doesn't get far. "You also speak out loud a lot without realizing, especially when you're thinking hard about something."

"What?" I gasp, laughing and trying to pull back to look at him, but he holds me tight. "I do not! You can't be serious."

"How do you think I knew all of your favourite foods

within the first week of our being together. You kept chattering out loud about how you wished for this and that. It's how I knew what to plant in our garden. How has no one told you that do this?"

He catches my hips in his hands and drags me down the bench until I fall, catching myself on an elbow. His eyes are on me as he slides his hands up my legs, from my ankles, to my calves, to my thighs. "I suppose no one's been brave enough to tell me."

"No," he says, hooking his fingers in the waistband of my borrowed panties. "No one told you because they didn't want you to stop. It's a beautiful and rare thing, finding someone who gives everything away. You are on the surface as you are underneath, beautiful and perfect."

Tears sting my eyes at his description. I'd never thought about the way I might look in another person's eyes. My constant drive to succeed and the little insecurities that make up most human beings has blinded me. But Diogo's adoration and unassailable love is hard to argue with. Looking at myself through his eyes makes me want to be the person he sees.

As he drags my panties down my thighs, I reach for him, hooking my arm around his neck and dragging him forward into my body. I kiss him with every ounce of passion and gratitude I feel. We are from two different words, two different childhoods and two different philosophies, yet I can't imagine loving anyone more than I love Diogo. His constant and persistent love is irresistible. I cling to him, pouring all of these feelings and thoughts into a single kiss. His hands tighten on me, holding me against him until we're practically fused. No end to him, no end to me, just the two of us together on an island, in an abandoned church, in an abandoned town.

"I need you, baby," he says against my lips, reaching between us, shoving my skirt up as he reaches for his own zipper. "More than I need to breathe."

I hold myself against him, kissing him, breathing in the scent of his skin, warm, male, sweaty and familiar. "Me too," I whisper in his ear before burying my face in his neck.

I forget where we are, what's happened to us, everything. I cling to his broad shoulders trusting him to take me to heaven. A place I'll only visit if my husband is by my side, guiding me every step of the way.

He parts my legs and surges between them, burying himself to the hilt in one thrust. I bite off a scream as I'm overwhelmed by the intense pressure of him forging a path into my tight body. His big body feels so completely right as it covers mine. We're connected physically, but our bond goes so much deeper. With each thrust our bodies strain, slide and cling. Our hearts beat in unison. My fingers dig into his arms while his are wrapped around me, holding me tight.

This meeting of our bodies goes beyond physical want. We are reaffirming ourselves and our marriage. He's claiming me and I'm giving myself up to him. The feel of his steely muscles under silken skin draws my hands down his flesh, eliciting a groan of ecstasy from him as he enjoys my gentle exploration. The juxtaposition between my soft touches and his near-brutal thrusts send us higher.

Our eyes connect in a moment of perfect understanding. This fleeting moment will end, the pleasure will end, but we won't. We're forever. Until death do us part.

"Taran!" he shouts my name as he buries his head into my shoulder and slams his cock deep inside me, his release quick and powerful.

I cradle him to me and whisper, "Diogo."

THIRTY-SIX

TARAN

"Heads up!"

Stryker's booming voice startles us both awake. Diogo sits up, immediately slamming his head into the bottom of the pew we'd fallen asleep under. After we had sex, Diogo decided it was the best place for us to be able to sleep together and have decent cover. He barely pauses to absorb the shock before rolling out the other side and leaping to his feet, knife in hand.

"Oh there you are," Stryker grunts. I sit up, blinking sleep from my eyes, just in time to see Stryker throw something at Diogo. When Diogo catches it, I realize it's a rifle.

"The fuck is going on?" Diogo demands, checking the weapon for bullets then cocking it in readiness.

"About a dozen Primitives headed our way, Commander. The guy you put on the edge of town sent up a warning and they appeared down main street a few minutes later. They weren't running like their next meal was about to peel outta town, but they definitely suspect humans in the vicinity. I told the lieutenant to watch our six, but he stopped responding. Think they got him."

"Motherfucker," Diogo growls. He sheathes his knife and pulls his sidearm.

He turns and hands it to me. I shake my head, but he shoves it into my hand. "I don't know how to use it!" I protest.

"How the hell did you get to your age not knowing how to use a damn weapon," Stryker growls. "You're like a helpless sitting duck. May as well go sit out front until the horde arrive."

"I've survived this long!" I feel the need to defend myself.

"Blessed are the fools."

"Hey!" Real anger rises up as Stryker insults me. "I've got skills, asshole."

"So did my grandma. Zombie's didn't give a shit about her knitting abilities when they took her out."

"Enough!" Diogo interjects. "Stryker, you're on the door. I'll cover the windows. Taran, you stay in the middle, use the pews for cover."

The words are barely out of his mouth when the shattering sound of glass fills the area and the high-pitched howl of a Primitive fills the air. We turn in unison to see the twisted body of a Primitive where it lies on the ground, having come through the glass window. We watch as it slowly turns over and pushes itself up, ignoring the glass cutting deep into its flesh.

It stands on the spot for a moment, heaving, the concave, emaciated hollowed out chest moving in and out. Slowly its eyes sweep the area until they land on us. It pauses as its malevolent, crazed gaze lingers, taking us in. Its nose twitches and then the eyes widen, taking on a wild look before it launches itself at us.

I yelp and stumble back hitting Stryker. He pushes me

to the side, toward the pews just as Diogo shoots the Primitive in the head, the boom of his rifle reverberating through the church. We don't speak as a moment of shocked silence passes through us.

"I think they know we're here," I point out.

Stryker snorts and heads toward the front of the church, hunching in the doorway between us and the lobby in an attempt to cover both areas.

"Don't engage, Taran. You just hide." Diogo gives the order just as several more Primitives come through the windows, sending shattered glass flying outward. Diogo's face lights up in some kind of savage victory. Like he's enjoying himself, savouring the moment. This is the Warlord shining through. The man who loves a battle and isn't afraid of death.

Shots fire all around us as Diogo and Stryker take out every Primitive that comes through the windows. Banging at the front doors tells me they're trying to get in that way too, but not having as much success as they are shattering the beautiful stained glass windows. Assuming the doors will hold, Stryker makes his way to Diogo's side. They continue shooting in unison, picking off everyone that comes through the window. Gradually the crowd thins until only a few stragglers are left trying to get in. The men cover each other when one needs to reload. I hold my pistol out in front of me, waiting for one to get by, but Diogo and Stryker are faster than the Primitives.

Then the inevitable happens and, with a resounding crack, the front doors are broken open. Stryker spins around, racing toward the Primitives pouring in through the doors. Five, six, seven! I lose count as they overwhelm him. Diogo pulls a knife from his belt and, after killing one more Primitive as it gets stuck on the windowsill into the church, turns to launch himself into the fray of Primitives attacking his man.

I back away from the writhing, screaming bodies, pointing my gun but unable to shoot because my husband is in there somewhere, killing everything he can get his knife on. The only warning I have that a Primitive made it through the window while no one was watching is a terrifying grunting sound and the clatter of someone scrambling over the pews.

I spin around just in time to see it launch itself over the last pew separating us. It lands on top of me, its heavy body slamming into mine and sending us both crashing backward into the pews. I scream and swing my arm up, trying to protect my face and neck. It sinks its teeth into my arm, biting down on the flesh at the same time as I bring my gun up underneath it and shoot it in the chin.

Blood sprays across me and I turn my head to the side so it doesn't get in my mouth and eyes. I try not to look at it as I push it to the side, its teeth dislodging from my flesh. I gasp down at my bleeding arm and cradle it against me.

"Taran!" Diogo shouts.

I look up as he disengages from the melee and hurdles toward me. The Primitives push Stryker back toward where I'm huddled, as if they scent blood and now want to get to me instead of killing Stryker. Diogo lands on his knees in front of me, his gaze first landing on the dead zombie at my side before taking in my bloody arm.

"Fuck, Taran!" Diogo grabs my shoulders and shakes me, sending a wave of dizziness through me. "Were you bitten again?"

I nod and thrust my arm out toward him. It's not nearly as bad as my neck wound had been but the skin is definitely broken, blood welling in the little dents caused by the teeth marks.

"You need to stop getting fucking bitten," he snarls as he wraps my arm using the bandana around his neck. I don't point out that his bandana is filthy and probably more likely to cause infection than just leaving the wound alone. I also don't point out that being bitten by zombies isn't a choice I make for myself, but rather a terrifying event that keeps getting thrust upon me. He's scared for my safety, and when he's scared he reacts in anger.

Looking deep into my eyes, he counts, first the seconds, then the minutes. "Thirty-seven, thirty-eight, thirty-nine..." I watch his lips as he counts, counting the numbers with him in my head, shaping them with my lips, though no sound passes through. We barely notice as Stryker protects our backs, staving off the last straggler Primitives who are driven to throw themselves on his weapons in an attempt to reach their prey. "Three minutes." Diogo says, and then starts his count again, "One, two, three, four, five..."

Though I was relatively certain I wouldn't turn, I still had a few doubts. But as Diogo ticks the seconds and minutes by, I become more and more certain. I will not turn. There is something in my blood that gives me immunity to the Death Kiss.

"Four minutes," Diogo persists. "One, two, three, four..."

The last Primitive falls, Stryker's knife buried in its stomach. He yanks the knife out and a quick flash relieves the zombie of its head. I flinch and look away. The small movement causes Diogo to grip my arms even harder, to shake me until I'm looking at him again.

"Talk to me, Taran," he demands. "Fifty-seven, fifty-eight, fifty-nine, five minutes."

I look at him, digging my fingers into his arms, catching him with my fingernails on purpose. I need him to feel the bite of pain, need it to ground his terror. "Diogo, I'm not going to turn."

He shakes his head and keeps counting. I look past him to Stryker who's watching the exchange with exhausted interest, blood dripping from the end of his knife, his pistol lowered to his side. My eyes meet his and a curious expression lights his gaze. Not worry that I'd been bitten, not fear that I could Turn. No, he looks angry, and that anger is directed at me, it glows hotter with each passing second. With each count that Diogo makes.

I shrink back into the pew behind me and close my eyes, willing the time to pass.

Finally, Diogo finishes. "Eight minutes," he says succinctly, stopping his count. Ignoring the torn flesh where I'd dig my fingernails in, he runs his hands up my arms. "You're safe now."

"Never doubted it," I murmur, steeling myself enough to lift my gaze past his shoulder, to meet Stryker's eyes again.

Instead of anger, I see resignation. He shutters his gaze and turns away, leaving us huddled on the floor together.

Diogo grips me hard and pulls me into his embrace. "This is the last time, baby. No more zombie bites. One more time and I'll spank the life out of you."

I laugh and sob at the same time, slapping a hand over my face as he holds me against his shoulder. "Yeah," I say, allowing the weariness to leak into my voice. "I'm good with that."

Maybe a solid spanking will give me incentive to stop getting bitten.

"I mean, on the upside, now we know that first bite

wasn't a fluke..." I trail off with a laugh, half hysterical half humorous.

Diogo just shakes his head and smashes me against his chest, holding me in a bone crushing grip that is exactly what I need in the moment.

THIRTY-SEVEN

TARAN

We leave the church immediately after the attack, gathering up our things and flinging them into the back of the jeep before piling in. I sit in between Diogo and Stryker. The tense silence in the car is building nearly to breaking point and I don't know why. Diogo is probably being vigilant, worried about another attack, a legitimate concern considering we're about to fuel up, something I'd learned from Talon is one of the most dangerous things survivors can do when traveling between cities.

It's Stryker's quiet tension that concerns me. From what I've seen of the man, he's usually relaxed and easy-going, no matter what's happening around him. He knows I was bitten, and he protected our backs while Diogo tended to me. But what does he think? Is he worried I'll still turn?

Or perhaps he's not even thinking about my immunity to the Death Kiss. Diogo trains his men to observe and react, but not to state their opinions unless asked for. Maybe Stryker's deliberating the best plan of execution for refuelling. I myself am pondering the same problem. There's almost no chance that the Primitives that hit the church were the only ones in the area. Yet, we can't wait to gas up. This is the only town with a working fuel station for at least 300 square miles.

He confirms my thoughts when he says, "I'm closer to the tank. I'll fuel while you cover. Your woman ain't half bad with that sidearm of yours, give her the gun and let her cover that window."

I want to protest but they both nod their agreement. Stryker takes Diogo's sidearm and fills the chamber with bullets. I want to tell them that I'm not a good enough shot to be given such an important job. Bullets are a commodity, one that isn't always easy to come across, but I swallow my protests. They need every person to take part. I'm protecting the man I love. With that thought I feel better about taking the weapon from Stryker and calmly holding it as we approach the fuel station.

Two Primitives throw themselves at the vehicle, one jumping onto the hood and smashing his hands against the windshield, while the other races toward Diogo's side of the car. Diogo places his rifle in the open window and pulls the trigger. I look away before I have to see the Primitive lose its head, the boom of the shot echoing through the car and against the surrounding buildings.

Stryker kills the one on the windshield and reaches out to grip the creature by a leg, dragging him off our vehicle and dumping him in the dirt. I will never get used to the casual acceptance of death. The immediate forgetting of the person that's been killed. No matter how many times I'm attacked, no matter how many Primitives are destroyed, I will never forget that they were people once.

I grip my arm, just over the fresh wound. Twice now I've been bitten. I could too easily be among their ranks. If I were to die a Primitive, I'd want someone to mourn. At least mourn the person I once was. I wouldn't want to be a forgotten corpse, left in the dirt, the exhaust fumes of a vehicle passing over me, the people inside forgetting my existence in the time it takes to blink an eye.

Moments later, we're at the fuel station, Primitives still lurching after us.

"Go," Diogo says grimly, hitting the brakes so hard that I have to reach out with my hand to stop myself from going into the dash. Both Diogo and Stryker leap from the vehicle while I crawl to the window, lifting the gun and placing it against the sill, waiting for an attack that I hope won't come.

We wait in tense anticipation. It's after sunset now and, except for a sliver of light provided by a crescent moon, visibility is next to nothing. Yet Diogo's sharp eyes pick them out of the darkness. His rifle barks and the echo of a shot rings out, the dull thump of a hit registering seconds later. He shoots three times in a row, each time hitting something I can't see. I'm shaking in fear, yet I continue to cover my husband's back as he protects us.

After what feels like hours, but is probably only minutes, Stryker shouts, "Done!"

Both men leap into the car, Stryker half through the window covering us in the darkness as Diogo peels out, leaving a cloud of dust in our wake. I twist in my seat, hanging onto the back as I watch the road behind us. My heart leaps as I see a single Primitive lurching through the dust, his hideous scarred features glaring in the light of the moon as he chases after us.

"Stryker, behind us!" I manage to yell, tapping the other man on the knee and pointing. He turns in the window, takes aim and pulls the trigger. I don't see where the bullet hits, but the Primitive stumbles and goes down in the dirt, not getting back up again.

A wave of nausea hits me as the jeep rattles along a broken road, going faster than it should considering the lack of light and the cracks in the road. If we get a flat tire out here on the road, we'll be sitting ducks. The Primitives can attack en masse, using sheer numbers to overcome our resistance.

It's Stryker that says something though. "Slow down, Commander. Nothing's chasing us right now and we need to put distance between us and that town, not strand ourselves out here with only a few bullets left and a couple of knives."

Diogo doesn't say anything, but the vehicle slows to a good pace. Squinting into the dark surrounding the vehicle I don't see any more Primitives. Still I keep a vigilant eye and so does Stryker, leaving Diogo to drive. We drive slowly through the night, Diogo carefully picking his path in the dark. I have never been in a vehicle in the dark and consider the whole experience frightening, with or without a horde of Primitives attacking. When all is quiet and we put enough distance between us and the town, Diogo takes the opportunity to explain road mechanics to me.

"When they existed fifty years ago all vehicles had lights on them so people could drive safely in the dark." He wraps an arm around me and tugs me closer to his side. "After the Great Fall, when vehicles became more and more scarce, lights were one of the first things to go. The bulbs themselves were difficult enough to find, but when the electrical circuitry that made them work failed, there were very few people left in the world with the mechanical know-how to fix them."

I very much doubt driving in the dark was ever safe, with or without lights. But I keep the comment to myself.

Instead I murmur, "It's a miracle we have any vehicles left. They're so rare and they fall apart so easily."

"Humans are nothing if not resilient," Diogo says. "We'll work with what we have and then try to better the things around us. Try to make our lives more convenient, more bearable. It's in our nature to survive using the best methods possible."

"That's surprisingly optimistic coming from you." I snuggle deeper into his side, enjoying the warmth passing from his body to mine. Cool desert air is flowing through the vehicle as we drive.

"Humans are fucking cockroaches," Stryker grunts. "They can't be killed."

I look over at the big man, slumped against the opposite window, a hat pulled low over his face. I thought he was asleep. "And that's a bad thing?" I ask softly.

He shrugs one shoulder and still doesn't look over. "Humans are responsible for the downfall of this planet. They were responsible for releasing the Death Kiss into the world, they were responsible for not stepping up when they should've to eradicate the disease -"

"Even if our ancestors had focused more on the disease than they did, you don't know that they could've come up with a cure," I interrupt. "I think the world we now live in was inevitable, but it's our actions and reactions that matter, that forges a path forward for us. We are responsible for ourselves and our own future, not a bunch of people that died fifty years ago."

He pushes his hat back just enough so that our eyes meet. I see a combination of deep-seated fury and accusation there, but also a softness, like his anger isn't directed at me. I wonder if Diogo sees the same thing I see when he looks at his man.

"You're too young to know what's inevitable in this world. Your optimism is cute, but misplaced. We live in a world where more people die than survive, where people either die violently or from an illness that could've been prevented shortly after the first outbreak." Stryker's words are bleak, even bleaker than the things I've heard Diogo say. He must've lost someone, and that loss has crippled his perspective, twisting it to something incredibly dark. He doesn't have my optimism, he doesn't have Diogo's realism, and his easy-going attitude is fake. He continues, "We could've come up with a cure fifty years ago if governments had gotten their heads outta their asses and helped each other, rather than focusing on the bottom dollar. Now we're outta dollars and everything else that makes this world bearable. We deserve to die this way."

I stare at him, wondering what happened to make him this way. We're all resentful of certain aspects of the apocalypse. I want safe haven for all, yet my dream will likely never come to fruition. Diogo wants a flourishing society.

"I'm sorry you feel that way," I murmur.

Stryker snorts and settles back into his seat. "Don't want nobody's pity. It means nothing."

"That's enough," Diogo interjects, his voice harsh and weary. He's been driving for hours, his eyes straining ahead as he picks out the safest, fastest routes to get us back home. Once in a while we pass one of his men on the road who falls in behind us.

Whether because of Diogo's order or because he has nothing else to say, Stryker falls silent and moments later his soft snores fill the vehicle. I smile, enjoying the feeling of having Diogo to myself. Enjoying the feeling of safety I get by just being near him, because I know he will ensure my well-being. With that kind of support at my back, I feel invincible, like I can do anything.

I must've drifted to sleep, my head on Diogo's arm, because the next time he speaks, he says, "Look, we're home." He nudges me awake.

Yawning, I sit up and look around. The first light of dawn is picking its path along the ground, lighting up the Western mountain range on the opposite side of the city. When I glance behind, I see the clouds of dust kicked up by Diogo and his men. It's an incredible sight, like an approaching storm, headed toward the city. I draw my breath when I catch sight of the city walls. Lighting a path across the top at key points are fires, as though guiding us home.

When I point them out, Diogo nods and says, "They're for us. A welcome to the Warlord and his lady."

Stryker coughs pointedly.

"And the Warlords guard," I add with a laugh.

"Damn right." Stryker leans his arm across the windowsill.

Diogo brings the vehicle to a stop in front of the gates. Though I'm exhausted, ready to be home, I'm still awed by the somehow significant moment. A guard rounds the front of the car and stops by Diogo's window.

"Welcome home. The Sanctuary is yours, Warlord Fuentes."

I drive through the gates of Sanctuary, happy to be home, but happier to have my wife safe behind the walls of our city. The Sanctuary that I own, that I control. The feeling is a dominant emotion within me, the instinct of having my woman in the place where I am king. Where I can protect her best.

I reach through the window and take a radio from one of the gate guards. Mine lost its charge while we were on the road. I lift it to my lips and start speaking, "Fuentes here. I need Doctor Bishop at the Tower immediately. Cruz, you'll need to come too. I want a full report of all activity since I was gone and a progress report on the wall rebuild."

"I don't need a doctor," Taran mumbles sinking into her seat and shooting me an annoyed look.

I glance pointedly at her arm where she'd been bitten, but don't bother speaking. She knows she'll be seeing the doctor. She was out of my sight for days, doing god knows what. Having god knows what done to her. She told me her version of the story, but I don't trust her to give me all the pertinent details, especially if she was hurt in some way I haven't discerned yet.

"Drop me at the station." Stryker nods to the road ahead of us, indicating the path to the guard station. Apparently, he means to get right back to work. Not that he has any reason to do otherwise. He doesn't have a wife to care for and he spent most of the night dozing in the passenger seat. He should be fresh as a daisy and ready to report to the wall.

I give Stryker a hard stare, one eye on the road and one on him. He stares steadily back. I wonder if he's thinking the same thing. That moment Taran got bitten. He hadn't been shocked or surprised. Hasn't said a word yet about how she didn't turn. I don't know where his brain's at, what he's thinking when it comes to her immunity. His knowledge could make him dangerous. And while I consider my men to be completely loyal, I don't like that someone besides me, Taran and Bishop know her secret.

Stryker knows what her survival means. Knows what her survival could've meant to his own wife if a cure could be developed from the people who have immunity to the bite. The existence of a possible anti-virus could be a game-changer. But even if a cure is developed, he has to realize it's too late to do anything about a woman who was bitten twenty years ago.

"What's happening?" Taran whispers, anxiety sharp in her tone.

I whip my head to the front and slow the vehicle down. People line the pavement, surrounding all of the most important buildings in sanctuary. The police station, guard station, water treatment and food distribution centres. The frowning desperate faces that we pass speak to unrest within the city.

"A riot?" Taran asks tentatively. "Like the food shortage riots?"

"Not yet," I grunt, guiding my jeep through the restless throng toward the guard building. "But something's definitely going on. They're preparing for some kind of protest."

I stop the car and without a word, Stryker gets out and walks toward the doors of the guard building. When someone tries to stop him he brushes them off, never breaking stride until he's safe inside the building.

We leave right away, heading toward Sector One and the Tower. She gasps and clutches my arm as we approach the checkpoint.

"I see it," I say grimly.

It's surrounded by people and they're arguing with the armed guards. She digs her fingers into my arm as the guard waves his rifle toward the crowd, causing them to step back.

"They're saying something."

We both fall silent, listening, and then our eyes meet as we realize at the same time they're chanting, *we want the Desert Wren,* over and over. She swallows hard and her eyes shine as she realizes the group at the gate are her rebel friends. They haven't seen her in months and they've come to demand her freedom. I frown at the excitement spreading across her face. I don't know what she's thinking, but her ties with the rebellion have been severed.

I'm about to shout for the guards to open the gate for us when Taran shouts, "Emery!" Before I can stop her, she flings the passenger side door open and leaps out of the jeep. It was still moving, albeit very slowly, so she stumbles when her feet hit the ground. Arms wrap around her and she's pulled into a bear hug with a man I don't recognize.

My blood boils as I park the car and reach for my own

door. Once again, she's putting herself at risk *and* she's hugging a male.

"It's Taran!" Voices shout from all around us.

I catch sight of her as she's dragged into the melee laughing and struggling to free herself from a bone-crushing hug. Once my woman is safely escorted away, I intend to return and break this man's arms, teaching him not to touch another man's wife, before disembowelling him to make sure it doesn't happen again.

"My girl!" Emery cries pulling Taran from the man and wrapping her in her arms. Tears stream down both of their faces. Emery takes Taran's face in her hands and examines her, her sharp eyes flying over Taran's body. "It's been so long since I've set eyes on you. I had to make sure you were safe."

"I'm doing okay, Emery," Taran reassures the other woman squeezing her hands.

I grab Taran, pull her against my side and walk her back to the car. I don't care that, for the first time in months, she's finally seeing the woman she considers as close as a mother. As far as I'm concerned Emery has brought danger to my gates in her selfish need to set eyes on Taran. I warned her to stay away, but she seems not to have heeded my warning. I may have to make my next warning more permanent.

"Listen to me." Emery grips Taran's hand in a hard hold, making sure they remain connected and walking with us as I drag Taran back to my jeep. Emery's words burst out in rapid fire, knowing she's limited to a few seconds. Once I shut the door between them, she'll be cut off from further communication, a satisfying thought. "There's unrest in the city. Without Xavier Gunther or the Desert Wren to lead us the slums are in complete chaos. People are scared and angry."

Fury rises, and I turn to snarl in her face, "The Desert Wren is dead. And all of her former rebel friends will be too if they don't stop pursuing my wife."

Ignoring Taran's gasp at my harsh words, I open the passenger side door and shove her inside. Completely ignoring Emery who smacks the doorframe with her palm and reaches for the locked handle, I return to my seat, start the jeep up and drive forward despite the crowd in my way.

Emery bangs on the jeep and shouts. "This rebellion is rising up. Make sure you're ready for it!"

"I'm sorry," Taran whispers, not loud enough for Emery to hear.

Emery's hand slides away. "Come back to us, darling."

I hit the gas and we shoot forward into Sector One. People leap out of the way of the vehicle. I turn to glance back through the window as guards shove the throngs of people back, shouting and pointing their weapons. Taran follows my gaze and frowns at the rough handling. I'm satisfied that my men will keep the rebels out.

"Was that necessary?" she snaps, turning back in her seat to glare furiously at me.

"You got out of a moving vehicle to confront an angry mob. Have you no care for your own life?" Any patience I had left slips from me as I remember the way she stumbled into the mob. My voice rises to a shout. "Do I have to handcuff you to me whenever we leave the apartment just to stop you from doing anything else stupid?"

She flinches back in her seat and stares at me, shocked. I'm not surprised, I rarely lose my temper, especially with her. Taran has forced me to find hitherto unknown depths of patience when it comes to dealing with her. I can see the gathering argument in her eyes, and while I'm still irritated with her behaviour, I can't help but admire her fighting spirit.

"You're wrong!" she snaps. "I may have my reckless moments, but I never do anything deliberately stupid. Those were my friends, I was never in danger."

"That is not for you to decide." The day I took her as my wife was the day she became mine to care for, whether she likes it or not.

"I'm not a child."

"You'll be treated like one until I know that you can comply with my wishes." I stop the vehicle in front of the Tower and turn to her, sliding my arm across the back of the seat and tangling my fingers in the ends of her hair. I breathe her scent her scent, touch her, savour the textures that make up her; her silky skin, her curly hair, her beautiful, small curves. They combine to calm me on a level nothing else can. "You are too independent, Taran. You get hurt when you're left to your own devices. I won't allow this to happen again. You're..." I trail off, searching her face for understanding. She looks back at me with those velvety grey eyes, with the intensity that is uniquely hers, as though she's truly looking at me and seeing every part, right down to my soul. "You're too fucking important to lose."

She sighs and relaxes, tipping her head to the side and rubbing it against my knuckles where my hand rests on the seat behind her. I feel the tension gradually release from my shoulders.

"I can never stay angry with you, even when you're being completely unreasonable." Her eyes water and she shakes her head, letting out a little laugh. "I cry too much."

I brush a tear from her cheek, curling it into the palm of my hand. "You cry the perfect amount." I lean over and kiss her, my lips lingering over hers, tasting the tears as they fall.

Then I murmur against her, "Just let me protect you. I can't lose you, baby."

She nods and smiles against me, her lips brushing mine, sending a wave of heat crashing through me. "Okay, you can be an overbearing pain in my ass for a while."

I take her wrist and pull her out my side of the car before reaching in to grab my bag and slinging it over my shoulder. I slam the car door shut and escort her into the Tower. "Unless you want the handcuffing option you'd better just settle in and follow the rules."

She laughs and says, "Let's start with some handcuffing in the privacy of our apartment first and then see if we like doing it in a more public place."

I grin at my wife's kinky suggestion. She never ceases to surprise or amuse me. I tap her ass as she hurtles past me to take the stairs at a run. She likes to do that. Thinks it gives her the momentum to get through the first ten floors. She makes it to twelve before she starts slowing down and then floor number sixteen when she starts clutching at a stitch in her side and looking a little green. Fuck, this is exactly why I wanted her to see a doctor. She's too fucking delicate for her own good.

I shift my bag and sweep her up into my arms, holding her against my chest. "Tell me what's wrong," I demand.

She snuggles against my chest and relaxes into me as I carry her the rest of the way up. "I'm fine, Diogo. Just a little tired from all that travel."

I grunt my disagreement, but she doesn't catch on to my concern. She used to be healthy enough to climb over a 90-story wall and back in the same day, in scorching hot desert conditions. But now she can't climb 20 floors on her own in a cool concrete stairwell. No, I won't believe my wife is in perfect condition until she receives a clean bill of health from her doctor.

Bishop, Cruz and Grayson await us just outside the apartment doors when we arrive. Grayson must've gotten through the crowds quicker than I did, to make it back to the Tower before us. I nod his way, pleased with my man for his dedication to Taran's safety. She reaches for his hand, a huge smile on her face.

"Grayson! You're okay."

He glances my way and gives her hand the fastest squeeze possible before dropping it like it's on fire. "Mrs. Fuentes, I'm pleased to have you back safe and sound. My apologies for the greenhouse."

"You did everything you could," she says seriously.

I break up the overly familiar moment between my lieutenant and my wife. "You wait outside while Cruz briefs me." I stalk into the apartment and through to the bedroom. I set her carefully down on the bed and turn to Bishop. "You need to examine every inch."

"Diogo!" Taran protests.

I don't bother arguing with her. We both know who'll win this one. I stare hard at my elderly doctor who's watching Taran with some concern. "I'll want a complete report when you finish."

I leave the doctor to tend my wife, leaving part of my heart in that room. I can't shake the feeling that something significant is about to take place. And while I suspect I know what it is, my gut clenches in fear while my heart soars at the possibilities.

"I thought I'd find you in here."

Rather than turn to look at Diogo, I glare forward into the basin of ripe tomatoes I'm picking. "It was a pretty good guess considering I'm on house arrest."

"For good reason, Taran." He approaches my back, but I still don't turn around. "Less than two weeks ago you were kidnapped."

"Yes, and my kidnapper is dead," I say irritably, blowing a strand of red hair from my face. "I'm perfectly safe now."

"You aren't safe." His voice takes on a stern note, an unyielding tone that tells me he won't give on this issue no matter what I say. "No one is safe right now. The city is exploding with protests and riots. Violent outbursts are cropping up all over the place. A part of the wall was set alight yesterday. There's no telling how bad this can get; I can't have you wandering the streets right now."

I roll my eyes at his overprotectiveness. Although, to be fair, I'm not sure if he is overreacting because I haven't been allowed out of our apartment since the day he brought me back into the city. "It's not like I'd wander the streets.

Not with Grayson watching over me all the time. I just want to go visit Bishop, or Milla and Dee, or the greenhouses."

"You're not going anywhere near the greenhouses," he says sharply.

I don't bother to remind him that my kidnapper was killed, therefore rendering the greenhouses safe once more. We'll work on that issue when I get him to lift some of his restrictions. "I'm sick of being locked up like some kind of criminal!"

A sharp chirp sounds from overhead, drawing our focus upward for a second. The babies are getting more and more demanding by the day. Soon they'll find their way out of our little shed and fly off on their own. They'll need to start hunting food and learning how to survive.

He kisses the back of my neck sending an annoying wave of tingles spiraling downward. Annoying, because I want to be mad at him and when he touches and kisses me, I lose my train of thought.

"Do I need to remind you how we met?" he asks, turning me in his arms and pressing his forehead to mine. "You are a criminal, baby. The sweetest kind of criminal."

"I hate you."

He chuckles. "That's just the hormones speaking, you don't hate me."

I pinch his arm until he yanks it back and grips my wrist to stop me from doing it again. "You don't get to say that to a pregnant woman."

"What if she is being hormonal though?" he asks, mock innocently. "Bishop said we should expect mood swings."

I end up snorting in an attempt to swallow my laughter. "You'd better lock up your weapons if you think it's a good idea to call a woman moody, pregnant or not. I will stab you.

Not fatally, because you're the father of my unborn spawn, but somewhere painful."

"Stop calling our baby spawn." He laughs even harder.

I shrug. "When the little beast stops making me throw up and feel like a sack of shit all the time, then I'll consider calling it baby instead of spawn. Right now it's the parasite that's made me hate canned peaches, which is really the big tragedy in all of this."

"If that's the biggest tragedy you can come up with, then I think you're doing okay, hormones or not."

I ignore his hormone dig and wrap my arms tight around his middle, pressing my cheek to his chest. "My dislike for peaches is about the only tragedy I can handle right now. I can't take any more losses."

He kisses my head, resting his chin on top. "I know, sweetheart." He runs his hand soothingly down my back. "You just focus on our baby and leave the rest to me."

"That is ridiculously misogynistic, Diogo." But it sounds really good right about now.

He shrugs. "Never said I was an advocate of equal rights."

His words sober me up. He isn't an advocate of equal rights. In fact, he outwardly opposes them. He thinks survival must be at the expense of the weakest members of society. How can we possibly raise a child in such a household of opposites, in a community at war with itself, within a dying world?

Despair hits me hard as it has many times over the past weeks. Finding out I was pregnant was a shock, but I also still carry with me the remnants of grief from losing Xavier and then losing my sister all over again. I feel like I'm in permanent shock.

"I'm scared for this baby, Diogo. I wasn't ready to be a

mom." We've had this argument several times over the past few weeks, but I can't seem to stop the accusation from leaking through once more. He wanted a child and I'd told him I wasn't ready.

"Our child will be treated like royalty. It'll never know the hardships you experienced when you were growing up. You have nothing to worry about." His never-ending patience grates on my frayed nerves.

"You can't know that," I snap, sitting on the nearby stool and rubbing the ache in my lower back. I'm barely three months pregnant, I'm not showing, yet the aches and pains are all real. "As a child my life was pretty good. Living in the countryside with my family back when my parents and brother were still alive. Primitives rarely bothered to come into such a sparsely populated area. We didn't have it easy, but we had each other and plenty of supplies. Then the illness came. Once my parents died, we weren't able to stay up North. The winters were just too cold and harsh for my grandparents." I pause, gathering my thoughts. "I guess my point is that you can't know what's going to happen. What if the rebels manage to overrun your forces and the city falls?"

"That won't happen." His hard voice holds an unassailable assurance.

I shake my head. "Sanctuaries are fragile, Diogo. They require a careful balance in order to survive. While never perfect, we were at least stable before the last few months." Before Diogo and I got together, setting in motion a chain of events that would destabilize the entire city. "Now, the city is in chaos. Every day that you leave I'm terrified you might be killed. Become a target for the rebellion. And I sit up here in my cage, helpless to do anything but watch an entire city burn."

Diogo's eyes darken in understanding. I almost hate him for it as he sees right through me, sees my concerns, understands my worries, but continues on just the same. Maybe it is hormones directing my thoughts, but my concerns are valid. Diogo is a target and I would serve the city much better on the ground.

"I want to help create a city where our child feels safe to grow up," I say passionately. "I can help, Diogo. I shouldn't be a prisoner, I should be an advocate for change."

"As the mother of our baby, the child that may possibly be the future leader of this city, you will be an advocate for change." He pauses, his expression hard and unyielding. He approaches, standing over me where I sit on the bottom rung of the ladder. Does he know how intimidating his hulking presence is? Even if I stand, I'll still only reach mid-chest. "You are not my prisoner, Taran. You have many freedoms and liberties that can be easily taken away. I show my respect for you by allowing you the freedom to express your opinions, whatever they may be. I allow you the freedom of the roof and access to all of the resources within. If you desire something all you need to do is ask. You've made yourself a prisoner in your own mind."

"Can I come and go as I please?" I demand, balling my hands into fists so I don't launch myself at him. "Or go see my friends without permission?"

"No." His response is immediate and uncompromising.

"Can I go to the slums?"

"Never."

"I want to visit my rebel friends. Have them brought to me if you won't allow me out to see them. Let me make sense of this mess in our city and try to help!" I know my arguments are pointless, but I can't help it. I'll argue with a concrete wall if it means I might have a chance at chipping away the immovable barrier. "I can help calm the rebellion if you'll just let me."

"Taran," he says sharply. "Stop it. You know I won't allow these things. I don't need your help with the rebellion, I can handle a group of riffraff troublemakers myself. You need to stay here and nurture our child."

"Thank you very much for clarifying my position within your household," I say scathingly, unable to hold back the fury bursting through me. "You have just outlined exactly why I am your prisoner, and every way in which we are not equal."

He looks down at me for a moment, his own features hardening into the professional mask I know so well. The Warlord. "I've never said we're equal, Taran. It is a fact that we aren't equal, nature has made it so."

I jump off my stool and poke a finger into his chest. "Nature has also given us the ability to reason and decide right from wrong. What you're doing right now is wrong."

He grabs my hand in a move so swift I try to jerk away. He jerks me back into his body, tugging my arm out to the side so he can press me closer. I tip my head up to glare at him. He looks down at me with a glacial expression.

"Right and wrong are human constructs we create to control masses of people."

"Says every evil despotic ruler ever," I snap, tugging on my arms, trying to free myself. I hate that the heat from his big body seeps into mine, igniting a visceral response from me. I want to relax, to melt into him and accept what his body offers. Even if I also want to stab him in the throat when he talks like this.

"You think I'm despotic?" he demands gruffly, sounding genuinely offended. My anger melts away even more, leaving me with the urge to laugh.

"Well, you are autocratic, tyrannical, oppressive…" I stop, trying to pull away from him and push my arms up his chest instead. His hands follow mine, capturing them and holding them against his body. His eyes flash amusement as he catches on to my playful tone. "You're also sexy and attentive. You keep the pantry stocked and you never steal all the hot water if you get in the shower before me. You're a strange mix of good and evil, and I don't know what to do with you."

"Love me," he says huskily.

"That's my problem, Warlord," I tell him, some of our earlier seriousness leaks back into my voice. "I do love you, and I'm starting to think I can't live without you."

"That shouldn't be a problem." He cups the back of my head in one of his big hands and leans down to kiss me. "Knowing I have your love makes me more selfish than ever. I will do whatever it takes to keep it, even if it means tightening my reign on this city."

I suck in a breath at his declaration. Sometimes his softness toward me makes me forget how harsh of a ruler he can be.

"You scare me when you say things like that."

"You don't ever need to be afraid of me, baby. You're the last person I would ever hurt."

"I'm not afraid for me. It's everyone else I worry about."

His expression darkens, and he says, "Good," before taking my lips in a fierce kiss.

FORTY

TARAN

"Your baby is healthy, you have nothing to be concerned about."

"Then why am I not showing yet, Bishop?" I ask worriedly, allowing him to take my hand and help me up from the bed. He's been kind enough to come visit me in the apartment since Diogo won't let me leave. "I'm almost five months along and nothing. Where did the baby go, if it's in there at all?"

He chuckles and pats the slight rise on my stomach. "Not everyone shows or grows babies the same. Not to worry, your belly will get bigger in no time and then you'll be worrying about where your feet went."

I narrow my eyes at him trying to stuff the impulse to start screaming at him deep down. I tell myself he wasn't always this annoying, that the baby is making me think things I wouldn't usually think. Like every person that talks to me is the devil and needs to fall off the nearest cliff. That list includes Grayson, Stryker, Dee, Milla, Bishop and most especially Diogo.

I take a calming breath and thank the doctor for the

exam and his expert assessment. "If this baby turns out to be a turnip I'm coming after you, Bishop." I rub my back, which has no real reason to hurt because my belly is non-existent. "It doesn't stick out and I only get the occasional flutter, which could be gas. The only way I can be sure it exists at all is that it makes me vomit, which you said would stop after the first trimester."

"I believe I said, the nausea should pass after the first trimester. Unfortunately, there are some women that are prone to sickness throughout their pregnancy."

Oh, fuck that!

"It is a turnip," I insist. "There's no way to know it exists except it makes me puke, and turnips make me puke. Therefore, I'm incubating a turnip. There's no other explanation."

Bishop smiles at my snarky silliness and picks up his stethoscope. "Listen," he says, placing the end against my belly and moving it around until he's satisfied. Then he pulls the earpieces from himself and hands them to me. I put them in my ears and dip my head, listening. It happens immediately; the gentle swish and whoosh of a heart rapidly beating. My own heart thunders in response, rushing blood to my head and obscuring the sound. I take a few calming breathes so I can hear it again.

I meet Bishop's eyes, my own wide with awe. I almost can't believe that my turnip is alive. Its heart is frantically beating away pumping life through its tiny half-formed body. A rush of something oddly close to affection hits me as I connect with the life inside me for the first time. No longer is it just a thing to worry about, a bundle of cells that makes me vomit on a semi-regular basis. Now it's real, and I ache to see what it looks like.

I dip my head again, swiping at tears as I pull the stethoscope from my head and hand it back to Bishop. I swallow hard and say, "Thank you. I needed that."

He smiles kindly and sets about repacking his bag. "I'm not surprised that you've been feeling disconnected, Taran. You've been through a lot in the past few months, not the least of which was a surprise marriage to our Warlord."

I smile at him, relieved that he understands and doesn't blame me for not wanting much to do with this baby. "I haven't even been able to bring myself to put together a baby room or think about things like baby clothes and diapers. Even women in the most deplorable conditions in the slums seem to look forward to birth more than I do."

He nods and sits on the edge of the bed, patting it, inviting me to sit with him. "In these tough times, babies are a reaffirmation of life. It's something normal and predictable in a chaotic world that changes as constantly as the wind. The joy of life is universal."

"Then why don't I feel joy?" Despair replaces my momentary feeling of wonder. "I feel like a ghost, like I'm going to disappear or fade away. I've lost almost everyone I've ever loved. I can't help but feel like... like I'm going to lose this family too. I'm already attached to Diogo, but it's not too late to distance myself from the baby."

He places a hand tentatively on my back and rubs a little in a comforting way. "What you're feeling is normal, Taran. Grief does terrible things to us, but it's a natural course in life and not an emotion to shun or hide from. It won't last forever, and there will be a light at the end of your tunnel, I promise."

"How do you know?" I whisper, swiping at a tear.

"Because I've seen this before. Depression during and after pregnancy, it's not uncommon. It's just not something people like to talk about. We're told that babies are joyous and we should be happy with each birth. Especially because each new life extends the overall lifetime of our species. But the plain truth is that women struggle, especially when they don't have enough support."

I feel better as he speaks, much less like a freak that can't love her own baby.

He continues, "Soon you'll have a baby to love and it will consume you. Every time it cries, every time it smiles, when it eats, when it says your name, you'll connect. It may take time and you may feel depressed and sometimes frustrated and overwhelmed, but I'll be here every step of the way with you. You call and I'll be on your doorstep." He winks at me, "And not just because you're carrying the future Warlord."

I give a watery laugh and nod my head, continuing to sit in his semi-embrace soaking up his calm assurance. I love my husband, but his dominant bulldozing way of doing things isn't what I need right now. I need the reassurance of a man that has seen many births and many new moms throughout his life.

Finally, I straighten away from him and stand. "Thank you for coming all the way over here, especially with such unrest on the streets."

"It's my pleasure." He stands and collects his bag. "Your husband gave me an escort. He wanted to make sure I made it through the protests okay."

"Are there fresh protests then?" I ask curiously, leading him from the room.

"Oh yes, what with the new arrests, the whole city seems to be up in arms. I believe this is the reason your husband was unable to make it to this appointment."

"New arrests?" I eye Grayson as I escort Bishop from

the bedroom. "Who's been arrested and why haven't I heard?"

Grayson stands to attention, his gaze sliding away from me. "Just some criminals, ma'am, nothing to worry about."

"I was considered a criminal until recently," I say sharply. "I want to know who has been arrested and why is it causing such an uproar?" When Grayson hesitates to answer I turn on the doctor. "I thought we were friends, Bishop. Friends don't withhold information and stress out pregnant women. I spend more time worrying about what I don't know than I do worrying over the things I do know and can't control."

It's a low blow, but I know exactly how to get the doctor to talk to me. He holds his hands up in surrender. "Rumour has it that your husband and his men arrested the new rebel leader and some top rebel advisors along with her. I believe they're being held for judgement, but the expected outcome is a charge of treason. Naturally, her arrest has caused a furor in the slums that seems to be rippling outward. Some young idiots nearly set my office on fire before Dee chased them away with a scalpel."

Fear rises up like acid, burning my stomach, throat and mouth. Emery! It has to be her. I can barely control the terror as I say goodnight to the doctor, kissing him on the cheek and thanking him for coming to see me.

"Any time, my dear," he says and leaves, either oblivious of my tension or happy to get away from it.

I turn my most scathing glare toward Grayson. "You can call my husband now and tell him to get his ass home." I really need to get one of these radios for myself instead of having to rely on Diogo's people to send my messages.

"Ma'am... Mrs. Fuentes," Grayson stumbles over his words as he tries to deal with my anger. "The Commander is in an important meeting right now, he gave strict instructions to not be disturbed unless it's an emergency."

"We've been through this before, Grayson. If you don't get my husband here, *now*, then I will create an emergency that will make a city on fire look like child's play."

He shifts on his feet and drops his hand to the butt of his weapon. Typical Grayson reaction. If he can't control it then shoot it. Although, in this case, he can't kill the object of his torment.

"One more chance, Grayson. I need you to radio my husband right this instant."

He clears his throat and holds up a hand placatingly. "Ma'am..."

I gave him his chance.

I gasp and grab my stomach without warning, pitching myself face forward into his arms with a pathetic moan.

FORTY-ONE

DIOGO

"Speak!" I bark, annoyed at the interruption.

"She tried to trick me," Grayson radios in. "Tried to convince me something was wrong with her, begged me to get her into the bathroom because she said she had to... umm... vomit." He clears his throat at this point before continuing. He's said enough though, I'm already heading out of my meeting and out the front door of the guard station. Cruz and the other lieutenants can wait, I have a wife to check on. And once I've assured myself she's fine, she will regret trying to trick her guard.

I will do anything to make sure my wife is safe. I will curtail all of her freedoms, have her watched 24/7, I will murder her friends if I think they're plotting to steal her back. I will do whatever it takes to make sure she lives.

Taran is my Sanctuary.

She'll be lucky to get away will a stern warning since I can't spank her while she's pregnant and she's already lost most of her privileges. "What did she do?" I demand as I step out of the building. I'm hit by a blast of smoke, caused by the many fires that've been lit throughout Sanctuary in protest of my recent arrests and the miserable living condi-tions. What the rebels fail to realize is conditions are bad everywhere. Each passing year stretches our limited resources. The technology we use to make life easier is breaking down with no one left to fix it. My purpose is not to supress any single faction or sector, but to make sure we all survive relatively unscathed. But explaining my motives to a group of people who have shown themselves to be dangerous is pointless. And I will not risk my wife so that she might reprise her role as the Desert Wren in order to soothe the masses. I draw the line at her involvement, though Cruz and several others have suggested I use her connection to the rebellion to calm the city.

I climb into the jeep and turn it on. It rumbles to life and I pull away from the curb barely a second later. I bring the radio up to my ear, listening to Grayson tell me how my devious little wife tried to escape her cage.

"After I helped her into the bathroom, she elbowed me in the stomach and ran out, slamming the door behind her. She tried to rush out of the apartment, but I cut her off, she didn't even make it to the front door."

"Fuck," I snarl, hitting the gas harder.

She could've slammed into the table on her way out and bruised her stomach. She could've fallen down the stairs in her rush to escape and lost the baby, or worse, her life. My anger rises with each step and peaks the moment I reach the Tower.

As I drive toward Sector One, ash settles on my wind-shield and all the buildings surrounding the area, turning the city to a dull grey. It's a grim site. If I don't bring this rebellion under control soon there may not be a city left to govern over. I'm trying to allow Taran's influence into my handling of captured rebels; handing out less harsh sentences, giving them the option of working on the wall rebuild or prison. But this morning we had a breakthrough, we found out who planted the bomb and were able to arrest her and a group of rebels she'd holed up with. I don't have a choice, I'll have to make an example of the bomber. I can't be seen as a weak leader, not in a time of such unrest.

When I reach the Tower, I take the steps two at a time until I reach the top. It takes me under three minutes, and I'm furious all over again as I arrive. If Taran had managed to incapacitate her guard and get out, she could've easily been grabbed on the streets. She's in no condition to run for her life, she's been sick for weeks. This pregnancy has obviously affected her judgement.

I stride into the apartment to find Taran pacing furiously across the floor, her arms wrapped tightly around her middle. When she catches sight of me, she sends me a fiery glare. I can't help it, some of my anger fades as her magnificence hits me. She shouldn't look this good with her dishevelled hair in an unbrushed tangle down her back and her clothes loose on her frame because she chose one of my shirts. But regardless of her drawn face and the tired puffiness to her eyes, she's never looked more beautiful.

"Come with me," I say, taking her arm. I don't give her a choice, I force her to follow me up the stairs to the terrace on the top of the building.

"What are we doing?" she asks sharply as we step out.

I take her hand in mine and push it out in front of us, waiting. It takes only a few seconds for a flake of ash to land on her. Then another, then another, until it coats us. Our hair, our clothes, our bare skin. She looks surprised and reaches up to brush some away from my nose. Then she brings her hand to her face and rubs her fingers together.

"Soot." She sounds shocked.

The ash started coming down this morning, flying up above the city, in a windy vortex, only to fall back down in a dirty, sticky coating, suffocating an already dying city. Taran must've stayed inside all day and not looked out the windows. She's usually very observant, but some of her edge seems to have been lost in a cloud of grief that hangs constantly over her. When I look at moments like this, taking in my distressed wife, I wonder if I made the right decision in leaving her sister behind. I could've taken Skye by force.

I didn't because I hadn't wanted the hellion fucking up my Sanctuary in a coup attempt. The woman had rebel leader written all over her. The last thing I need is a competent, fierce woman taking over our already annoying rebellion. She would become the new Desert Wren, only with enough cold-blooded intelligence to do a more effective job than her predecessors.

Taran walks toward the edge of the building, staring out at the falling ash and then up at the clouds above. The sky is grey, but the ash isn't coming from the clouds. It's coming from a city on fire.

"Look." I point into the city, where a blaze glows bright orange.

"The slums!" she gasps worriedly.

"The gates, to be more exact," I say grimly. "Rebels are setting fires at the major checkpoints between sectors, creating chaos and making it easier to slip through. They've infiltrated every part of the city, Taran. Setting buildings alight along the way. Not all of those buildings are abandoned. In the past several weeks, many of our residents have lost their homes. I've had to divert resources to relocation efforts instead of stopping the fires and apprehending the culprits."

Guilt flashes across her face as she realizes it's most likely her friends causing all this damage. I don't want her to feel guilty, I want her to wake up and take her own safety into consideration. "Taran, if you'd gotten out of the building today, you could've walked straight into this mess. I don't care who you're connected to, the danger is real."

She sighs heavily and settles a hand on her lower back, kneading it without thinking. I brush her hand away and place one of mine on her front and the other on her back, rubbing her in the way I know she likes best, using my stronger fingers to dig into the tense muscles just above her butt.

"I wasn't going to leave," she admits. "I just wanted to get your attention. Grayson said he required an emergency before he would call you. I created an emergency. To be honest, I'm way too exhausted these days to be climbing those damn stairs by myself, up or down."

I chuckle, relief easing the last of my anger. Taran is an intelligent woman, but she's also driven. I have no doubt if she'd decided she needed out of the building she would've found a way.

"What happened that you couldn't wait for me to come home?" I turn her so that I can see her beautiful expressive eyes when we talk.

"You arrested the rebel leader... a woman." Her voice is an accusation, but I don't know why. She would have to know that the fires are driving arrests. "Bishop said you'd probably have to execute..." her voice trails off as emotion chokes her.

Now I understand her urgency. She's afraid for her friend. "I haven't arrested Emery." Again. But she doesn't need to know about the first time.

A small frown creases her brows. "Who did you arrest?"

"A woman named Allison Blanshard. You know her?" I watch her carefully as she ponders the name.

She shrugs. "Only a little. I'd seen her around at the meetings, but I was more of a field person. I liked working with people on the ground, I wasn't as much into the intrigue as some of the others... Xavier included."

Something inside me releases at her admission. I'd known she was deep in the rebellion, but we haven't had the tough conversations yet. Where I grill her on her involvement in the rebellion like I should've the first day we met. I'd never had the heart to ask the hard questions, and part of me didn't want to know the answers. Didn't want to know if she was instrumental in the extremist methods used by some of her fellow compatriots. Now that I've gotten to know my pacifist wife I see the impossibility of her being involved in anything overtly destructive. I don't know what I would've done if she'd turned out to be more extreme in her beliefs.

No, that's not true. I know exactly what I would've done. I would have restricted her even further, allowing her almost no freedoms and I would have kept her, just the way she is now. Miserable but alive.

"You're worried about Emery?" I ask, holding her against me and running my hand up from the small of her back to massage between her shoulders.

She sighs and tips her head forward. "I saw her every day for years, Diogo. She was like family to me, a surrogate mother. I can't imagine her not being part of my future. Not being part of this baby's future."

"Alright," I relent on the issue of her rebel colleague. "I'll see if she'll come here to talk. I can't take you out of the Tower. The risk is too great, but I can bring her here if she's willing to talk."

"Oh my goodness, yes please!" Taran tips her head back and laughs excitedly. "She's going to be blown away by this place! And she doesn't know about the baby yet. Oh, I wish I was showing so I could really surprise her."

My heart aches as I listen to my wife ramble excitedly, becoming more animated than she's been since her kidnapping. She sounds happy. The more she talks, the more I realize how close she is to Emery. I'd misjudged their relationship or misjudged how easy it would be to separate them. By keeping her from the things she's close to I've exacerbated her sense of disconnection and grief. The thought doesn't settle easily. Like many decisions I have to make in the course of my leadership, I'd made a snap judgment and held to my convictions without looking at the deeper truth. Though rebels, Taran has made some deep connections within the community. And I tore her from the people that care about her.

"I'll meet with her tomorrow and see if she's willing to come."

"She will!" Taran yells and throws her arms around me. Standing on tiptoes she kisses my jaw. I realize I haven't shaved in days. Her soft lips could become abraded against my rough skin. I'll have to be more cognizant of her needs.

I gather her closer against me and kiss her full on the lips. They part beneath mine as she accepts the intrusion of my tongue against hers. No matter how many times I hold her, kiss her, make love to her, I still want more. My body aches for hers constantly. Not just sexually, I also crave her warmth, her smell, her delicate touch.

I reach down and sweep her legs out from under her, thinking how light she feels in my arms. Like holding nothing. Then worry hits me as I remember she's supposed to be gaining weight. I should be holding a healthfully curved wife with baby weight giving her some extra girth to hang on to.

"What did Bishop say about the baby?" I ask nonchalantly as I descend the stairs.

She laughs, reading my mind and my concerns. "He told me everything is fine and to stop worrying, that different women carry their babies differently."

Relief rushes through me. Bishop wouldn't lie to Taran. Not even if a lie would help ease her mind. He'd a deeply moral man that doesn't believe in sugar-coating. And he would tell me if there was a problem.

Taran takes my face in her hand and gently turns it toward hers. "Diogo, I heard the heartbeat today."

I can't explain the emotions that hit me all at once. Elation that Taran got to experience such a wonderful moment, happiness that my baby is nestled deep within her body and doing well, and sadness that I missed such a significant moment.

"You'll be there next time, love." Once again, she reads me well. "This baby isn't going anywhere."

I set her down on the bed and tug her clothes off. She sits up, helping me by lifting her arms first so I can pull her shirt over her head, then lifting her hips so I can drag her pants and underwear down her body.

Lately, Taran has been too sick for us to be intimate. But now... now... as I stand back, looking down at the subtle changes taking her from young woman into motherhood, I'm more turned on than ever. Her hips and the tiny rise of her belly call to me like a siren's lure. I fall to my knees on the floor and drag her to the edge of the bed, spreading her hips with my shoulders.

"Diogo!" she gasps, knowing what I want and already

reacting with passion. She grabs her face and twists as I drop my head between her legs.

I drop a kiss on each hipbone, loving the gently sloping dips with my tongue before I follow a path up to her stomach. I spend the majority of my time worshipping the slight rise. She giggles as I thrust my tongue onto her bellybutton. She tries to roll away, but I grip her hips and hold her still, delving into the tiny recess. She needs to know that no part of her will ever be off limits. She belongs to me, from the top of her wild red hair, to the dip of her bellybutton, to the space between her pinky toe and the next one.

I make my way further down, kissing her intimately between the legs, sliding my tongue right into the spot I want to taste most. I can tell that she hasn't showered yet this afternoon, her taste is not the soapy taste she prefers I get when we I fuck her with my mouth. She usually complains when I go down on her after she's been working all day but before she's showered. I want the real her though. The woman who has worked, moved, been my Taran all day long. I want to taste her and only her, all woman, all mine.

She shouts her pleasure, her beautiful voice singing to the ceiling as I force her higher and higher, then change the pressure of my tongue so she'll drop away from the imminent orgasm. Only to pick her back up and carry her once more to the pleasurable peak. And again, as she approaches it, her voice filling the room with cries of ecstasy, I step back.

She screams her frustration and sits up, shoving her hair back angrily and pressing her knees together. She glares at me in protest as I strip out of my military uniform, allowing each piece to fall to the floor. Then I fall on the bed, kneeling at her tiny feet. I grip her knees, parting them and crawl up her body.

"You don't get to come without me," I growl into her ear before surging into her.

Her scream and the claw of her fingernails against my shoulders is music to my ears. I gather her in my arms and hold her against my chest as I thrust into her, taking us both out of the world and onto a path to heaven.

I pace the apartment in agitation as I await news of Diogo's meeting with Emery. I know he's met her, and I just hope he sees the sweet woman beneath the tough, sometimes abrasive exterior. She's not one to hold back her opinion if she thinks a person has done something they shouldn't. But she's also very sweet, exactly the person I need to be with right now.

The door opens and Diogo strides in, his cloak of arrogance firmly in place. The implacable grim look on his face causes my heart to sink. The meeting didn't go well. She said something he didn't like or maybe even refused to come. After all, the Tower is a key building in Sanctuary and it firmly belongs to the Warlord's side.

I'm about to demand an explanation for my missing friend when she pops out from behind Diogo. His broad body was blocking my view of her.

"Emery!" I grin and launch myself at her.

She meets me halfway around the table, clasping me against her body and holding tight. We rock back and forth and cry for a few minutes while Diogo watches, his face softening a little. He knows how important this moment is to me and he made it happen. I love that Diogo will always try to make me happy. Even if it goes against his core beliefs, he will find a way. He didn't want me to leave the Tower, so he brought exactly what I needed to me.

"I have to go," Diogo announces. He gives Emery a little nudge, forcing her to step back while he reaches for me, cupping the back of my head and leaning down for a kiss.

"Thank you," I say, telling him with my tone just how much I mean it. "Please, be safe out there."

He doesn't answer. He releases me and strides out the door, barking out a few orders to my bodyguard; don't let me leave, watch over us, keep us inside, no one enters the apartment except Diogo, etc. The usual safety commands. Today I care less than I did yesterday. I may be trapped in a cage, but the addition of my beloved friend will make the time pass quickly.

The moment Diogo leaves, Emery announces, "You're pregnant," and then launches herself at me again.

I'm so shocked I don't know how to respond. I just stand with my mouth open as she grabs me and hauls me into another tight hug. Then her familiar embrace calls to me and I melt into her. Emery feels like home in a way nothing has in a long time. Like the fond remembrances of child-hood; fuzzy memories, nostalgia, and good intentions.

"How did you know?" I finally manage to ask when she breaks the hug.

"Your face is a little rounder, so is your belly and you look pale and tired, like you haven't eaten properly or slept in weeks."

I frown. I didn't think I looked that bad.

"How far along are you?" she asks and then looks around. "Where shall we sit?"

I laugh as she gazes first at the table then off to the side where our bedroom is. The place is not really set up for guests. Diogo was a long-time bachelor when I moved in and I haven't had much of a chance to make changes yet. I can now see the apartment's deficiencies through Emery's eyes. Very little furniture. Just a table that dominates the room next to the door. One bedroom, and the rest is just open concrete with big windows. We're going to have to have walls built so we can add a baby room.

In comparison to Emery's crowded comfortable home, with mismatched furniture and useless old electronics that don't work anymore, this place must look completely bare.

"I suppose we'll have to sit right here until I find some suitable furniture." I wave her toward the table and she pulls out a chair and sits. I follow suit, pulling out the chair that Diogo usually sits in and moving it closer.

We both look pointedly at Grayson.

He clears his throat. "Uh, think I'll just step out. I'll be just outside the door if you need anything."

When he leaves, I laugh and turn back to Emery. "At least he's no longer worried I'll climb out a window and scale down the side of the building."

"Please tell me you wouldn't do that!" Emery admonishes me.

"Well, not anymore. I don't have the stamina for it now and the baby might not like heights. The last thing I need is to throw up while I'm climbing down a twenty-story building."

Even though she knows I'm joking, she still shakes her head. "Maybe becoming a mother will settle you down a bit. You were always a bit of a wild child, impossible to keep in one place. Always climbing this or that, giving me a heart attack with your shenanigans."

I grin at her description. I'd never thought of myself as difficult before. When I lost the last of my relatives I became fiercely independent, outspoken and unabashedly idealistic. As far as I was concerned, there was nothing holding me back from achieving the things I wanted in life. Xavier encouraged this behaviour as he saw it as my rebellious streak shining through. When I'd moved in with Emery, I hadn't made any real changes, though I knew she worried about me. She tried to mother me. At the time I hadn't had much patience for her, but now I'm grateful that she persisted.

"I'm sorry if I caused you any heartache." I reach out to grip her hand. "You took me in when you didn't have to. You've always been kind and generous, providing for me and never making me feel like some stray that you picked up."

"You have no need to apologize. You were a teenager, and though you were certainly rebellious at times, you never caused me heartache. I was proud of you then and continue to be proud of the woman you've become. I'm grateful that I've had the opportunity to watch you grow and to stand in as a surrogate parent when you needed one."

It takes me a moment to find my voice in a throat swelling with emotion. "I'll always need you, Emery."

She squeezes my hand. "Good, because I'm not going anywhere according to your Warlord husband. He's informed me that a suitable suite will be made available on one of the lower floors and that I'm welcome to visit with you whenever he's not here."

"But that's not fair," I cry, though I'm grateful that Diogo has created this possibility. As always, he's using his dominant force to get what he wants, which is ultimately what I want. "He should've asked, not demanded. And what about your beautiful little home? All those antiques and memories."

She shakes her head. "Not to worry, I wouldn't have agreed if it wasn't what I wanted. He's having my things moved over. I do love that home, but memories aren't in places or things, they're in our minds. It's up to us to preserve the things we love by remembering them. I can't see or touch my mother anymore, but I remember her clear as day. I don't need a house to remind me that she existed."

Though she denies it, I know that house means a lot to Emery. It's been in her family for generations. Her mother raised her in that house alone and then died of the flu before Emery was full grown. A common story, one that I can relate to.

She must sense my continued concern, because she says, "Commander Fuentes told me that he'll have the house boarded up and protected from squatters. I told him not to, that I would like to invite some of the families living in deplorable conditions in the slums to move in. I haven't told him, but I intend to offer it to Kelly and Joanne Hunt and their children."

The Hunts are a refugee family, struggling to get by without jobs or food vouchers because they were escorted into the city illegally by me and don't have documentation. I was arrested shortly after helping them into Sanctuary and unable to see to their immediate needs.

"Thank you, Emery. They deserve more than they found when they arrived in Sanctuary. I'm happy they'll be more comfortable. Maybe I can convince Diogo to give them papers to."

She shakes her head and laughs. "A few months ago, I

would've thought you'd be killed where you stood for suggesting the Warlord give legal status to illegal refugees. Now I've seen the regard the Warlord holds for you, I believe you can make it happen."

I don't know that I entirely agree with her on that. There's still plenty that the Warlord won't allow me to change or become involved in. If the task includes leaving the Tower, I may as well forget about it. Unless I'm escorted by my husband and several armed guards, I won't be leaving the premises. The new greenhouse plan has been almost entirely abandoned.

I light up at the thought as an idea hits me. Emery has always had a green thumb, is always planting seeds in her yard and nurturing them. She's passionate about feeding the less privileged in our city and is one of the many that gives away her own food rations in order to feed others. The greenhouse project is perfect for her!

I outline the expansion plan and she quickly agrees, eagerly offering her own advice as we chat. If she takes to the project, perhaps she could even replace poor Mr. Sharp as greenhouse manager.

"Let's not get ahead of ourselves," she laughs. "I'm not sure I want to take on a project that big."

"You will," I say confidently.

She gives me a fond look. "You always were one that liked to get your own way."

"No," I protest with a laugh. "I can just predict the future. And I know that you'll become our new greenhouse manager."

"Whatever you say."

As we talk, another bigger idea hits me. All along I've struggled to get Diogo to see my point of view, to integrate some of my ideas into a Sanctuary driven by survival and held together through harsh security methods. The lack of resources is one of the major setbacks in making changes to things like food, clean water, medical aid and education. But we're missing out on a major resource right here in our own city. People! If we can get Diogo's people to work with the rebels instead of against the rebels, we can put a group of passionate well-intentioned people to work to better our city.

It's a long shot, and even I can see the ridiculously idealistic idea for what it is; an unlikely dream. But I have to try. Now I can use Emery as my mouthpiece. I can send her out to talk to our rebel friends, get them to see the merits of working with the city elite instead of against them. We can pair people from the slums with medical and first aid knowledge with Bishop and Dee, generate ideas and spread resources. We can pair educators from the lower classes with people like Milla.

When I outline my idea to Emery, she takes some of the steam out of my plan. "Are you forgetting that this city is at war? The rebels blew up the wall. Your husband isn't likely to forget or forgive something like that, and to be honest, even to a rebel like me, I don't think he should. He'll look like a weak leader if he just forgives such a huge transgression. As far as I'm concerned, I was lucky to get off as light as I did."

"That was an extreme action taken by extreme people," I argue, eager to make my plan work. "We both know that the majority of the rebels are peace-loving people that just want to see changes for the better. Diogo was able to accept me, and now he accepts you too. He'll accept others once he sees that they don't pose any kind of danger."

"He only accepts me conditionally and because of you," Emery points out.

"Then he'll accept everyone else because I tell him to," I say firmly, drawing a laugh from Emery. I do sound arrogant in my assurance that I can get Diogo to do what I want, but my plan is reasonable, there's no reason he should say no.

"I've missed you, sweetheart, and your wildly optimistic ideas."

FORTY-THREE
TARAN

Although Diogo has asked that I stay indoors, I can't help but be drawn to the roof. Every day I drift toward the rooftop terrace, looking out into a city covered in grey ash, the only splash of colour the fires that continue to burn, choking Sanctuary. The ash doesn't rain down daily, only when the wind is high, but often enough to coat our city. Today the flakes land on me and on the terrace, landing like the snowflakes of my childhood. Light and fluffy, but not nearly as innocent as snow. It darkens the sky, obscuring the buildings around me. Even the fires are harder to spot through the thick ash.

I've been doing the same thing for the past two months, since Emery came to live in the Tower. Since I offered Diogo a way to unite our city. Coming to the top of the building and watching our city as it wars against itself. Buildings burn, cars, homes, everything. Nothing and no one is safe. This is what I've tried repeatedly, and failed repeatedly, to tell Diogo. I am not safe up here in my tower. The rebellion will push forward, despite his brutal attempts to squash it. I should be down there, on the ground, at his side. I should be arguing for a united city. People will listen to me.

The city is particularly smoky today. When the West wall was set alight, the billowing smoke lasted for days. I wonder if it's the wall again or if it's something closer. The sharp acrid smell suggests the rebellion has finally spilled into Sector One.

"Taran, what are you doing out here." Diogo's urgent voice startles me.

He rushes toward me and drags me back into the stairwell leading down to our apartment. I yelp at his tight grip, but he doesn't release me. Instead he spins me around to face him and starts brushing at me with his gloved hands. I gape at him while he dusts me off. He's wearing a bandana over his face. He continues to beat at me until I shove his hands away with a shout.

"Stop it, Diogo, that hurts!"

"I'm sorry, baby," he says, but doesn't stop. He reaches for the buttons on my blouse and rapidly starts to undress me. "All this ash, it's no good for you and the turnip. You can't stand outside anymore, it'll get into your lungs."

I'm caught somewhere between amusement because my pet name for our child has caught on and annoyance. Can't go outside anymore? The roof is one of the few pleasures I have left during my enforced captivity.

"I was checking on the nest, to see if Skye's come back yet." I sound dejected, even to my own ears. Those first few weeks after I'd found out I was pregnant I'd gone to visit her daily, talking about birth and parenthood. Asking her the tough questions that I was too afraid to ask anyone else. Did she love her babies? How did she know she loved them? After all, they're noisy, smelly, demanding and ungrateful. Was she terrified that they would die?

Was she afraid to let them learn to fly, to go off on their own?

And then the inevitable happened. One day I went up to see her and the nest was empty. I was terrified that the something had happened to them, but Diogo assured me that she probably took them out through the hole in the greenhouse. That the babies were old enough to leave the nest.

"She'll come back, baby," Diogo reassures me.

"How do you know?" For some reason I can't just let her go. I'm invested in the bird, she's part of our growing family.

"Because she always does," he says simply, taking my hand and leading me down the stairs.

Relief surges through me. "She's done this before?"

"Yes, several times. Our Desert Wren is a seasoned mama." I smile at his word choice. He continues, "She'll probably leave the city entirely until it's safe to return. The fire is driving out any wildlife that manages to get inside."

"I like to go up to the roof to watch the fires," I admit, as we step out into our main living area. "I need to know what's happening out there, especially in the slums."

"You shouldn't be worrying about them," he says sharply. "Stress isn't good for the baby."

I snort. "I'm still aware that the fires exist when I'm inside. We do have windows, Diogo. I worry constantly about the rebel flareup and you telling me not to worry isn't going to stop me being anxious. Until I'm on the ground, talking to my loyal followers and smoothing the unrest, I'll continue to worry." Diogo has consistently refused my requests to try to integrate rebels into the elite systems, insisting it's too dangerous and that pardoning rebels to play key roles in the city would set a bad precedent. I don't agree with him and like to remind him on a semi-frequent basis.

He growls and turns me in his arms so that I'm facing him. "You know I can't do that, Taran. You and the baby are too vulnerable. There's a traitor passing information along to the rebels. Until I know who it is, until we can stamp out this rebel uprising, you need to stay here, stay separated from the danger."

"I don't understand," I say. "How do you know there's a traitor?"

He shakes his head allowing some of his frustration to show. "Every time we get a handle on this rebellion the tide changes. Like they know exactly where we're going to be and when. The only way for that to happen is if one of my top lieutenants is dirty. We only discuss our plans in private, with a total of eight people in attendance. I'm about ready to execute the lot of them and start over with a new, more loyal group."

I gasp at his harsh words. "Diogo, you don't mean that."

"I do," he growls. "Whoever it is has put you in danger. I won't tolerate such disloyalty."

I hug myself to him, my arms wrapped tightly around his waist. I stand on tiptoe to kiss the edge of his jaw, my protruding belly pressing against him. "I'm perfectly safe," I insist. "You've made sure of it."

"You aren't safe. The rebels have crossed into Sector One. I rushed home to see you, make sure you were okay. Make sure they hadn't made it to the Tower yet."

I open my mouth to respond, to reassure him once more when the door flies open and slams against the wall. Diogo pulls his weapon and steps in front of me. The move is so reminiscent of the time Garrett had burst in on us that I have to fight tears as I remember his violent death.

"Fuck, Truss," Diogo snarls. "I could've killed you."

Grayson ignores Diogo's annoyance. "Commander, something's happening. You need to come right away."

"What is it?" he demands. "I don't want to leave Taran."

Grayson shakes his head. "You need to hear for yourself, Commander. Bring her, it involves her sister."

"No!" I gasp covering my mouth.

"Just tell me man and stop upsetting my wife or I really will shoot you."

"I can't explain what's happening, sir, because I don't understand it myself. Boss gave me a partial message but there's some kind of interference with the radios. He said you're needed in the control room without delay, that Santa Fe Sanctuary is calling in with an emergency."

Diogo interprets my confused expression. "The control room is where we can receive long-range transmissions. They're not easy to finetune so we don't often get calls, but it's how we keep in touch with other Sanctuaries."

"I didn't know that was possible." I can't keep the accusation from my voice. Why wouldn't he tell me it's possible to call my sister, to talk to her, listen to her voice, reassure myself that she's still alive?

I can't read his expression, but the look in his eyes tells me all I need to know. He's sorry I'm hurt by this knowledge, but he wouldn't change his actions even if he could.

"We'll talk about this later," I say coldly, heading for the door. "For now, let's go find out what's wrong with my sister."

"You're not coming," he says just as coldly, grabbing my arm and spinning me around.

I raise my eyebrows. "You've done some questionable things since we've met. Forced me into marriage, locked me up in this apartment, arrested and threatened my friends.

I've forgiven a lot, Diogo. But I can promise you, if you don't let me go and listen to Skye's voice, especially if she's in trouble, I won't forgive you."

He growls and slams his fist into the table then reaches up and grabs his head while he thinks. He knows I'm just as safe with him as I am trapped up here. I've manipulated his feelings to get what I want, but I don't regret it. Diogo is a bulldozer, running over everything in his path to get what he wants. I need him to stop and listen. I need to hear Skye's voice.

"Okay, let's go," he relents, but grips my arm and gives me a little shake. "You follow my every command the moment it's given. I tell you to duck, you duck. I tell you to run, you run and don't look back. Understand?"

I nod solemnly and assure him, "I won't put our baby at risk."

He insists on carrying me down the stairs for safety. Part of me wonders if he just doesn't want to go as slow as I tend to move these days. My heart skips a beat in trepidation. I haven't left the building in months. I'm both scared to death and thrilled to be back on the ground again. I've had one terrifying experience after another and they seem to keep happening when I leave the apartment, but I still want to know what's happening out there, to see for myself.

As we reach the lobby, several guards fall into step around us. I gape at them. I hadn't known they were down here. I suppose it makes sense though. The Tower is well known throughout Sanctuary, it would become a target of rebel extremists if they made it this far. As we step out onto the sidewalk, Diogo covers my head with his hand, pushing it into his shoulder. I catch only a glimpse of a mob as the guards start shouting angrily and pushing them back.

Some voices do filter through.

"Desert Wren!"

"The Warlord has our girl."

"Let her go!"

I want to shout back, to tell them they're wrong. That Diogo is a good man, that he protects me, and he protects the city. That they're not doing themselves any favours by rioting. Diogo shoves me into the back of his jeep before I can draw a breath, let alone speak.

"Head down, Taran." He shoves my upper body down into the seat. I curl against the worn leather and cradle my head in my hands in case anyone is stupid enough to shoot out the back window. I'm starting to think leaving the Tower wasn't such a good idea. For weeks I believed that Diogo was exaggerating the riots, that he was being overprotective. Now that I see them with my own eyes, I understand.

I lift my head from the seat, sorrow washing through me. "Diogo," I whisper. He's sitting in the passenger seat covering us while Grayson drives. At first, I don't think he hears me, and then he turns his head, his eyes meeting mine for just a second before he looks back out the window. "I'm sorry," I tell him sincerely. I am sorry. Sorry I didn't believe him, sorry that I'd complained so much about being cooped up, sorry that his city is falling down around him.

He seems to understand what I mean in those few words. He keeps his eyes forward, but he reaches back with his free hand, the one not holding a gun, and places it over my head, the gesture both protective and reassuring.

I watch from my limited position as we pass through checkpoints, some of them surrounded by blazing fires and armed guards warning off rioters as we pass. The fires and smoke grow thicker as we head to the guard station. I realize the control room must be there.

"Come on," Diogo says grimly, getting swiftly from the vehicle and reaching back to help me out. He covers me with his body and rushes me into the guard station.

"You," he snaps at the nearest guard. "I want more men over here while my wife is in attendance. Pull them from police duty if you have to. Triple the guards on the doors and roof."

"But Commander, the men are already stretched - "

"Dismissed," Diogo cuts him off. "You're off the elite guard. Leave your weapons and go. If you hesitate, you'll be arrested for insubordination."

He turns to the next man and raises an eyebrow. The guy snaps to attention and gives Diogo a sharp nod. "Consider it done."

Without another word Diogo pulls me down a nearby hallway. I twist around trying to catch a glimpse of the guy he just fired. "I don't think that was well done, Diogo. He was just giving you his opinion. A pretty valid one probably," I admonish him.

He doesn't bother looking back when he says. "I'll invite my men to submit their opinions when I'm ready to hear them. When It comes to the security of my family there can be no hesitation."

Perhaps if I didn't have a turnip nestled under my breast, I would argue his autocratic statement, but the baby has changed my views on many things. If Diogo wants to go overboard on safety, who am I to argue?

We enter what I assume is the control room. A man sits at a desk next to a radio. He swivels in his seat as we enter.

"Bossman, report," Diogo barks.

"Commander." Boss stands, his back ramrod straight and his arms straight by his sides. "I'm getting strange messages from all over the country."

I can tell right away that this is unusual. The tension in the room goes up as the men look at each other. Behind us Cruz, Stryker and a few others pile in.

"What kind of messages?"

"Well." He turns back to the radio. "The first message came from Santa Fe Sanctuary. Hang on, it's coming in on repeat, almost like a recording."

He flips a switch and turns a dial. I don't know much about radios, but I know enough to realize he's changing frequencies. At first we hear nothing, then some intermittent static. Then, finally, a voice bursts through.

"Mayday, mayday, Santa Fe Sanctuary has fallen. Repeat, Santa Fe has fallen."

I gasp and reach for the radio. My sister's sanctuary! Boss shakes his head. "The message is on a loop. I don't think anyone is actually picking up our signal anymore."

"What the hell has happened?" Diogo demands. "The city was stable when we were there. How can they have fallen so quickly?"

"It's not just them. Sanctuaries from all over the East are calling in and requesting Sanctuary for their citizens. From what I can tell there was a catastrophic failure at one of those old power plants, which seems to have caused a chain reaction. There have been at least four meltdowns that I know of so far at power plants in completely different places."

"How is that possible?" Diogo demands.

Boss shrugs. "Can't tell. They shouldn't be connected in any way, yet there's a definite cascade pattern. One goes and a few hours later another."

Diogo paces the room. "The plants are mostly out East?"

"Yes, Commander. Our ancestors were smart enough

not to put too many of them in the Western earthquake zones."

"Good," Diogo mutters.

"Not good, sir," Boss contradicts him. Diogo gives him a sharp look. "We have three plants in a close enough vicinity to cause some major damage. Two were safely shut down directly after the Great Fall, but one still functions automatically. They can run for years without human interference, but if something interrupts the system, or the circuitry wears out, a failure can occur. Whatever is happening out East can possibly happen here too."

"If something happens, will we be in the exclusion zone?" Diogo demands.

"Yes, Commander," he replies emphatically.

Diogo's eyes meet mine. Although I know he worries about me, protects me with everything he has, I've never seen fear in his eyes. Not until today.

"I don't understand what's happening..." My voice trails off.

His stern gaze holds mine and I can tell he doesn't want to tell me. I stare steadily back at him, giving him no choice.

"I've been hearing rumours for years. More than rumours actually, a theory proposed by scientific historians," he finally tells me. "Do you know what a nuclear power plant is?"

"No." The words aren't even familiar to me.

"They used to be how people would draw energy for electricity, power, everything," he explains.

Now those words I have heard of.

"But the power can be dangerous. Historians have talked about the terrible consequences if that power loses containment. The power plant reactors can go into meltdown. The devastation can reach far across the land, can affect people in cities far away from the power plant."

"Okay," I say slowly. "And what happens to the people affected by this?"

"When a reactor goes it generates massive amounts of radiation, which can't be contained. Imagine the hottest day of summer out in the middle of the desert, only a thousand times hotter. That's what's happening inside one of those reactors. The heat generates radiation, and high doses of radiation can poison people, animals, plants, everything. A nuclear meltdown will kill everything far and wide in the exclusion zone and poison the area for years after. Eventually the radiation can mix with the soil and water and end up in the atmosphere, mixing with weather patterns and moving around the world."

I'm shocked that I've never heard any of this before. It sounds so devastating. I suppose since humans don't use nuclear energy anymore, we have no reason to learn about it. "Has this not happened since the Great Fall. How are these places allowed to still exist if they're such a threat to humanity?"

Diogo shakes his head and comes over to place a hand comfortingly on my shoulder. "Baby, there is no safe way to get rid of these places entirely. When the Primitives attacked, the stations that weren't safely shut down were abandoned by the workers. The meltdowns are inevitable. What I don't understand is why they're happening in a cascade."

Boss pipes up. "Near as I can tell, there seems to be massive Primitive horde attacks on Sanctuary cities after each failure. It almost feels as though they've figured out a strategy and are using the plants to their advantage."

"How is that possible?" Cruz points out. "Primitives

are... well... Primitive. They lack the ability to reason to that capacity."

No one speaks for a moment.

"Don't they?" Cruz asks.

A chill goes through the room as we all imagine the possibilities inherent in Primitives that can think and reason, but still contain the vicious drive to hunt prey. Are we wrong in our beliefs or are they evolving? Bishop is right, there hasn't been enough research done on these creatures.

"But wouldn't a nuclear meltdown kill them too?" I ask.

Boss shrugs. "Who knows. Don't think anyone's ever experimented with zombies and radiation before."

I turn to Diogo. "I want to try to contact my sister's Sanctuary. If a Primitive horde is attacking them, I need to know."

He nods to Bossman who hands me the receiver. I grip the radio so hard my fingers feel stiff. I choke back a sob and speak as calmly as I can. "Santa Fe Sanctuary, we're receiving your transmission. Please tell us, are there any survivors?"

Static feedback greets my desperate question. I sag back against Diogo a sob catching in my throat as we wait for confirmation. The more time that passes, the more I despair. My voice high with terror, I repeat the transmission. When no one answers, I turn in Diogo's arms, the radio slipping from my fingers. He catches in and holds me tight against his body. I feel him shift, bring the radio to his mouth.

"Santa Fe Sanctuary, please report. Do you have any survivors?"

More static.

Then, "Yes. The survivors of Santa Fe request Sanctuary."

"Granted," Diogo says without pause, his arm wrapped tight around me.

I shiver against him, releasing a tense sob. "Thank you," I whisper, my voice breaking. I know his philosophy on refugees and how they will strain our resources.

"If there's any chance that your sister is among the survivors then I won't take the chance of having her die in the desert."

I smile through the tears and hug him hard, placing my ear against his heart. "I love you, Diogo."

He kisses the top of my head. We turn to leave when the radio crackles again. We turn back to look at Lieutenant Bossman.

"Is that Santa Fe?" Diogo demands.

"No Commander, the signal is coming in on another frequency. Hang on..." Boss makes some adjustments.

Suddenly a voice bursts through clear as day. "Mayday, mayday. Nashville Sanctuary is down, overrun with Primitives. We request Sanctuary."

Boss looks toward Diogo who shakes his head. Instead of responding Boss turns to another channel and another voice fills the room.

"Please, anyone, Little Rock requests Sanctuary."

Another channel, another voice.

"Jackson is down, we're... under attack. Please... are there any Sanctuaries left?"

We look at each other.

"All the Eastern sanctuaries." I point out what we're all thinking.

"Mayday, mayday."

"Austen down... request Sanctuary."

"Atlanta has fallen... Sanctuary."

It hurts to listen to the desperation in the voices. To

listen and know what exactly is coming our way. A wave of refugees from fallen sanctuaries, too many for us to accommodate, with hordes of Primitives following close behind.

"Turn it off," Diogo says quietly, and Boss turns to comply, relief written on his face. The voices are an eerie, heartbreaking foreshadowing of our possible future.

Just before he can flip the switch, one more lonely voice, broken by static feedback, filters through...

"Mayday... Sanctuary...."

FORTY-FOUR

DIOGO

"She's going to be okay, baby."

I hold Taran on my lap, her face pressed against my shoulder as I cover us. We're on our way back to the Tower. I'm worried about Taran and the baby. She hasn't said a word since our visit to the control room. I shouldn't have let her go, but I'd had no idea what was coming. I thought perhaps her sister was calling in. Had changed her mind about breaking from her Warlord and was requesting Sanctuary with us.

Instead, we'd heard the pathetic, terrified and dying voices of almost every Sanctuary East of us. Still, Taran doesn't speak but the slow steady shake of her shoulders and the growing wet spot on the front of my jacket tells me she's crying.

"Hush, baby, you're breaking my heart," I murmur, holding her tight against me.

Grayson meets my eyes, his darting quickly down to her. I can tell that he's concerned. I'm pleased that he's bonding with my wife, something that will sharpen his care of her. Though, I also wish he wouldn't look at her, talk to her or think about her. Since I can't have it both ways, I content myself with giving him a fierce glare. He turns back to the road and doesn't glance at her again.

Once again, our path into the Tower is obstructed by shouting rebels. My men fall in around us, creating a human shield. Taran is so lost in her own grief that she doesn't register the disturbance. Not until a shot rings out, startling everyone in the vicinity. Both Grayson and I react without hesitation. He reaches for me at the same time as I shove Taran into his arms. He turns, protecting her with his back and rushes into the Tower while I pull my gun and turn back to the crowd in time to see one of my men go down, his hand clutching his shoulder.

"Stop!" I shout, amplifying my voice. It echoes across the buildings.

Everything seems to stop as they hear their Warlord give a command. Even if the rebels don't agree with my hold on the city, they've been trained to fear my presence. I'm using my voice to hold back a potential massacre. If my men start shooting, there will be no rebels left in the vicinity. And while I'd dearly love to stamp out this irritating rebellion, I don't want to have to kill half my city in the process; part of the reason I'd been hesitating in taking decisive action against the rebels. I need to sort out the true ringleaders before prosecuting.

"You will disperse or face lethal consequences." Once I've made my statement, I nod to the most senior of my men guarding the Tower and stride through the door.

I find Taran is sitting on the steps leading up to the top floors, a concerned Grayson hovering over her like a mother hen watching his chick. I'd find more amusement in the analogy if Taran wasn't so pale, her body shivering in the aftermath of shock. My poor girl has been kidnapped, attacked by zombies, kidnapped again and now shot at. I'm starting to wonder if she wouldn't have been better off if we'd never met.

No, if we'd never met, one of my men would've eventually arrested her and she would've been executed. She's better off in my care. We live in a brutal world, where terrible things become an unfortunate norm. If I could protect my wife from every potential hurt, I would. Since that's not realistic, I'll just have to do my best to change the world around her until she's achieved some sort of peace.

My desire to fix her world doesn't look like it's going to be happening any time soon if those transmissions were accurate. My Sanctuary will destabilize even further if I'm not able to bring it under control before the masses of survivors descend upon us with a horde of Primitives on their tail. Because where the live humans go, the undead follow.

"Let's go."

I pick Taran up and hold her against me, climbing the stairs as fast as I can. As we walk, I bark orders at Grayson to secure the building and make sure the rebels have dispersed. I'm uncomfortable with having Taran here, but unless we leave the city, there's almost no place where she'll be safer.

I vow to remain by her side. If she has to, then she'll come to work with me in the morning. For now, we both need a good night's sleep. I carry her into our apartment, Grayson behind us, on his radio, relaying my orders.

Before entering the bedroom, I say to him, "Make sure each floor is secure and double the guard in the lobby. I'm going to turn my radio off so Taran can sleep. If anything happens, bang on the door."

"Yes, Commander." He turns and leaves.

"Can someone please check on Emery?" Taran asks, her voice strained as she speaks for the first time since the guard station.

"Of course, baby." I set her down on the bed and leave to relay her wishes to Grayson who immediately agrees to go check on Taran's friend. We set her up in an apartment three floors down so the women could have easy access to each other. The arrangement seems to be working well. Taran has been more settled since receiving daily visits with Emery. She's even taken to making requests for the nursery, a big step in her willingness to see our baby as real.

When I get back to the bedroom, Taran is gone. "Taran!" I say sharply.

"In here." Her voice drifts out from the washroom.

I quickly go to her, the need to keep eyes on her, make sure she and the baby are safe, has become a compulsion. When we're apart, I'm uneasy until I've made my way back to her side. An exhausting prospect considering the chaos erupting all over the city. I've had to delegate tasks and trust my men in a way I've never done before in an effort to spend as much time with Taran as I can manage while still keeping my hold on the city.

I stand in the doorway watching her as she slowly disrobes, peeling the layers away and revealing her beautiful body. I've always loved looking at my wife, but now, as her curves fill and her belly grows, I'm more in awe of her than ever. She doesn't look like the underfed urchin I first arrested. Now she's lush, the bones of her ribs and breast no longer visible through her skin. She struggles to pull her pants down, unable to reach her toes anymore.

"Let me help." I reach for her, kneeling at her feet and tugging the soft cotton legs of her pants off each foot. When she's completely naked I place a kiss on her belly, then rise up to stand next to her. I pick up her wrist and examine the bite mark on her arm, now faded to just a few marks. I kiss her arm over the bite and then run my hand up to her shoulder, pushing her hair away and touching the mark on her neck. This one is much more vicious, the skin stretched and distorted, badly scarred. I drop a kiss onto the scar and then trail my lips up to her hairline, kissing just behind her ear. She shivers against me.

I reach out and turn the taps on, taking my own clothes off while the water heats. We get into the shower together. She stands quietly, allowing me to wash her, massaging her skin as I glide the soap over her body. She shifts obediently when I nudge her legs apart, giving me access. I run the soap through her folds gliding my fingers through and dipping briefly inside her before finishing up.

By the time I'm done washing her entire body and her hair my cock is standing tall against my belly. I've never bothered hiding my reaction to her. It's always been like this, she looks at me, touches me, breaths near me and my body responds. The feel of her soft skin is almost more than I can take, but her health is more important. She's exhausted and emotional, she doesn't need a rough, scarred up Warlord pawing at her.

"My turn," she murmurs taking the soap from my hand.

"Taran," I say warningly, catching her wrist. I can handle touching her, can hold myself back from ravishing her. But the true test of my good intentions will be when she touches me.

"Diogo," she says and tugs her wrist from my loose hold. I'm not going to protest too much. Who wouldn't want those soft hands gliding all over them, even if the experience is going to be excruciating in the best way possible?

She washes my chest, then my back, her soapy hands

sliding over my bare skin with purpose. She washes my neck and then leans over to wash everything below my waist. I catch her arm and pull her back up. I don't want her bending like that or going to her knees in her condition.

"But – " she starts to protest.

"No, baby, not tonight." She needs rest and I'm determined to be chivalrous, though the effort might cause a permanent hard-on. She hands the soap back and tries to smother a yawn. "Come on, let's get you to bed."

She nods and allows me to pull her from the shower and dry her off. I linger over her, rubbing each part of her delicate skin, touching her here and there until she's nearly asleep in my arms. When we're both dry, I give her one of my shirts to put on. She drags it over her head, leaving half the buttons undone as she crawls into the bed and collapses on her side, this time not even bothering to cover a huge yawn.

I smile in amusement and tug at the blanket underneath her, pulling it over her and tucking it in around her. She frowns and pulls up an edge. "Come to bed," she orders.

"I have to check in with my men. Make sure they saw to Emery and dispersed the crowd outside. I'll be back in a few minutes."

"Okay..." Her voice drifts off and the tension leaves her body as she falls asleep in the blink of an eye, exhaustion overwhelming her. I kiss her just above her eyebrow, retuck the blanket around her and leave the room.

FORTY-FIVE
TARAN

Something wakes me up. Something violent and sudden. I sit up with a gasp, clinging to my blanket and searching the dark room for my absent husband. It takes a moment for my brain to register a loud booming sound coming from the depths of the building. Seconds later I realize the room is shaking causing the things on my vanity to rattle and a brush to fall off the edge clattering to the floor.

"Diogo!" I call, hoping he's nearby as I struggle to throw off the blankets and crawl to the edge of the bed.

Just as I'm dragging myself to my feet he comes flying through the door, banging it against the wall. His eyes land on me with relief. He rushes to my side and helps me stand.

"We have to get out of the building, baby. Are you okay? Were you hurt?"

I shake my head. "What's happening down there, DIogo? Is it really bad?"

"An explosion," he says succinctly, pulling me out of the bedroom.

"My clothes!" I protest.

He doesn't look at me, just continues toward the door

leading to the stairwell. "No time. The building is on fire, we have to get you out right now."

Grayson holds the door open for us and follows as Diogo runs through and starts down the stairs. Grayson moves out ahead of us his weapon out and at the ready. I hide my face in Diogo's shoulder unable to handle the dizzying pace as he descends the stairs faster than we've ever gone before.

"Taran!" I look up when I hear Emery's voice. She's on a landing in front of us with a few of Diogo's men.

"Move!" Diogo snarls. "There won't be a way out of the building unless we get the fuck out now."

Everyone hurtles downward, Diogo's men flanking us as we go, protecting us. I struggle to keep my eyes on Emery, praying that she's keeping up with the group. Around the fourteenth floor the air begins to thicken with smoke. A bad sign considering all the doors are fire proofed. If the explosion happened in the lobby we'll have to find a different way out. Perhaps underneath the building, through the old parking garage.

Eventually the smoke becomes so thick I can barely see through it. Everyone is coughing as their lungs fill with the sharp, acrid smoke.

"Commander!" A voice shouts eerily from below us.

"Here!" Diogo shouts back, his voice hoarse from the smoke.

The man leaps up the stairs to our level and then stops, doubling over to cough. He tries to catch his breath, but his lungs only fill with more smoke. Tears run unchecked down his face, a visceral response to the lack of oxygen.

"The bottom floors are completely... destroyed." He struggles to get the words out. "I just barely made it out before the fire engulfed the lobby."

"Fuck," Diogo snarls. "How many did we lose?"

"Don't know for sure. Dax was killed in the explosion. I lost sight of the others."

Diogo's fingers clench around me as he takes in the news. It's hard to imagine the big tough guys he recruits into his military being killed. I hope they somehow managed to get out. Our own situation is starting to look bleak.

"We can't go back up," Diogo announces. "There's no way out of the building up there. We have to go as low as we can and see if we can make it to the ground another way."

I cling tighter to DIogo as he runs down the stairs, struggling to breathe with each step as we inhale the poisonous smoke. He pushes my head into his shoulder telling me to keep my face averted as much as I can. I want to tell him to put me down, that I'm slowing him down and making it harder for him to breathe, but I know he'll refuse. Besides, I won't be able to take the stairs as fast as everyone else.

Finally, we reach the point where the smoke is too thick, and the heat of the fire is reaching up through the lower floors.

"Through here," Diogo barks, flinging a landing door open with his shoulder. He carries me through and I'm able to take my first deep breath as fresh air from the broken windows of an abandoned floor hits us.

"What floor is this?" I ask fearfully.

"Six," Grayson answers grimly, coughing.

"Emery!" I twist around in time to see one of Diogo's men, his arm wrapped around Emery's waist, half dragging her, half carrying her through the door. She falls to her knees coughing.

"How do we get out?" I ask, as Diogo sets me on my feet, makes sure I'm steady and then heads to the windows, looking out over the side of the building. All the windowpanes are missing on this level, causing a sharp wind to rush through. When he turns back to look at me, I know we're in big trouble. Though his face doesn't change expression, I can read the terror. He's afraid. Not for himself, never for himself. He's afraid for me and our unborn child.

I curve my arms protectively around my stomach and walk toward the windows. Diogo holds me as I lean out the open window and look down. A rush of smoke and heat hits me, and I have to blink before I can see anything. Flames shoot out of some of the windows of the lower floors as they reach up toward us. I can't even see the ground, but I know it's down there, about 60 feet away. Shouts reach through the darkness, the occasional gunshot echoing through the night. It sounds like Diogo's people are fighting the rebels.

Then it really hits me. There's no way out of the building. My eyes connect with Diogo's and the message is clear; we're trapped.

"I'm so sorry, baby." He grabs me by the neck and drags me into his body. He lowers his head to speak in my ear. "I won't stop fighting for you. We'll find a way."

"I know," I whisper back smiling tremulously.

"She can climb." Emery's voice snaps us out of our moment. She stumbles toward us. "Out the window, she can climb down to the ground."

Fury flashes in Diogo's eyes as his arm tightens around me. "Absolutely not. In her condition she'll fall."

Emery shakes her head and persists, "I've seen this girl climb in almost every condition. In pouring rain, deadly heat, wearing multiple layers of clothing. Twenty extra pounds won't slow her down much."

Emery is exaggerating and we both know it. But she's also right. I'm the only one with the skill and experience to make it out of the building.

I grip Diogo's hand. "I can do it! I can make my way down and go get help."

He opens his mouth to refuse, I can see the negative in his eyes before he even speaks. Emery cuts him off. "Don't let her die along with the rest of us."

Her words stop Diogo and for the second time I see that flash of fury. Only this time I don't think it's aimed at my friend. It's aimed at himself, at the situation. "I should have fucking executed every last rebel when I had the chance."

He takes my face between his hands and holds me for a moment, looking at me. Seconds tick by as the fire rises through the building consuming everything on its way up to us. Smoke surrounds us, choking Emery and Diogo's men as they reach for the windows, trying to breathe.

"You will not fall." Diogo's voice is passionate, angry, despairing.

"I won't," I promise him fervently.

"You will survive."

"Yes!" Tears are running down my face now as I realize I'm about to leave my husband in a burning building.

"Our child will survive," he says fiercely, his grip on my head becoming almost painful. "Promise me."

"I promise." My voice is shaking, and I can barely see him through the tears.

"I love you." He smashes his lips down on mine, kissing me with passion and anger. I hang onto him, kissing him back.

"Commander!" Grayson shouts. "She needs to go now, or she won't make it through the fire. It's bursting all the windows on the lower floors."

We break apart. Without pausing Diogo lifts me onto the window ledge. I cling to it for a second, looking back at his grim face, the beloved lines. He hasn't shaved in days, his life completely consumed by me and the rebellion. He looks more handsome to me, lonelier and more unreachable in this moment than I've ever seen him. He is the Warlord. And he's saying goodbye. He doesn't believe they'll make it out.

A sob bursts from my lips as he leans out to place a gentle kiss on my lips. "Goodbye, Taran."

"I love you, Diogo."

Blinking away the tears I start my descent, climbing away from the open window and down into the raging fiery inferno below. My last view before I have to pay attention to what I'm doing is of Diogo's face as he's forced to watch his 7-month pregnant wife scale a building. He watches over me as I pick out the best path to the ground. When I look back up again, I see nothing more, my view of the others completely obscured as the building is engulfed in smoke and flames.

"Diogo," I whisper.

TO BE CONTINUED…

"I won't leave." My voice catches on a sob. I bury my face in Silas' lap, clinging to the sides of his chair.

The fortress is in chaos and has been from the moment the ash started falling from the sky, landing in thick heaps on our city streets. Wolfe knew immediately what was happening, confirmed it with Sanctuaries on the East coast. Sanctuaries that don't stand a chance of outrunning the nuclear horror settling down upon all of us. They will be worst hit, but we aren't much better off.

In an effort to follow their prey and outrun the fallout, Primitives from all across the land are attacking the walls of our Sanctuaries. We can only stand for so long against such an onslaught. Our own Sanctuary is weakening as the wall crumbles and the Primitives find their way through.

Reports come in of attacks all over the city, of Primitives driving people from their homes and out into the panicked streets. We've allowed many of the more vulnerable citizens into the fortress, but we've reached our capacity. Soon the Primitives will find their way inside and we'll all be doomed. Even my own immunity to the bite won't save me from being torn apart.

"You must go with Wolfe, my love." Silas gently runs a shaking hand over my head, the way he knows I love to be touched.

"I won't leave you!" I snarl fiercely into the fabric of his pants.

Gentle hands wrap around me from behind and tug.

Hannah tries to pull me to my feet, but I resist. "Stand up, my darling, we need to get you out of here. Sanctuary is falling, and the people need you if they are to escape."

Silas has made it clear that he is unable to travel any kind of long distance. I tried to suggest we just make it into the mountains where we can hide out, but he refuses. He thinks he only has a few weeks left anyway and he doesn't want to spend the last minutes of his life on the road, uncomfortable and in pain. I refuse to allow him to spend the last moments of his life alone.

"No," I snap, "I'm not leaving him, just go!"

I look up in time to see her exchange a look with someone behind us. I lean over and look around Silas' chair. Wolfe is standing at the ready. I thought he left when the fortress staff abandoned the building.

"Darling, it's time for you to go now," Hannah says softly, stepping back. Wolfe rounds the chair and tugs my clinging hands from Silas, lifting me right of my feet and into his strong arms.

I shriek and resist, thrusting an elbow back into his neck. He tightens his hold and turns away from Hannah and Silas.

"He won't be alone," Hannah assures me, standing next to our husband and placing her hand on his shoulder.

"No!" I scream. "Silas!"

Coming soon in The Last Sanctuary

"How long are you going to keep me here?" Allie finally decided to brave the questions she knew needed asking.

His eyes sharpened on her face. "You're here to stay, Allison," he said implacably using her full name, which he did when he wanted her to know he meant what he was saying.

She shook her head. "No, I'm not."

"This isn't a negotiation." His voice was hard, his eyes harder.

Anger and a dose of panic rose up in Allie. She knew when Jay decided something he was immovable. "Jay, I can't stay here with you. I'm still married to Derrick. I still have a job. I have to go home. I can see exactly what you've done. You've built this beautiful home and filled it with things that you know I love. But its too late for us, Jay. Even a beautiful prison is still a prison. You can't just keep me here forever!"

Something frightening flared in Jay's eyes, stopping the flow of Allie's words. He stepped toward her. Allie stepped back. He stalked toward her until only inches separated them. She felt the electric attraction jump between them, stronger than ever, and gasped. He didn't touch her, yet every part of her felt alive from his nearness. It had always been there, the thing that lay between them, but Jay had suppressed it before, sending her away. He was doing nothing to hold himself back from her now. Her head spun from the knowledge that he was done hiding his attraction.

"You've always belonged to me, Allison," his quiet voice sounded guttural with need. "I should have taken you when you were eighteen, but I didn't. For better or worse, I sent you away instead."

She nodded mutely, eyes wide on his face.

"I let you go once."

Her lips parted and her breath escaped in a shudder.

"It'll never happen again."

Allie whimpered, half in fear and half in arousal, as he pinned her with his possessive grey eyes. He looked as though he wanted to reach for her, but was ruthlessly holding himself back so he wouldn't hurt her. His long fingers curled into fists and his cruel lips compressed into a line. Allie shivered as he stepped away from her. Some of the tension diffused.

"Get some rest," he said.

He turned and left the room, locking the door behind him.

Keep reading today! Now available on Amazon!

EXCERPT: FIRE & VICE BOOK 4 – SAVAGE VENDETTA

"I asked you a question, Sitnikov," she spat his name like it was a curse. "What do you want?"

His thin lips curled up in a cruel smile – though, to be fair, she didn't think the hard slash of his mouth was made for anything other than cruel expressions. "Ah, Jane, now *that* is a question with many answers. Few that I think you would enjoy quite yet." He leaned back, his chair creaking against the worn tile of her kitchen floor.

Jane rolled her eyes. "I'm definitely not in the mood for word games, Sitnikov. Why *the fuck* are you here, in my home? One would think that you'd prefer to keep your distance from the cop that's about to take you down."

His eyes narrowed slightly, but otherwise his expression didn't change. "You have a smart mouth, Jane, you should be careful what you say with it, lest a concerned citizen step in to shut those lovely lips," he remarked quietly. "Call me Vladimir."

"Not in this lifetime, *Sit-ni-kov*," she sneered, pronouncing each syllable of his last name deliberately. "Also, I'm pretty sure that was a threat you were uttering.

You might want to step lightly while in the presence of a police officer and her gun. I'm pretty sure it wouldn't be too difficult to claim self-defense if a suspected mob boss were shot in my apartment."

A muscle in his strong jaw jumped. The sudden tightening of his body was barely perceptible, except to the eyes of an experienced cop. She'd spent enough time in the interrogation room to know when a man was stopping himself from lunging across the table toward her. She almost smirked at the thought of getting a reaction out of a man like Sitnikov. She really did have a remarkable tendency to piss people off. It was how she had made detective at such a young age. Her dogged determination combined with her take-no-prisoners attitude had impressed the higher ups. Plus, she pissed off her beat sergeant to the point where he was happy to see her promoted and out of his department.

"I have an offer for you," Sitnokov said, his dark eyes drinking her in.

She arched her eyebrow. "This should be good."

"Be my mistress."

Jane sat frozen in her chair caught between laughter at the absurdity of his proposition, and terror. "That's the stupidest thing I've ever heard. You would let a cop get that close to you? Just to scratch an itch? You like to live dangerously, don't you, Sitnikov? Sure, yeah, let's do it. Can we go back to your place now? Can I have the code to your safe before we get down?"

His lips curled in a quasi smile at her sarcasm. "No, I would not allow a police detective access to my private life," he said calmly.

Jane frowned. "I don't understand. Supposedly you want to have a fling with me, *a detective*, but you don't plan on letting law enforcement near you. I'm not sure how long it's been for you, but usually that kind of intimacy requires a physical presence. Not that I'm even remotely entertaining the idea of any kind of relationship with you. Not happening, *Russian*." She spat the last word.

He didn't seem to enjoy the way she spoke to him. His body was rigid in the seat and he seemed to be struggling with himself. She was happy to have a weapon close at hand. She suspected that no one spoke to the Boss the way she just had. Or if they did, they quickly found themselves without a tongue and having silent conversations with fishes. She had to bite her own tongue just from pointing out her original assertion that she tended to annoy people.

"Listen to my offer, then give your opinion, *woman*." He deliberately sneered the last word. His posture was relaxed, but his eyes were sharp, taking in every expression that crossed her features. "You will quit your job and come to live with me. For a time, we will share a home and a bed. I will pay you a monthly fee that will make your current salary look like a child's allowance. I will also give you a generous settlement and a house once we have finished our association."

Jane's breath caught in her chest and pain blossomed. She felt sudden and intense hatred for the man sitting across from her. It made her feel out of control, something she hadn't felt for years. Not one to hide her feelings, Jane reached out and picked up the gun. She pointed it at him, flipped the safety off and said, "We're done with this conversation. You can go now."

His dark eyes snapped in fury before he hid it under his usual icy visage. "You do not like my terms, though they are more than generous? Name what it is you want then, I may be willing to negotiate."

Jane clenched her teeth and spoke in a furious voice. "I

want you to admit to the murder of Dennis Yankovich. On record. Then I *want* you to go rot in a federal prison somewhere for the rest of your life. In the mean time, you can take your offer and go fuck yourself."

He thought for a moment, his body straining in his seat, and then shook his head slightly. "I don't think I will accommodate that request, no matter how attractive I find you. Put the gun down, Jane. I don't want you to get hurt."

"Fuck you, Sitnikov. Get out of my apartment. Now!" she snapped. "The answer is no. You don't get to touch me, *ever*."

Sitnikov stood, his long limbs unfolding with the fluidity of a lion rising from its rest. Jane stood also, not wanting to feel small or trapped around this predatory man. He stalked around the table toward her. His lean, muscular body tensed with lethal intent. Jane brought the gun up, her grip steady and professional. She snapped, "Stop, don't you come near me!"

Rather than waste time responding, Sitnikov stepped swiftly to the side, forcing her to bring her gun arm around. Before the gun settled on him again, he reached out and gripped her wrist in a ruthless hold that made her cry out, and yanked the gun from her grip with his other hand. He moved so quickly Jane didn't have a chance. He flipped the safety back on and tossed the gun in the direction of her couch.

"No!" she gasped as he took hold of her arms and hauled her bodily up against his hard chest.

Jane struggled in his hold, but was easily subdued. He was nearly a foot taller than her and outweighed her by a fair amount. His skill in subduing an armed opponent was undeniable. He held her easily, heat radiating from his much larger body into hers.

"You promised you wouldn't hurt me! I don't want your offer, my answer is no. Now go away!"

His fingers tightened around her arms and he lifted her up until only the tips of her bare toes touched the floor and she was forced to brace her hands against his hard body for stability. She felt the flexed pectoral muscles under his expensive shirt. His heart beat steadily against her fingertips. He dropped his face towards hers, his lips inches from her mouth. Their breaths mingled as tension snapped in the air around them. He smelled like mint with a hint of cigar and vodka. She braced herself against his chest, her fingers digging into the muscles, as she tried ineffectively to push him away.

"I have no intention of hurting you, Jane. Not tonight, anyway." His voice was deep and steady. "But you mistake my intention in coming here. The offer is not contingent on your acceptance. The offer is a bonus for what is inevitable. You *will* become my mistress."

Keep reading today! Now available on Amazon!

ALSO BY NIKITA SLATER

If you enjoyed this book, check out some other works by #1 International Bestselling Author, Nikita Slater. More titles are always in progress, so check back often to see what's new!

Angels & Assassins Series

Book One – The Assassin's Wife

The Queens Series

Book One – Scarred Queen

Book Two - Queen's Move

Book Three - Born a Queen (coming 2020)

Alejandro's Prey (a novella)

Fire & Vice Series

Book One – Prisoner of Fortune

Book Two – Fight or Flight

Book Three – King's Command

Book Four – Savage Vendetta

Book Five – Fear in Her Eyes

Book Six – Bound by Blood

Book Seven – In His Sights

Book Eight - Burning Beauty (Coming 2019)

The Driven Hearts Series

Book One - Driven by Desire

Book Two - Thieving Hearts

Book Three - Capturing Victory

The Sanctuary Series

Book One - Sanctuary's Warlord

Book Two - Sanctuary on Fire

Book Three - The Last Sanctuary (coming soon)

Standalone books

Because You're Mine

Mine to Keep (a novella)

Stalked

After Dark

In collaboration with Jasmin Quinn

Collared: A Dark Captive Romance

Safeword: A Dark Romance

Chained: A Mafia Marriage Romance

Good Girl: A Captive BDSM Romance

Hostile Takeover: An Enemies to Lovers Romance (coming soon!)

Visit **nikitaslater.com** for more information

and the latest updates!

STAY CONNECTED WITH NIKITA!

Don't miss one sexy moment. Keep in touch with Nikita for the latest news and updates about all of your favourite characters.

- Follow me on **Amazon** for all of my book releases!
- Follow me on **Instagram**
- Like and follow me on **Facebook**
- Follow me on **Twitter** (**@NikSlaterWrites**)
- Connect with me on **Goodreads**
- Follow me on **Bookbub**!

Sign up for the newsletter today at receive exclusive updates and access to ***bonus content and chapters*** not available anywhere else!

www.nikitaslater.com
nik@nikitaslater.ca

ABOUT THE AUTHOR

Nikita Slater is the International Bestselling dark romance author of the Fire & Vice series, Angels & Assassins series, The Queens series and several standalone novels. Her favourite genre is mafia romance, the bloodier the better, though she loves to write about every subject under the sun. She lives on the beautiful Canadian prairies with her son and crazy awesome dog. She has an unholy affinity for books (especially erotic romance), wine, pets and anything chocolate. Despite some of the darker themes in her books (which are pure fun and fantasy), Nikita is a staunch feminist and advocate of equal rights for all races, genders and non-gender specific persons. When she isn't writing, dreaming about writing or talking about writing, she helps others discover a love of reading and writing through literacy and social work.